DEAD RIGHT

DEAD RIGHT

TIM SUSMAN

Dead Right
Production copyright Argyll Productions © 2024
Text copyright © Tim Susman 2024
Published by Argyll Productions
Dallas, Texas
www.argyllproductions.com

Cover art by Royz Ilya
Cover design by Christine Foltzer
Interior design by Argyll Productions

Print ISBN 978-1-61450-639-3
eBook ISBN 978-1-61450-640-9

First Edition Trade Paperback

For all of our ghosts

CHAPTER
ONE

The living room of my one-bedroom apartment looked out over two blocks of low-rise buildings and strip malls to the concrete walls of Chicago's Wolftown. They rose four stories tall, so I could see a section of them over the liquor store and laundromat, bracketed by a ten and a fifteen-story apartment building. Behind those walls, in an area a little over two square miles, resided an estimated 80-85% of the extranormal people in Chicago: a lot of werewolves, some vampires, other shapechangers of all kinds.

The first Wolftown was built in the fifties in New York, and there were a dozen or so across the USA now, almost seventy years later. There were also a lot of people who didn't think extras should be confined to a walled neighborhood anymore. I hadn't thought much about that until about seven years ago—Wolftown was just where I went when I snuck out to visit my friends who were extras—but the Wolftown issues, and getting better treatment for extras in general, were a lot more on my mind these days.

My boyfriend stood behind me, also looking out the

window. "There," he said, lifting his grey-furred arm past my shoulder and pointing with a finger tipped with a claw. "You can see some of them gathering."

Through gaps between buildings, a small crowd of extra-normal people were visible, keeping their extra forms outside of Wolftown. Mostly they were werewolves in their half-shifted phase: human body and proportions with a wolf's fur, head, and tail, just like Czoltan was behind me. This allowed them to make use of their heightened senses of smell and directional hearing while still able to, y'know, use language and tools. Best of both worlds, or it would be if it didn't freak out many people who couldn't shift.

Not me. Obviously.

"How long before Carla gets here?" I asked, turning around.

"Dunno. She said she wanted to watch the coverage before we left, but I don't know when that starts. Want to call your mother before she gets here?"

My nose came up to his shoulder, so I had to lean my head back to look up into his green eyes as I linked my hands around behind his back. He wasn't wearing a shirt—most werewolves didn't when they were shifted—and so I pushed my fingers through the thick fur above his tail. "I really don't," I said, pressing a little closer.

He grinned and lowered his muzzle to touch his nose to mine and then kissed me. His paw reached down to my rear. "Is that so?"

"You're going on the march today and then leaving tomorrow," I complained. "That only leaves tonight and tomorrow morning."

There was the smallest hitch in his reaction, because I wasn't coming on the march with him, and he knew why, and he also knew I wasn't asking him not to go, but all that took a half-second to process before he bumped his nose into mine again and said, "That's not enough time?"

I could tell from the way he pressed against me that he was wondering too, and what had started as a half-joke now became an actual thought, *Do we have time before they show up?* Not for everything we liked to do, but a quickie, maybe?

I leaned my head against the coarse fur of his shoulder and breathed in the comforting smell of him. "We probably shouldn't," I said.

"Probably not," he agreed, but our bodies kept making the counter-argument, and as long as we stood here holding each other, it felt like any future was possible.

But of course, just as I was thinking we should move away from the window and to the couch or bedroom or something, the door buzzer sounded. We looked at each other, and then Czoltan moved his paws to my shoulders, kissed me again, and let me go. "Tonight, I promise," he said. "A nice dinner in and a quiet time together."

He walked to the door to buzz in his friends, and I tried to compose myself. Carla was a thunderbird, not a werewolf, so I wasn't worried about her smelling our arousal, but she probably wasn't alone.

Czoltan shot me a smile and adjusted himself as well, and then went to the bathroom where I heard the spritz of his cologne, light enough to not offend wolfy noses but strong enough to cover scents you might not want people to catch. When he came out he was in human form, with olive skin and dark hair instead of fur. Same green eyes, same lovely body, though. "Carla can't be shifted indoors," he said. "So we go skin, so she doesn't feel alone."

· · ·

Sure enough, when Carla came in, she was in human form. So was her companion, a young man with an attractive physique and sharp golden eyes who introduced himself as Gabriel, and said he was a nagual* (were-jaguar) from El Salvador. Carla stood an inch or two taller than Czoltan, with shoulder-length black hair and an all-business expression, and Gabriel, more my height, wore silver studs in both ears and his nose. As he passed me I caught a distinct cat-like aroma that was probably a feline version of Czoltan's cologne. His black hair, a little longer than Czoltan's close cut, sported frosted tips in a rosette pattern, or at least close enough to one that I could tell that's what they were meant to be. Gabriel wore a short-sleeved collared shirt completely unbuttoned, and Carla wore a spandex halter top that would either stretch or easily unfasten if she shifted.

Gabriel and Carla went right to the couch as Czoltan turned on the TV. "Channel 7," Carla instructed. "D said they were doing live coverage."

The nagual plopped down on the couch as Czoltan, standing beside it, switched to the local news. He waited for Carla to take the other side of the couch, but she stood behind it, so he sat next to Gabriel.

I stayed by the front door, leaning against the doorway to the small kitchen. The one-bedroom apartment was plenty spacious for me living alone (or with a ghost, which I'd had until my former ghost partner had moved on five months ago), but whenever Czoltan visited from Detroit, the place became cozily close. Sure, we shared a bed, but when we weren't doing bed stuff, there weren't many places we could be, and even my

---

* In Mesoamerican religion, sometimes a nagual (or nahual) is a were-jaguar; sometimes it is any person who can shift into their guardian animal spirit's form. In Wolftown, they are were-jaguars.

poor human ears could hear noises made anywhere in the apartment. Having extra people here made the close quarters feel even closer.

But they wouldn't be here for long. Carla, Czoltan, and, I assumed, Gabriel, were members of the National Organization for the Protection of Extranormals, or NOPE (they had an ongoing campaign with signs and banners that had phrases like "Is it okay to discriminate against werewolves? NOPE" — excellent use of an acronym). This was the largest nationwide extras-rights group, and the one that had the most publicity and recognition. They marched, they lobbied politicians, they printed up information. Today, they were taking part in a large march to demand changes to local laws to make it easier for extras to get homes outside of Wolftown. They generally wanted better integration of human and extra society, but without giving up the Wolftowns, which, despite their concrete walls, had developed into vibrant communities.

There was another, less public movement called Teardown, an underground activist network that wanted to eliminate Wolftowns entirely. They generally went in for showier, more destructive acts like smashing parts of the Wolftown walls or vandalizing construction sites of housing companies with discriminatory policies. Publicly, NOPE disavowed the Teardown movement, because they were considered terrorists, and that meant they got thrown in jail or—if you were an immigrant like Czoltan—deported. Czoltan told me he didn't have anything to do with them here in Chicago, and I hadn't asked about Detroit.

(If you believed the right-wing news networks, there was a highly dangerous, organized movement called For All, or 4All sometimes—the news liked to flash up the same three pictures of graffiti with a 4 in a circle—that wanted to turn humans into extras, usually werewolves.

But so far, only one person had been definitively connected to that group, if it even existed. Czoltan said it was bullshit; he'd met one or two extras who'd say "things'd be better if everyone was extra" over a couple drinks, but that was it. Every couple years, an extra would be arrested for an illegal turn, and the right-wing media would find any instances of the number 4 in their life and claim they were part of this group. Nobody outside their sphere really bought it.)

We watched the newscast for about twenty minutes as they talked about the politics behind the march, mentioning NOPE and a few other organizations, but not Teardown. The anchor in the studio, a blond woman in a green suit, listed the main demands: access to better housing throughout the city, laws specifically forbidding discrimination against extras in workplace and housing. Sometimes human reporters characterized the extras rights movement as "wanting special treatment," but this team were more objective journalists, and their commentary didn't get more than an "Uh-huh" from Carla, Gabriel, or Czoltan.

When she'd given the background for the movement and the reasons for the march, she spoke to a human-looking— probably not an extra, though you never knew—man in a blue jacket and yellow tie standing in Federal Plaza, currently empty. He spoke in a carefully neutral news-personality voice. "The protest will arrive here at Federal Plaza around noon," he said, "and march through downtown after speeches by local civic leaders."

"Hey," Gabriel said, leaning back to Carla, "that's you."

A map came up on the screen showing the route. "The rally will end—"

"That's good," Carla said. "You can turn it off."

Czoltan tapped the remote and the TV went black. "I

thought you wanted to hear what they were going to say about us."

"No, I wanted to make sure they got the route right. Two years ago they showed the wrong one and we didn't know why the cops were directing us along different streets. It's all good."

"Anyway," Gabriel said, "at least this time they didn't say we were 'a small minority of extras.' That shit pisses me off every time. Lots of people agree with us, they just don't want to walk a couple miles and get shit yelled at them." He rubbed his shoulder. "Thrown, too, sometimes."

"Messaging is Danielle's department anyway," Carla said. "I'm logistics. I care about the route." She scrolled through her phone and tapped out a message. "You boys ready?"

Gabriel stretched on the couch as if he had no intention of leaving, but Czoltan stood and looked at me. "Watch us on TV?" he said.

"Course."

Gabriel turned with interest; I could almost see his cat's ears perk up. "You're not coming? To support your boyfriend?"

"I, ah, I get a lot of referrals from the CPD," I said.

"And he's worried that showing up at a protest could make the cops, you know, not like him as much," Czoltan explained.

The nagual looked from him back to me. "Takin' money from the cops is like working for 'em," he said.

"I'm not taking money from the cops," I said. "I take money from people who go to the cops with their problems and the cops don't want to go into Wolftown so they send them along to me. They don't have to do that."

Gabriel squinted. "You used to be a cop?"

"Army," I said, "but I know a few cops. Hey, I try to get work through other channels, but these assholes keep going to the cops, so I have to stay in good with the cops. Anyway, if I hadn't, I'd probably be in Detroit jail right now."

"Wait!" Gabriel stood up from the couch fluidly and smoothed his hair down. "That thing in Detroit where the chick got poisoned and someone had to turn her to save her? There was a Chicago cop or something there. That was you?"

"Not a cop, but that was me."

"Daaaaamn. Zo said you were famous for a hot minute but I didn't think I woulda known you. That was crazy! I watched that vid like a hundred times. She was all like dyin' and shit, and that guy was high on wolfsbane and just bit her, like whoa. I never saw someone turned before."

"Yeah," I said, "it was pretty intense."

Gabriel paced toward the TV and then came over to me. "How'd you know she was poisoned? Some of my friends said the guy who turned her got arrested after, but Marce said it's legal to turn someone if it'll save their life."

"How would you turn someone into a nagual?" I asked, because I didn't want to get into the story.

"Can't." Gabriel puffed out his chest. "I mean, I can't. Naguals have nagual kids, but we don't turn regular people. The jaguar is my connection to my god. If someone feels that connection real strong, then a priest can maybe free the nagual in them and turn them, but we can't just bite someone."

"That's why there are so many more werewolves than any other extras," Carla said. "Just need a little wolfsbane."

"That and the wars." Czoltan looked at the floor.

I walked over and hugged him, and he let me, and then hugged back. "I'm fine," he said into the awkward silence. "Just history."

I didn't think Carla and Gabriel knew he'd been orphaned in the Second Kosovo War, and they definitely didn't know that he was probably fine talking about it. Maybe that was just with me; we'd talked about his family a lot when we were first going out six or seven years ago, and we'd talked about them a little in the past two months after getting back together. But I didn't want to say anything in front of them, and they didn't know what to say, so finally Carla looked at me and said, "But you support the Teardown, right?"

Czoltan was the one who now made the "my ears would be perking up if I were in wolf form" face. I caught his eye and saw how ready he was to jump in if I said the wrong thing. "Of course I do," I said. "I just have to be careful how publicly I support it because, you know, the cops are always watching."

"Oh, we know it," Carla said, and returned to her phone. She seemed satisfied, and Czoltan relaxed.

Regardless of the pros and cons, I'm very aware that I don't have a lot of standing in this argument. I'm sure as hell not going to argue nuance with Carla, who's devoting most of her life to it. Fundamentally, at the core, I support the movement to get rid of the walls. I think the Teardown folks are being a little hasty about it, but also, would they have as much momentum if they weren't? That's not a subject anyone (except Czoltan) really wants to hear a human's opinion on. Especially not one of the five top people in an affiliated local movement, and extra especially not five minutes before they're about to go organize a march.

"Right," Carla said, looking up from her phone. "You two ready? We need to get going."

"Ready, boss." Gabriel snapped his fingers.

"I'm gonna say goodbye to Jae," Czoltan said, "if you don't mind waiting outside."

Gabriel made finger guns and a "chk-chk" noise which, accompanied with a wink, seemed to indicate that he thought we were going to fuck when they left the room. If only. Carla just said, "Fine," and walked out the front door into the hall. After a quick, "Nice to meet you, Jae," Gabriel hurried after her.

When the door had closed, I reached out for Czoltan to hug

him. "I'm not going to tell you to be safe," I said. "But I'll hold onto your phone if you want."

"Nah." He grinned and stepped into the hug. "I backed it up already. If things get rough I'll just power it off."

Most extras I know only unlock their phone with their shifted face, even though you can have multiple faces set (finally), because it's illegal to force someone to shift forms. So if they get arrested, they stay in human form and there's no way the police can wave the phone in front of their face and unlock it. It's—as Czoltan says—extra safe.

It was a little strange to feel that human face next to mine and not fur, but there was something in the form of his body and the scent of him that remained the same, that told me this was him even though he might look and feel different. "Be careful," I said.

He laughed. "I thought you weren't gonna tell me that."

"I can't help it." I pulled my head back, arms still around his chest. Even human, he's a little taller than me, just enough to be sexy. "I'm going to worry until I see you all safely at the end of the march. Protests like these are a big target."

"This one's ten times smaller than the march on D.C.," he said, "and that one went fine."

"Yeah, but this is Chicago. There's a lot of crazy people here."

Czoltan stepped out of the hug and poked my chest with a smile. "I know it. Hey, listen, you gotta call your mother."

"I know."

"I know you know, but today you gotta do it, all right? The wedding's in like a month."

"Yes." I took a deep breath and let it out. "I promise."

"Great." He leaned forward and kissed me. "And if I can't be around, that's fine. Or if I have to stay human, that's fine too."

"I *know*." I kissed him back. "So you're going to keep yourself safe, and I'm going to call my mother, and I'll see you tonight. Chicken tagine okay?'

"Fantastic. You need me to get figs?"

"No, I'll run out."

"All right." He kissed me one last time, squeezed my hand, and then hurried out to join his friends.

It wasn't fine if he couldn't be around, despite what he said, and that's why I'd been putting off calling my mom. A friend of hers was getting married in Chicago and she'd already accepted the invitation, but she was waiting for me to confirm I'd be around so she knew when she could fly in and back. Ideally she wanted to stay several days and do lots of "things" around Chicago, which she was leaving it up to me to pick (from a list she kept adding to). Those things might include Czoltan or might not, and whether they did or not hinged on whether I was going to tell my mother that we were dating. I'd been putting that off because—well, let's just say she doesn't call Wolftowns "zoos" anymore, but mostly because she knows that's a thing racists say. In one sense, it's not really her fault; she grew up in a pretty tight Korean community here, and back in Korea, gumiho (their native shifters) didn't have a lot of rights or acceptance at the time she and her friends here left. They didn't have to interact much with extras here, so they haven't been pressed to change their views at all.

"I've never seen your place," my mother said when I Face-Timed her.

The feeling of being a teenager flooded back into me, the vague apprehension sitting in the pit of my stomach, the urge to pull my arms in against my body and sit up straight, the sense of a love I couldn't ever return adequately, all of it so familiar as to be comforting. "You see it all the time." I moved the phone around. "See? There's my living room, there's the bedroom."

"Tch. You know what I mean. I can't wait to visit for the first time. You've lived in Chicago for six years and it will be the first time I've visited."

"You hate to fly," I reminded her. "You asked Judy Park if you could Zoom in to the wedding."

"Oh, I didn't mean it seriously," she said. "It was a joke, and Judy laughed, I will have you know. Now, if it was your wedding, I wouldn't have even joked."

"Of course not," I said.

"So you do have room for your mother to stay in your apartment? I can stay on that couch behind you. I won't be any trouble."

If she stayed her, she'd take the bed, and we both knew it. I stood up for a last, futile attempt to talk her out of staying with me. "I'm on the South side," I said. "Your wedding is up in Lincoln Park."

"Is that far?"

As though she doesn't Google Map with the best of them. "It's twenty minutes if there's no traffic, and there's always traffic. Probably half hour to an hour depending on the time of day."

"It's fine. We'll go up for the rehearsal dinner and then the day of the wedding. We'll just be driving up, staying the day, and coming back. I won't need to keep going back and forth to your apartment. Vella's getting a hotel room and she said I could use it to change."

"Why don't you just stay with Vella?"

"Because she'll make me watch Bridgerton. Besides, she snores."

I spent a few distracted seconds wondering how my mother knew that. "I'm not sure you'll be comfortable here." I moved to the window. "See those walls behind me? That's where Wolftown is."

"Pssh," she said. "I can see the football stadium from my bedroom window, but that doesn't mean I ever go into it. Is there a reason you don't want me to stay with you, Jae?"

"No," I said automatically; I couldn't envision any scenario in which I would say "yes" to that question. Floods, fire, riots? If I were comfortable here, then my mother could come stay. "I'm just thinking of your comfort."

"You're coming to the wedding, so you'll have to drive up there anyway. This way I get to save a bit of money and I get to spend time with you."

Money wasn't an issue to my mother, who managed a small local chain of restaurants, but she often acted as though it was. She knew that I knew this, and there was no sense in pointing it out unless I wanted to divert the conversation into one of those arguments that had gouged a rut so deep that it ran by itself with barely any guidance from us. She knew that too; I could see it in her expression.

So I was left with two choices: leave it and put off telling her about Czoltan, or say "there will be someone else here" and start a whole conversation that would not at all run by itself.

Before I could make that decision, Mom's face changed from determined to curious, and she asked, "Whatever happened to your old captain, the ghost? I don't think you ever told me."

Changing the subject so the previous matter would be considered settled was another of her tactics. And this subject hit with all the subtlety of a mortar round. I got up and paced over to the window. "I, ah, haven't taken care of him yet. He's still in police custody in Detroit."

"You told me a month ago that you were going to Detroit."

"It was three weeks ago that I said that," I reminded her, "and some work came up. I've got a really big job opportunity."

"What opportunity? Why haven't you mentioned it?"

"Because I'm not allowed to talk about it and I knew you'd ask for details I can't give you if I mentioned it."

"Hmph. Well, how long is it going to take to settle him? Can't you go get him while you're doing your other work? You had a ghost partner for a long time."

"It's different with Richard. I knew him when he was alive, so it's hard interacting with him as a ghost." This was at least partly true. There was also the small matter that as an unbound ghost, he'd tried to kill both me and his wife—or widow, I guess—Desiree. I knew that unbound ghosts had trouble holding onto their sanity, and he'd apologized for that several times already, but it's not the kind of thing you can just accept an apology for and wipe it out of your memory. I'd prefer not to have to deal with him at all, but Desiree had specifically asked me to take charge of him, and refusing that would mean that she would have to, and I didn't want to put that on her. I just didn't really want to put it on myself, either.

"I understand that. But he's a friend, right? Is it hard for him being in police custody?"

"No," I said. "He's got a ghost expert there to talk to. He's not floating in a void."

"That's good." She paused. "What will happen when you take charge of him? I thought you were going to keep him as your partner, but if you're not comfortable talking to him, what will you do with him?"

That was the big question, wasn't it? Ideally I'd help Richard sort out his business so he could pass peacefully on to the afterlife, but the only clue I had to what was keeping him here was that he was afraid of losing Desiree—who was currently sleeping with a werewolf. There was a group called

Moving On that helped ghosts resolve their business, but Richard hadn't even wanted to go to the free therapy offered by the VA after the war, so I didn't think he'd go for Moving On. But that was an obstacle I'd put in my own path, not something I'd actually asked him about. "I'll find a place where he can be happy," I said, which was the simplest true answer.

"That's good. Of course my boy will do the right thing for him."

This was more of a reminder that my actions reflected on her, even if she didn't know about them. "That's why his wife left me in charge," I said with considerably less annoyance than I felt both at Desiree and at Mom. "His widow, I mean."

"You can tell me all about how it turns out at the wedding," Mom said. She gave me a big smile. "I'm looking forward to having a whole weekend with you. As long as you can take the time off."

"I can manage it," I said. "Of course I will."

Good old Mom, reminding me that the Kim family honor rested on my shoulders. That was a little sarcastic, but I also kind of mean it; reminding me that my treatment of Richard reflected on her spurred me to get online and book a flight to Detroit for the next day. Czoltan was flying back then and it'd be a nice surprise. I could stay with him while I figured out Richard's deal.

And sometime, I'd have to tell Mom about Czoltan. The wedding gave me a deadline, at least. He'd been very understanding, but the memory of breaking up five years ago because I couldn't tell Mom about him hung over both of us. I'd promised both him and myself that it wouldn't happen like that this time, but "it won't happen like that" is a conveniently cowardly way of avoiding pointing a finger at who, exactly, is responsible for making sure it won't. There was only one person, and that was me.

Czoltan and I had at least gotten to the point that I could book the flight without asking him if it would be all right (though I did text him to tell him I was buying it). That brought a smile to my face even as I bought a ticket I didn't really want to buy. It was the right thing to do, though. The big job was still in the research phase, and even if one or two of the inquiries gave me a firm lead to chase down in the next week, I could do that while taking care of Richard. Probably.

But the big job had to be the priority. It was a lot of money, and not only that, it was the promise of four or five more related jobs for the same pay if I did well on this one. If that all came in, then with Czoltan's salary, we'd be set up to get a bigger place in Chicago next year, one we could both live in. Together.

Yes, yes, cart before horse and all that, but I'd run the numbers and our options for living together were: somewhere near Wolftown Detroit where I would have to build up my contacts from basically zero, this too-small apartment that would drive us crazy eventually, a nicer place an hour outside of Chicago, or for one of us to start making a lot more money. I didn't like any of the first three options, and while Czoltan probably wouldn't have minded the first one, he wouldn't like the others much either.

Full disclosure: Mom sends me money now and then. I keep that money in a separate account, an emergency fund in case things get bad (or in case things get bad for Mom and I'm able to help her out financially, every son's dream). But having this job, and the future jobs that would definitely come along if I proved myself on this, would mean a lot to Czoltan's and my future. "Move into a nice place" was underselling it: this job would allow us the freedom to move our relationship forward however we wanted (I couldn't quite think this thought without feeling guilty that I wasn't telling Mom about him, but

I would do that...soon, when I was sure she could accept him). We didn't have to move in together, but right now we couldn't do it even if we wanted to. This would change that faster than anything else I could think of.

That all sounds great, right? So there had to be a catch. There was, and it was a big one: this job was for the FBI.

I know, I know, I *know*. I'd just made that point to Gabriel about not taking money from the cops, and here I was with a proposal from the uber-cops. I hadn't wanted to take the job when they first approached me (it was right after that business with Desiree, because they'd been looking for a human who knew Wolftowns), but then they added twenty percent to their offer and mentioned future jobs, and—heck, you might not know this, but a private investigator isn't salaried. I get paid when people ask me to work. So a single job that equaled what I'd make in a few months of process services? That was huge.

But. Czoltan definitely wouldn't like me taking money from the FBI, which was why I'd been putting off telling him. And anyway maybe I wouldn't be able to do it and that would be the end of it. But I figured I'd evaluate it first, and then if it looked reasonable, I'd have a conversation with him and I'd lay out the future I saw and we'd decide together whether taking money from the FBI was worth it.

It had taken months to get to this point because they'd had to interview me a couple times and then run background checks. I thought my time in the Army would make that easier, but I forgot that the only thing worse than one bureaucracy is two bureaucracies. After two months of people sending me emails to let me know that they were requesting a document, or considering sending a document to the people who had requested it, or actually sending it, or had received it, they finally sorted out everything and a week ago had given me the introduction to the assignment.

After looking through what they'd sent, I thought I could do it. I wanted to do it. I'd even browsed apartment listings for places that would work for the two of us, nice places with big windows and lake views in apartment buildings that had some extras living in them. Flush with excitement over some of the listings, I'd promised Agent Jefferson a "go/no-go" email by the end of the weekend, and this time alone was a perfect time to decide if I wanted to present the job to Czoltan.

The guy they were looking for was an extra, known to be in Wolftowns in the northeast—New York, Philly, DC, and Boston. He was good at staying under the radar, so they thought that I, with my Wolftown connections (few though they were in those particular cities), could do a better job than they could.

This was, to put it mildly, not usual. The FBI often contracted with specialists when they needed expertise in some field or another, but they did not often give out the name of a person they were interested in finding. I'd had to sign an NDA to see this, one that detailed the number of months I could spend in federal prison if I violated it (it was not a small number).

So I kept the scant information the FBI had given me in a password-protected folder on my computer, and the paper stuff (some of it they didn't want in electronic form) in a locked drawer in my desk. Czoltan didn't ask much about my work as a rule, for which I was grateful, but I still felt bad about hiding it from him. Another of my excuses for not telling him about this job yet, one that I knew was thin but had convinced myself was valid, was that I wasn't even sure I'd be allowed to tell him that I was working for the FBI.

Whether I was or I wasn't, there were going to be difficulties.

TWO

You would think that the FBI would have plenty of surveillance to track down people, and they do, but if you're an extra who doesn't use credit cards or a cell phone and doesn't often leave Wolftowns—where there are laws about cameras and surveillance—then there's only so much they can do. Someone like me, who has some connections in the extra community and experience in finding people, can actually do more with phone calls and referrals.

But it took a lot of phone calls to get even a small bit of information about a werewolf, even for me. The FBI said they wanted to talk to him in connection with a wolfsbane smuggling ring, but I had my doubts about that. Not that wolfsbane smuggling wasn't a problem—it was, and New York was one of the places it came in—but the more people I talked to about this guy, the less it felt like a smuggling case. It felt more like he was part of the Teardown movement.

I wasn't surprised the FBI wasn't up front with me about that, if it was the case. For one thing, if they were going after a terrorist, it was often easier to get them on smaller charges, like the Al Capone-tax evasion thing. And for another, they knew I was dating an extra, so they'd be wary about sending me after someone with extras-rights ties. I was worried about what it would mean for me to help them find the guy, if that was the case, but the Teardown movement was big and it wasn't likely this was the guy in charge—it wasn't even likely there was one guy in charge—because the way the FBI built cases was by going after lower-level people and working their way up. Yeah, I was clinging to the very thin justification that they hadn't actually told me anything other than the wolfsbane story, and that I hadn't proven that he was an activist yet, but the money was so good, I had to at least try. My preliminary work had convinced me that I had a good chance of finding the guy.

On the TV I had live coverage of the protest march, and every so often I'd look up and try to pick my grey wolf's head out of the hundreds in the street. He'd be up near the front, I figured, but the cameras were too far and too shaky for me to ever be certain where he was.

I was composing my email to Agent Jefferson to move on to the next stage of the job, and I'd just typed the line, "Is it okay for me to tell my boyfriend that I'm working for the FBI," and had paused there to think about whether I was phrasing that right. Should I add "but of course no details"? Should I mention the NDA to show that I was aware of it and taking it into consideration?

Movement on the TV distracted me, and I looked up to see the march stalled, people milling around in confusion. Shit. I scrambled for the volume, staring at the people there to see if anyone was hurt. The thought that Chicago contained a lot of shitty bigots flashed through my mind, and then I got the volume up.

"—sounds like some kind of screeching. I can almost make

out words, but you have to stop and listen. Nobody seems to know where it's coming from specifically, but it's definitely from Wolftown."

The person talking wasn't on screen, as the cameras continued to cover the march, and then I saw Carla's thunderbird urging people forward. As the reporter paused, I heard what sounded like a female voice wailing. I turned the volume up to hear it better, but just then the reporter started talking over it again.

"We're trying to get someone from Wolftown on the line. The march organizers have confirmed that this is not associated with the march. I have Jamie here, who's an expert on extras. Jamie, what do you think could be causing this noise?"

I went to my living room window and opened it as Jamie said, "Well, even extras have big speakers, and it might be someone playing a punk song to encourage the march. But we can't rule out the possibility that it might be a siren."

The marchers weren't visible from my window anymore, and I couldn't hear the singing from where I was. If I remembered the route correctly, they were up on the northwest side of Wolftown, which meant it was coming from somewhere near there.

It was possible that someone had hooked up a mike to some powerful speakers on a roof at the edge of Wolftown and was blasting screams out into the city, sure, but there were a few extras who could project sound pretty well. Sirens, like Jamie had said, though the Chicago community was small compared to L.A. and New York, and there were definitely regulations about the levels where they could use their voice (these regulations did not apply in international waters, which was one reason the coastal cities were home to larger communities). Also, although the screeching did sound like singing, it wasn't particularly good singing, so it probably wasn't a siren.

The possibility that nagged at me was that it was a ghost. Ghosts could project like that, and that howling half-singing sure sounded like a new ghost, unbound and trying to make sense of its situation. They weren't usually *that* loud, but they could be.

I turned the ring on my finger that had held Sergei for five years. Then I texted my friend Yumi, a yuki-onna (Japanese snow spirit) who was a captain in Wolftown's internal peacekeeping force. She didn't respond right away, so I texted that if it was a ghost, I might be able to help, and a minute later a Google Maps pin popped up in reply with the message "no CPD."

The pin was at an address in Wolftown, on the far side from where I was. I stared at my computer, at the unfinished email to FBI Agent Jefferson, and then got up and walked out.

Outside, all that reached my poor dull human ears were the sounds of traffic: cars on my street and the drone of the expressway a half mile over. That soundtrack, interwoven with the murmurs and hustling of people on the sidewalks and punctuated by the occasional plane overhead, followed me down to 71st.

Chicago in late summer is prone to savage thunderstorms and brutal, punishing heat, with the lake contributing to air so humid it feels like fingers clinging to you as you walk through it. Along 71st, there was a brisk breeze, but very little shade apart from the occasional tree, many of which were barely taller than I was. By the time I got to the Visitor Center that led to the only entrance to Wolftown, my short-sleeved collared shirt was damp enough that the air conditioning felt icy.

Most of the people at the security checkpoint know me

from years of having to stop with Sergei to get screened. This time, I hadn't brought my gun (I rarely carry it), and the ring didn't register on the scanner without a ghost bound to it, so the guard waved me through without secondary screening. One metal door and two glass doors later, I stepped out into Kennelly Plaza, the first sight most people saw of Wolftown.

It's a medium-sized plaza by Chicago standards, about a hundred to a hundred and twenty feet around, with the wall and security entrance on one side and five streets radiating away from it like spokes of a wheel. The buildings facing the plaza are some of the oldest in Wolftown, but the old red brick and sandstone are kept clean—cleaner than the flagstones of the plaza, anyway, but what can you do with the places where tourists walk?

The plaza was cleaner this morning because tourists don't visit Wolftown as much in the height of summer, at least not from late morning to evening. The sun and humidity give the place a distinct aroma any time of year, but in summer it's more pronounced, a musky sharp smell that unkind people say reminds them of a zoo. It reminds me more of a park inside a city, except that it doesn't smell as much like a toilet.

Here in Kennelly Plaza, there weren't that many extras in their shifted forms, not as many as you'd think you'd see upon walking into Wolftown. There were a couple werewolves in their fur, wearing green vests bearing a pin with a picture of a camera and a green checkmark to indicate that you could take your picture with them (they would take the vests off for the actual picture), but nobody was taking them up on that offer currently.

The t-shirt sellers, food cart workers, and guides were all fully human-looking except one who was wolf-shifted, standing over a freezer with wheels and a sign on the side showing all the ice cream treats for sale. Several of the windows overlooking the plaza were open, and out of two, werewolves looked down, one sipping a Coke through a straw.

I hurried through the plaza, waving briefly to the young woman behind the churros food cart, a First Nations raven shifter named Carey. "On a job?" she called as I sped past, and I gave her a thumbs up in acknowledgment.

As I walked, I texted Yumi that I was in Wolftown and on my way. She sent back a thumbs up but no other details.

Still, I had to believe that my guess that it was a ghost was right, or she wouldn't have called me at all. I had the spell to bind the ghost on my phone, the ring where I'd kept Sergei to hold the ghost when it was bound, and I had my stories.

A dying person became a ghost if there was some kind of trauma holding them here, something so powerful that they wanted to wait around in this world to resolve it ("powerful," of course, was relative to the person; I read about one ghost who stuck around for five years until someone could find the last series 1 Star Wars card they needed to complete their collection). The problem was that without a living body to anchor them, they lost the ability to regulate their thoughts, and could go from terror to anger to rage quickly. Sergei had been a ghost for over a century, and he claimed not to remember whether he'd killed anyone as a ghost; these days, deaths from ghosts were rare because there were plenty of experts to handle them, but a century ago, they could kill a couple people before someone showed up to banish them.

I wasn't up to banishing, and these days that was considered cruel anyway, depending on who you asked. But I'd done a couple bindings already and was licensed to do them. Most importantly, Yumi knew and trusted me, and I would get there faster than calling the Bureau of Extranormal Affairs, who were legally responsible for new ghosts but also were famously slow to arrive to take charge of them.

A few blocks in from the plaza, I ran past wolves standing still with ears perked, looking in the direction I was hurrying. A block later, I heard the screeching in person for the first time and encountered others walking toward it as well. A crowd had gathered, moving in that direction, thick enough that I had to weave around and through them, taking care to avoid swinging tails.

The screeching grew so loud that I thought I must be almost there, but when I checked my phone, I was still several blocks away. Then I rounded a corner and saw the peacekeeper barricades set up and a thin crowd standing around them.

At the front of the barricade, after I'd pushed my way through the gawkers, a large brown wolf with black ear tips stood with his arms folded, surveying the crowd. None of them were leaning close enough to the barricades to warrant his direct attention, so when I came up to the wooden boards, his ears and yellow eyes snapped to focus on me. Peacekeepers weren't cops, but sometimes their hackles came up when they had to deal with humans.

"No entry," he said sharply.

I dug out my P.I. license. "I'm here by request of Captain Yumi Hachimura," I said.

His ears splayed and he narrowed his eyes. "Hold on." He got a small radio off his belt and flicked it on. "Vic for Hachimura," he said.

It took a minute or two for her to come onto the radio, while the ghost's screeching resolved into what sounded like a punk song she was screaming. I couldn't make out all the words from here; it sounded like I was standing outside a club where a very loud concert was going on. Beyond the barricade, in the street, two more peacekeepers, a werewolf and a kishi (a were-hyena), called to people to stay inside their homes. If peacekeepers were patrolling all the streets around this ghost, then the entire twelve-person force was here.

The radio crackled, and as the wolf lifted it to his head, Yumi snapped out a terse, "What?"

"I've got a, uh," the wolf motioned for my license again. "A Jae Kim, says you asked for him?"

She shouted her reply loudly enough that his ears flattened. "Let him the fuck in here."

"Right," he said, and clipped the radio back to his belt, then stepped back to get out of my way and bumped into one of the sawhorses. He turned quickly to grab it before it fell. "Uh, you can go in."

"Thanks." I walked through the space he'd left for me.

The street, echoing with the unearthly screechy singing and empty except for the officer, felt like stepping into the early minutes of a horror movie. My arm hairs prickled for the first time; I didn't think I should be walking toward this sound. But Yumi was counting on me, and maybe so was this ghost.

When I came up to the house where this was happening, Yumi was waiting outside, a rail-thin woman nearly a foot taller than me with a pale white complexion and straight black hair past her shoulders. The house looked similar to the other houses on the block, but a sign in the front window read, "Unified Society Alliance" in block letters.

"Thanks for getting in touch," she said as I walked up. "You got stuff to bind a ghost with?"

"Yeah," I said. The screeching was still indistinct, though now I could make out some words: "plastic face" and "rotten." The rest was incomprehensible. "What's the story?"

"No idea." Yumi had a tablet in one hand and typed my name into it, then checked the time and added it. "Started screaming an hour ago, maybe less. How did you hear about it?"

"It was on TV," I said. "The march just went by on the other side of the wall."

"Well, thank frost for that, because I'm not sure I'd have thought to call you." Her face relaxed. "I've been here half an hour and the best we can do is keep people out. We haven't found a body, but we haven't really looked hard because— well, you'll see when you go inside. Rather, you'll hear."

"I can hear it now."

"Yeah. It's worse inside." She drew her blue jacket around herself. "I'll stay human as long as I can when we get in there. If I need a break, I'll go snow, but it'll only be for a minute."

"Does it hurt to go snow when it's ninety degrees out?"

She gave me a baleful look. "If you bind the ghost, I'll buy you a drink and you can ask all about my seasonal affective disorder. First things first. You got everything?"

"You already asked me that." I showed her the ring and then took out my phone. "The spell's here. And the story..." I took a breath. "I'm going to have to listen."

"Won't have a problem with that." She squared her shoulders. "Come on."

I followed her up the stairs to the front door. She paused there a moment, then took a breath and pushed it open.

CHAPTER
THREE

The noise assaulted me as soon as the door opened, the screaming physically pulsing against my eardrums. Reflexively, I put hands over my ears, followed Yumi into the house, and shut the door behind us.

We stood in what had likely once been a living room, now repurposed as a welcome/meeting room. A big "Unified Society Alliance" poster hung on one wall over a table where a bunch of brochures lay in some disarray, as though they'd been in stacks before someone jarred the table. On another wall hung a corkboard with a collage of photos familiar to any activist organization: bright, happy, mostly young people smiling for the camera in front of a sign at various rallies; the same people sitting on the floor in an office; one middle-aged person shaking hands with a man in a blue blazer and power tie. Dates and small descriptions accompanied each photo, but I didn't examine them more closely.

The noise was distressing, but I understood what Yumi had meant: it wasn't just the volume. Here, close to the ghost, the anguish in the screaming gripped me. Its rawness and lack of focus confirmed that this was probably a recent ghost, someone who'd died overnight or this morning and "awoken" in a disembodied state with nothing to grasp but the visceral emotion that had kept them here. Left unchecked, they'd soon be able to lash out at people psychically, which was often more dangerous than throwing physical objects around.

I'd had practice with ghosts, so the waves of emotion were something I knew how to deal with. Yumi was having a harder time, her hands over her ears like mine, her white face creased in pain and eyes squinched shut, now looking like the central figure in Munch's Scream. I tapped her shoulder to get her to look at me. "Go ahead and snow," I yelled over the screams. "I got this."

She nodded, grateful, and a moment later her body was a flurry of snow, a small white whirlwind hovering in place. But she stayed in the room with me, which was nice of her, and not only because it dropped the room temperature by ten or fifteen degrees. I turned my attention to the words the ghost was screaming.

Though much louder, I could make out more of them now. "YOU SHOW THE WORLD YOUR PLASTIC FACE BUT UNDER-NEATH IT'S ROTTEN," beat, then: "YOU HANG ON TIGHT TO THAT BRIEFCASE BUT WHAT HAVE YOU FORGOTTEN."

"Hello?" I called out tentatively, to no effect at all.

"YOU CLIMB THE FUCKIN LADDER WHILE THE ONES BENEATH YOU SMOTHER," she screamed. "AND I'M SO FUCKIN' MADDER I'LL NEVER CALL YOU MOTHER."

Mother. There was something to latch onto. If the ghost wasn't going to talk to me, that was all I was going to have to go on. I got my phone out and called up the binding spell.

Binding a newly-released ghost is easier than binding one that's been around for a while. Not only have they not had time to learn the kinds of tricks ghosts can get up to—emotional manipulation, tossing furniture around, possession—they're also confused and inclined to reach for any kind of support they can muster.

That's what the binding spell does. It offers them stability and support. But the caster has to supplement that with an actual emotional hook, something the ghost can relate to as well. There are some ghost binders who are professional actors, good enough at improvising that they can craft stories to match a ghost's trauma almost on the fly, even if they've gone in with no prior knowledge of it.

I'm not an expert, but give me a little preparation and I can come up with something. Most traumas deep enough to keep a ghost here are going to be related to parents, romantic partners, or kids, the people in our lives we feel closest to. I don't have kids, but I've got the rest covered: guilt over leaving my partner five years ago, the horrors of the war that orphaned him, a father who left when I was seven and died overseas.

And of course, I've got Mom.

The last time I'd tried a binding, with Richard, I'd drawn on our shared war trauma. I wouldn't have anything quite so visceral or precisely targeted this time, but that wasn't usually necessary with new ghosts. You wanted something steady and comforting, but with enough tension in it to get them to trust you and go with you. They were going to be confused, but the story in the binding spell gave them something else to think about for a bit, and most of the time, they'd clutch onto it.

As I spoke the words of the spell, I built the story in my head. I was fourteen, and around me was the living room of the Seattle home I'd grown up in. I remembered the wallpaper, the vertical red stripes on the cream colored background, the Korean flag on one wall, the grandfather clock that my mother thought was elegant even though it never kept the correct time. There was the tear in the wallpaper that I'd made when I was five, the stain on the ceiling that was too small to be worth painting over, the corner where the carpet hadn't quite been fitted properly. The scene had the quality of a dream, one of the real-seeming ones that lingers for a few moments after you wake up, making you startle out of bed to escape the mortar attack your dream warned you about. The reality was only a veneer, but holding it, believing it, was critical.

My mother stood there, holding an oven mitt, looking the way she looked then, strong in my memory: about the age I am now, her black hair not streaked with grey, her face clear and smooth, but those same red plastic-framed glasses perched on her nose. "That's right," she was saying, "everyone has the right to live in the world."

I stood in the doorway of our old living room, my heart beating. I knew that she believed what she'd said. I'd also heard what she'd said over the years about extras, calling them "monsters," even when she was saying, "I'm sure they're not all monsters." I knew she wouldn't react well to me asking to go visit my new classmate, but I had to ask her.

(Years later, telling this story in college, a white friend of mine asked, "Why didn't you just go without asking?" and let me tell you, I didn't even know how to answer that question.)

It was into this tension-filled space that I made room for the ghost, stepping to one side and looking at the doorway to see who appeared.

In the background, the ghost's screaming died away. Echoes remained, but maybe they were just in my head; when that's where the spell was being cast, it was sometimes hard to tell the difference. And in the doorway, an image appeared, faint at first and then clearer, as if it were being projected onto smoke that was gradually thickening.

The figure was shorter than me, white, with mousy brown straight hair past the shoulders and a large vintage Kurt

Cobain t-shirt over distressed jeans. Bracelets on both wrists, thin gold things, and a necklace with some kind of pendant. She was skinny, with a young face, brown eyes and a serious straight-lipped mouth with lipstick. Based on that and the singing/screaming voice, I thought of her as female. Subject to change with further information, of course.

"What's happening?" Her speaking voice sounded almost nothing like her singing voice. A Chicago accent pulled the "a" out of its usual alignment, like "hyeahppening."

"I'm glad you're here," I said. "I need your help."

"I don't understand." She looked around. "I was...I think I was having a bad dream. Am I still dreaming?"

Best not to engage with that. Dreams didn't usually explain that they were dreams, and I wanted her to focus on what she and I had in common. "It's my mother," I said. "She claims that she supports everyone's right to exist."

"I do," Mom said, diverging from my memory to say what I believed she would've said. "We came here from Korea and made a life for ourselves."

"But," I told the ghost, "I don't think she'll let me go visit my new school friend. He's an extra and she can't look past that. Can you help me convince her?"

"I..." She still looked uncertain.

"What's your name?"

"P-Penny."

"Hi, Penny," I said. "I'm Jae."

I waited. Her eyes jumped around and then met mine. Her features settled. "Hi, Jae."

"My mom hates extras," I told her.

"I don't hate extras," Mom protested. This was a line she'd actually said to me, along with what came after. "They're very happy living in the zoo, and I don't see why they want to come out and mix with humans."

"Zoo?" Penny's brow creased.

"Thirty years ago," I explained, "there was a scare. A terrorist who wanted the walls torn down blew up a government building."

"In California," she said, her eyes clearing. "The Ontario something. I learned about that."

"That's the one. Then for a while, some people called the Wolftowns 'zoos,' until it stopped being okay again."

"Political correctness run amok," Mom said dismissively. "It's just a name. You know what people called me when I was growing up?"

She would stop using the term sometime around when I went to college, at least in front of me. "But Mom," I said, "Andy's really nice. His family just moved up here from L.A. and he doesn't know anyone. We got paired up in biology and he likes Real World too."

"Where does he live?"

I turned to Penny. "This is the problem," I said. "I can't lie to Mom. But if I tell her he lives in Wolftown, she won't let me go."

She reacted the way I'd hoped she would: with sympathetic anger. "Lie to her," she said roughly. "My mom's the same way. She says she wants to help people, but she doesn't do shit about it beyond what she has to."

What she has to indicated that her mother was in some kind of service job; I filed that away. "So what should I do?" I asked.

"Just go. Leave. Don't ask her." Penny's face was set. "She'll try to stop you, but she can't stop you forever."

"Jae wouldn't dare go anywhere without my permission," Mom said. "He's a very good boy."

That was true, once. I extended a hand to Penny. "I don't think I can do it alone," I said. My heart sped up a little. The last time I'd done this had been with Richard. "Will you come with me? Will you help me?"

"I..." She looked wary, for the first time looking around here. "Where is this? Where am I?"

"You're in a safe place," I said. "And I need your help with my mother. You can help with that, right? Your mother's the same way. You know what I'm going through."

"I do, yeah." The wariness flickered, uncertainty behind it. If I'd woven the spell well enough, she'd feel the outside as a scary, chaotic mess and would want to come inside with me. If I hadn't, well, she would lash out, and that could hurt, but I didn't think she had the experience to possess me; she'd probably just break the spell. But she related to my struggle, that was clear, so even with what little information I had, I'd made a good scenario. The Korean mom was probably a little too unfamiliar, but without knowing her race, I couldn't have made it any better.

Penny took a step forward into the room and then took my hand. Here in the spell world it felt solid and real, and that was enough. *Come with me*, I offered, and she came along as I completed the spell. My mother melted away, along with our living room, but Penny's presence stayed firm and strong next to me. Once again I was standing in the main room of the Unified Society Alliance, a small snowstorm spinning in the air next to me.

"It's done," I said, turning the ring on my finger.

I wasn't sure how well Yumi could hear me in her snow form, but at any rate the snow gathered itself and then fell away around the shape of Yumi in her uniform.

Wha—what's going on? Penny asked in my head. *I see the living room, but it doesn't feel right. I can't move my arms.*

Having a ghost bound to you and talking to you is a strange sensation, but I'd had Sergei as a partner for five years, so I was used to it. Their presence is like when there's someone right behind you and you know they're there, but you can't see or hear them. You just *know*. And when they talk to you, the voice comes into your head like you're wearing earbuds, only you can't shut it out by putting fingers in your ears (which didn't stop me from doing that theatrically when Sergei was being annoying). But the voice also comes with background noise, images and feelings that swim into your mind, and that can be disorienting if you're not used to someone else's thoughts butting up into yours. I hadn't had to deal with it in five months, and it was a little unsettling going back to it.

"What happened?" Yumi asked.

I held up a finger for Yumi, and answered Penny first. *You're a ghost*, I told her, as gently as I could. *You died, probably recently, and when someone dies with something weighing on their mind, they stick around and become—*

I know what a ghost is, she snapped. *Fuck! I can't be dead. I've got to—*

I waited, but she didn't elaborate. *What do you have to do?* I asked.

None of your business. Was that really you in that dream? Oh shit, it was. And that was your mom.

I had no idea if she'd already accepted her death or was never going to, and I wasn't a therapist, so the best I could do was roll with whatever she was feeling. *Hey*, I said, *you're going to be okay. You're safe with me.*

And who the hell are you? The question brought up images of me chasing people through Wolftown, serving process papers. *Oh shit*, she said, *you're a cop.*

Okay, you know what ghosts are, so you know that we need to have boundaries. I'm not going to go poking around in your mind, and you don't go poking into mine.

You bound me, so why shouldn't I poke around in your mind a bit, huh? That's right, isn't it? That's why I can talk to you, because you bound me?

Yumi's radio crackled, and she walked into an adjacent room to answer it. I stayed put and talked to Penny. *That's right. But if you do go into my mind like that, you expose yours as well. It's like we're sharing a small apartment, and we can talk through a doorway, but if you make that doorway bigger to look at my side, I can also see your side. So if you want me to know all your secrets, go right ahead. I already got a picture of an older woman. Is that your mom?*

Silence.

You'll figure out how to manifest, I said, *and there are some electronics you can affect. I can help with some of that.*

I know people who can help, she snapped. *I don't need a cop. As soon as you can get me to my friends, they'll take care of me.*

I'm not a cop, I said. *And legally I can't take you to your friends. It has to be a relative, next of kin ideally.*

You sound like a cop. You're here with a cop.

I'm a private investigator. And Yumi's a peacekeeper, not a cop.

Yumi returned. "Jae," she said, "does the ghost know where its body is?"

"Her name's Penny." *Do you?* I asked, noting that she didn't correct my pronoun use.

She didn't reply. *We're pretty sure it's in this house,* I said. *If you tell us where it might be, then we won't have to go look for it.* When that didn't get a response out of her, I added, *If you tell me, I can tell Yumi, and then she'll go confirm and you won't have to see your own body.*

Or else what? Or else you'll go through the house and make me look at it?

I understood her anger and responded calmly. *I won't do that.*

Well, I'm not interested in helping out the cops. So she can just search all the rooms until she finds me.

I shook my head to Yumi. "She doesn't like cops. She won't tell me where her body might be. But it's probably in this house."

"Is she an extra?"

Are you—

No.

"No."

"Can't she manifest and tell me herself?"

"She doesn't like cops, like I said, and she doesn't how to manifest yet. She's only been a ghost for a couple hours."

"I'm not a cop."

"I know that. But I don't think she cares about the difference."

Penny's silence either confirmed my suspicion or indicated that she wasn't listening anymore. Yumi tossed her head with an exclamation of disgust. "We try to separate ourselves from the CPD, but people still don't fucking trust us. We're extras! And every time the CPD fucks up with an extra outside the walls, people come and yell at us."

"I'm not a cop either," I said, partly for Penny's benefit.

"All right, take her outside, and I'll have a team search the house. They've been talking to the other people who lived here, so maybe they'll have an identity for me by now."

Nobody else lived here, Penny said.

"She says nobody else lived here."

Yumi looked around the room again. "I wasn't sure about that. Worked here, then. Ask her why she was living here."

I did, and got silence. "She's not saying."

"Cheh. All right, I'm going to go look for a dead body, and you try to get that ghost to talk." Yumi smiled at me, showing blue crystalline teeth. "I think I have the easier job."

"No argument." I nodded to her. "I'll go outside and wait. Maybe if we're not in the house where she died, it'll be easier for her to talk."

It won't be, she told me, and I could feel the confusion and fear she was holding back. Dying was bad enough, what with losing your body and needing to be bound to keep your mind together. Worse than that, the part I wasn't sure Penny had quite yet grasped, was that as a ghost she was no longer considered a person. She was legally something more like a pet, with a few laws against cruel mistreatment that were rarely invoked, and a legal requirement to be bound to some-one. When I'd acquired Sergei, he was already familiar with this status, and though he'd complained about it from time to time, he'd been resigned to it. I was going to have to remind Penny that she was no longer considered an autonomous person, and I didn't know what words to use to even start that conversation. But I walked outside anyway.

The house hadn't been air conditioned, but it had been cooler than outside even before Yumi had chilled it, so coming back out into the heat and daylight was a little bit of a shock. "Oof," I said aloud as the heat crawled over my skin, and scanned the empty street.

At the end of the block there was some activity: two peace-keepers walking toward me. One was the brown wolf from the barricade, Vic, I think his name was. As they neared the house, a few un-uniformed people (two wolves and a human-looking one) straggled in behind them, peering down the street but keeping their distance.

If you know how ghosts work, I told Penny, *then you know that I have to find your next of kin and turn you over to their custody. The faster you tell me how to find them, the quicker you can be done with me.*

I'd hoped that getting away from me would be a good

motivator, but she remained silent. I could feel her presence the same way I'd felt Sergei's, and I was surprised at how much relief I felt to have another ghost as company in my mind, even silent. Sergei had been with me for five years, and after his departure, I found myself talking to him anyway, reaching for the space adjacent to my mind that he'd formerly occupied. I tried playing chess against myself, doing Sergei's voice for the other side's moves, but that felt so hollow that after four moves I swept the pieces into their box and hadn't taken them out since.

Gradually I'd gotten used to the emptiness, which is how I'd lived for thirty-some years before I got Sergei anyway. Life, like flesh, re-forms around wounds and leaves only scars to remember them by.

It's not permanent, I told myself. She's going to her family soon enough. But that made me think of Richard, and whatever the hell I was going to do there.

I saw that image of the older woman again at the same time as Penny spoke. *Who's Richard?*

Who's that woman? Is it your mother?

I felt rather than heard her frustrated exclamation. So I said, *I'll tell you about Richard if you tell me about her.*

That's not a fair trade.

How do you know?

Because nobody's threatening to send you off to be looked after by Richard, are they?

All right, I said. *You don't have to tell me her name or your name or anything, just tell me what happened between you.*

My negotiating skills were pretty good, but not good enough to deal with a stubborn teenager, I guess. There was no response, nor did I get any more images from her. All right. I turned toward the street and found myself nose to nose with the wolf from the barricade. Not actually nose to nose, because he was half a foot taller than me, but anyway he was right there. "Hey," he said. "What happened to the ghost?"

"I bound her." I held up my hand.

His ears went back. "You?"

"Yeah." I stood a little straighter.

He reached up to scratch behind his ears, which did not come back up. "Huh. Then who's this other guy?"

"What other guy?"

He turned back to the end of the street, where the other wolf now stood with a man in a dark blue suit and tie that made me sweat just looking at it. I couldn't make out the man's features at this distance, but he had dark hair and his whole stance screamed "professional asshole," the kind of guy that makes your spine stiffen with just a look because you're sure he's going to say something annoying. He was talking to the grey wolf standing with him, and though I couldn't hear them, I felt instinctively that he was asking to talk to the manager.

"Look, when Captain Hachimura said she called you, I figured you were gonna handle it. But then this guy shows up from the BEA and insists—"

I missed the rest of what he said, because Penny shouted into my head, *NO! NOT THE BEA! GET OUT OF HERE.*

"Sorry," I said, one hand to my head. It had been a long time since a ghost had shouted at me. "Vic, right? Can't you just tell him to go away? It's been dealt with."

"I guess." He scratched his ears again. "I told him someone else was here, and then he said he had to inspect the scene anyway. Are you sure you got the ghost?"

"Do you hear it anymore?"

His ears went up and now he looked relieved. "No. But maybe it just calmed down."

"Ghosts don't usually 'just calm down,'" I told him.

"I know." He looked annoyed.

WHY ARE YOU STILL STANDING HERE?

I've got this under control. I've dealt with the government before.

I'm a teenage girl ghost, she said.

I know.

THE BEA SELLS TEENAGE GIRLS TO RUSSIAN BILLIONAIRES.

I winced. Vic frowned. "You okay?"

"Yeah," I said. "Look, can you tell Captain Hachimura that I went home and I'll follow up with her later? I've got a real bad headache."

"The guy's right there," he said. "Just explain you took care of the ghost and then he'll go home."

"Right there" was no longer the end of the street; the guy and the grey wolf were halfway down it toward us. I half-turned to face them, and Vic turned with me, standing at my side. I had no illusion that that meant he was actually *on* my side.

Penny's volume ascended toward the levels it had had when I'd first heard her. *GO! GO GO GO!*

Jesus Christ, calm down, I said. *I'm not going to hand you over to him. I just need to explain that, and then we'll get out of here.*

NO—

But I can't do that, I interrupted over her yell, *if you're screaming in my head the whole time. Quiet down and let me handle this.*

Don't tell me to calm down and be quiet, she snapped at a more reasonable volume. *That's how men have been silencing women for centuries.*

You can talk to me, I said. *Just don't scream. If I'm not handling it right, tell me. Okay?*

There was a beat, and then she said, *Fine.*

CHAPTER
FOUR

U p close, the Fed brought back other memories for me. He was probably six-foot two or so, taller than me and the grey wolf escorting him, and his short black hair stayed unruffled in the breezes that swirled through the street. He wore blue glass sunglasses—Oakleys, I saw now that he was closer—over a mustache and goatee that looked like he was trying to be cool ten years ago. The suit he wore was only remarkable in that it was a dark East Coast suit in a Chicago summer, but it looked neatly tailored, and the tie, red with black diamonds on it, felt like a standard-issue government tie.

He looked exactly like the guys in college whose parents were paying their full tuition, who didn't have to work at their classes because their family would have a job waiting for them when they graduated. That's unfair, I told myself. Maybe he's a government lifer, or maybe he's one of the exceptions to the usual morass of nepotism and incompetence that swirls around in the BEA.

Then he opened his mouth.

"Hi there," he said, addressing Vic. "I presume you let Ms. Hachimura know I'm here."

The brown wolf's ears twitched and went back a centimeter, just about the amount Czoltan's go back when he can't control his annoyance but is trying to. "I think Captain Hachimura is still inside. I was talking to Mr. Kim here."

The agent sighed, a little too dramatically. "All right, I'll just go inside, then." And he turned, still without looking at me, and took a step toward the door.

I wanted him to go inside so I could leave, so I kept my mouth shut. But Vic, trying to be helpful maybe, said, "You don't have to. Mr. Kim here bound the ghost already."

My stomach sank as the guy stopped. He didn't turn right away; he stopped like a guy in a movie hearing something shocking. Then he did the slow turn and lowered his sunglasses to really look at me for the first time. He probably thought that was intimidating somehow, like he was deigning to notice me and I should be impressed with how much he didn't need to pay attention to me, but I just found it really fucking annoying.

"Mr....Kim?"

"Hi," I said, pushing back the bright-hot anger coming from Penny. "Jae Kim. And you are...?"

He took a step back toward me. "On whose authority did you bind the ghost?"

"Captain Hachimura is the officer in charge and she requested my assistance. I provided it." I tried to make my emphasis on "in charge" not subtle at all.

The agent stopped in front of me, sunglasses back in place, and looked down at me. "I'm sure that was very neighborly of you," he said. "But the BEA is here now, so you can hand over the ghost."

Don't!

Don't worry, I told Penny. I hadn't believed her story about government agents selling teenage girl ghosts, but this guy was making it seem more credible.

"It's no trouble," I said. "Captain Hachimura is going to identify the ghost and then I'll turn it over to its nearest living relative, as is the law."

He frowned. "I know how you people work," he said. "All 'I know the law' and then you turn around and sell the ghost to a dealer who can give you a fake document of relationship."

"I'm not—"

"Jesus Christ, it's so exhausting, too. Every time we arrest one of you, two more pop up. Your dealers are worse. Just hand over the damn ghost and don't make me go through the paperwork."

"First of all," I said, digging in my pocket, "I don't know who you think I am, but I'm a private investigator." He got tense, so I picked out my wallet carefully and showed it to him —Christ, he really thought he was an action hero, like I was going to pull a gun on him in front of the two werewolves— and pulled out my license. "See?"

He peered at it and then straightened. Before he could say anything, I went on. "Second, you want to provide some iden-tification to me so I know you're not what you're accusing me of?"

Vic looked confused as the agent dug for his ID in his jacket pocket. "What is he accusing you of?"

"Ghost chasers," I said. "Like ambulance chasers, but worse. They hang around and bind newly-released ghosts and sell them to people who want ghosts."

"Shit. That's for real?"

"Sure. There's a big black market in ghosts. Problem is, you can't always tell when someone's death is going to make them a ghost, so they usually hang out near wars, hospitals, places like that." I side-eyed the agent. "If the BEA always showed up this quickly, they'd be out of business."

The guy didn't show any sign of having heard my jibe as he folded back his badge holder and showed me the card with his picture and the name "Rock Zawada" under the heading "Bureau of Extranormal Affairs." It looked legit to me.

"Shit," said Vic. "Fucking ghouls."

"Ghouls are something else," Agent Zawada said. "Regardless, you don't have authority to take possession of this ghost now that the BEA is on site. Please hand her over."

I swear to God if you give me to him I'll scream so loud—

Don't worry, I told Penny again. *He's trying to intimidate me, but I know the law.* To Zawada, I said, "The BEA has jurisdiction over unbound ghosts when it arrives at a scene. But this ghost isn't unbound. Federal law says that the person who binds a ghost has the right and responsibility to deliver it to the next of kin, and that's what I'm doing."

Vic turned and talked into his radio in a low voice. Zawada took off his sunglasses, his brown eyes fixed on me. My skin chilled a bit. The problem with guys who think they're action heroes is that to them, you're either a bystander or a villain, and they tend to gravitate to action-hero-type solutions to conflict, which are big and flashy and often violent. I felt like I was being pushed into the "villain" category. "While that's the letter of the law," he said slowly, "the BEA retains ultimate authority over ghosts, and I can take her from you."

He can't, I told Penny quickly, though I wasn't entirely sure about that.

"So why don't you save me the trouble and just hand her over?" he went on.

"Funny thing," I said. "Whenever someone asks me to 'save them the trouble,' it turns out that the 'trouble' they're talking about is something they can't actually do. So no, I don't think I will 'save you the trouble,' Agent Zawada. If you want this ghost, I'll give you the number of my lawyer, and you can negotiate with him."

In my head, Penny's anger and fear settled. That allowed me to take a breath and calm myself further.

Zawada didn't say anything for a moment. He looked baffled that I hadn't just done what he asked. I waited while he composed himself, and then he said, "I'm recommending this for your own protection. Handling ghosts can be a dangerous business. Often in ways you don't anticipate."

"I had a ghost partner for five years," I told him. "I think I can handle myself. But thanks for the warning."

"Show me your license again."

He held up his phone while I got my wallet out and snapped a picture when I held it up. I didn't like it, but there was no way to stop him; I have to show the license when asked, and he can take a picture of it for his records. If I wanted to be a dick, I would've asked to take a picture of his badge, but I remembered the name and that was all I needed.

The door of the house opened just as Zawada lowered his phone, and Yumi came out. She stopped on the front porch and assessed the situation, then walked to Vic and nodded a head toward Zawada. "Vic, who's this?"

"I'm Agent Rock Zawada of the BEA." He put on a smile and strode toward her, hand out. "You must be Ms. Hachimura."

"I'm Captain Hachimura, yes." She took his hand, shook it once, and then released it. "What's the BEA doing here?"

"We got a call that there was an unbound ghost in the area, and we're just coming down to see if we can be of any assistance. I'm the local ghost expert, so the office sent me over."

Yumi nodded. She glanced at me and then returned her

attention to Rock. "Pretty quick. Who called you? Was it one of my officers?"

"You know," he said, still smiling, "I don't know. Ginny back at the office took the call. I can find out for you, though. I just got over here as fast as I could. I know unbound ghosts can be quite a handful, and even well-meaning amateurs can find themselves in over their heads pretty quickly."

"Fortunately," Yumi said, "Mr. Kim here is a professional, so you don't have anything to worry about on that score."

"Hundred percent," Zawada said. "And I'm so grateful he was able to bind the ghost. But the BEA has the top facilities in the country for handling ghosts, so she'll be taken care of better with us than anywhere else. If you could just let Mr. Kim here know that it's okay to turn the ghost over to me."

One of the nice things about Yumi is that she has a pretty good bullshit detector. She didn't even have to check with me again. "I trust Mr. Kim's judgment," she said. "So if he wants to take charge of the ghost, I'm inclined to let him."

Vic and Grey Wolf looked at each other, Grey Wolf looking a little more confused by that statement than Vic, who already didn't like Zawada. Zawada didn't let his smile flicker even a little bit. "But—"

"Agent...Zawada, was it?" Yumi interrupted. "I'd really like to know who called you to this site. Because you know the federal government has to contact the peacekeepers before undertaking any action here. As the head of the peacekeepers, I can confidently say that no such contact was made."

Now the smile looked plastic, still frozen and fixed. "Under the Emergency Provision, federal services are authorized to operate inside the walls without consultation."

"Oh!" Vic said, stepping forward. "Actually, a couple years ago the courts restricted use of the Emergency Provision to cases where the Wolftown authorities are incapacitated.

Remember Hurricane Loni, when FEMA tried to evacuate the Miami Wolftown? What was it, like '08 or '09?"

Yumi kept her eyes on Zawada. "In any event, I'd hardly consider one unbound ghost an 'emergency.' In fact, if you will recall, we had two unbound ghosts at the same time three years ago, and the BEA didn't even show up for that. So unless you want to tell me why this one ghost constitutes an emergency, I think we'll call this situation handled. Mr. Kim is more than capable of locating the ghost's family. If he needs any help, he knows who to call."

"Rock Zawada of the BEA," I said.

He turned to me, and now the smile showed teeth. His demeanor slipped for a moment. "You two have no idea what you're dealing with. Just give me the fucking ghost already," he said, in a sharp tone loud enough to make me take a half-step back, and Vic a half-step forward.

"I don't think you wanna threaten Mr. Kim," the werewolf said. "Or Captain Hachimura."

"Vic," Yumi said quietly, and the werewolf's hackles went down, but he didn't back off.

For a moment Rock just stared, and I could see him wrestling with what to say next. All I could think was that he hadn't expected to have his authority challenged, but it was clear that Penny was important to him for a reason he wasn't willing to divulge to anyone, and he was sorting through his remaining strategies. His smile relaxed, and that worried me because it looked like he thought he'd figured out his next move. "Fine," he said. "When you need help, I hope you'll remember that the BEA has many resources available that can make your life easier."

"I'm well aware," I said. "Do you have a card or should I just call the BEA and ask for the Rock?"

He slipped his hand into an inside jacket pocket and out

again with a card so quickly it felt like a sleight of hand trick. "Here," he said. "But asking for Rock will work too."

I took the card and put it into my pants pocket. "Thanks for arriving so quickly, Agent," I said. "You don't have to share, of course, but it would be helpful if you told me what you know about what I'm 'dealing with.'"

But his plastic demeanor was back. "It was causing a commotion audible outside the walls."

"Of course," I said. "Everyone heard that. Thanks for your help, agent. I hope I won't have to call on you."

"Oh, I'm sure our paths will cross again." He looked around at everyone else present and seemed to clock that there weren't any allies for him here. "Mr. Kim, I expect you will call me when the ghost is in custody of its family. Just so I can close the report on this one."

I didn't want to, but at that point it would be out of my hands. "Sure."

"And feel free to call if you find yourself in trouble."

"With the ghost?"

"Any kind of trouble. There's all kinds of trouble a lone private investigator could find himself in." He flashed another smile, a tight, angry one, and then took out his phone and started typing on it as he turned and walked away.

The four of us waited until he was at the end of the street, where a few other pedestrians were now wandering around, and then Vic said, "What a dick."

Yumi shook her head. "Just a typical government dick, not like an extra dick."

"I dunno," I said slowly. *Penny, did you know him at all?*

"What do you mean?" Yumi asked.

No.

"First of all, he kept telling me I could end up 'in trouble.' Felt like a threat."

49

"If he was going to threaten you," Yumi said, "why didn't he just arrest you?"

"Would you have let him?"

"No."

"That's probably why, then. You'd already challenged his authority. But there's another thing that bothers me. Before you came out, when he was talking to me about Penny, he referred to her as 'her.' Later, when I asked whether he knew anything about the ghost, he went back to 'it.' I only called Penny 'it' the whole time I was talking to him. I was very careful about that."

Gee, thanks.

It was to avoid giving you away, I told her.

I know. I'm just... There was a raw edge to her voice as it trailed off.

"Her voice sounded female," Yumi said. "That doesn't mean he knows something."

"Not on its own. But how'd he get down here so fast?"

"The BEA has an office in Wolftown," Yumi said. "But he didn't look like someone who works out of that office. It's mostly accountants and bureaucrats. And anyway, it's over by Kennelly. Could you hear the screaming there?"

Singing, Penny objected, but flatly.

"No. But maybe he saw the TV report, same as I did, and came down right away..."

"He said someone called," Yumi reminded me.

I shook my head. "It's all plausible, but it feels hinky, doesn't it?"

Grey Wolf wasn't sure, but Yumi said, "Yeah," and Vic nodded. "All right," Yumi said, "Vic, you escort Mr. Kim out of Wolftown. I'm going to go back to searching the house. I didn't find anything yet, but I'd only barely gotten to the second floor."

No chance you want to tell Yumi where to look? I asked.

No reply. "All right," I said. "I'll get her home. By the time I get back, maybe you'll have found a name or something."

"Thanks for coming around, Jae," Yumi said. "I appreciate it, and that ghost will appreciate it too, even if she doesn't know it yet."

As I set off down the street, the only acknowledgment Penny gave that she'd heard that remark was a low, sarcastic snort.

FIVE

Vic walked along with me down the street, where people were starting to filter back in now that they'd opened the barricades. We'd only gotten a block before Penny said, *Shit.*

What? You did know him?

No. But...I'm dead. I mean...I'm dead.

Delayed reaction to trauma was something I was used to from the Army, especially when there was a situation that required their attention before they could afford space to process their trauma. Penny had been bound and then almost immediately, the BEA guy showed up to take over her brainspace. Now he was gone, and as she relaxed, she was assessing her situation and starting to process it. *Do you remember how it happened?* I asked gently.

I thought I'd wake up this morning and go see my friends, and... I'm never going to see them again, am I? They're probably at Starbucks right now.

You can still see them, I assured her, trying to help.

"You okay?" Vic asked, and I realized I'd slowed down.

"Yeah, I'm just talking to her. To the ghost."

I'm never going to have a latte again. I'll never have a blueberry scone. My friends are wondering what happened to me and I'll never be able to tell them. David's going to... She didn't finish the thought, but I caught a brief flash of a young-looking werewolf and a confusion of emotions.

I felt wildly unprepared to counsel a newly-dead person on their change to ghosthood. I didn't even know if those were the right words to use. *This is just a change,* I said, working to block the bleed over of thoughts and emotions. *In time you'll be able to manifest and talk to people.* But as soon as I said that, those words felt like they were brushing off the problem. She was *dead*. I thought about what that would mean as I passed the barricade and walked back out into the Wolftown street, trailing Vic's swaying brown tail.

He did keep glancing back to check that I was following him as we walked into larger crowds. *I was going to help people,* Penny said, her voice fading in and out now. *It's over. I'm over.*

You can still help people. The fading of her voice spiked my adrenaline, sped up my footsteps as though I could save her if I could get home quickly. How was I supposed to comfort someone who'd just died? Sergei had been dead for a century; he'd come to terms with it. Even Richard had been dead for months before I talked to him. *Listen,* I said, *this sucks. It's awful.*

Can we go to the Starbucks? she asked. *I just want to see them.*

Sure, I said. *I can pass on a message from you if you want.*

No. I don't want to see them. I can't. I can't deal with that. A moment later, she asked, *Is it possible that I could just be in a coma? Is there some way that people's spirits can leave their bodies and go back?*

The people around me felt less substantial than the ghost in my head, at least for the moment. They were physical obstacles to navigate around, but Penny was real. *I don't know of anything like that,* I said. *I'm so sorry.*

"Still doing okay?" Vic turned to ask.

"Yeah. I mean, no, but I'm fine. Thanks for helping clear a path."

He dropped back to walk at my side. "I'm glad you got the ghost and not that guy."

You're not an expert, though, right? Penny said. *So that could happen, maybe? They didn't find me yet. Maybe I'm just in a coma.*

I'll look it up when I get home, I said. *But I've never heard of that happening.*

Go back! Tell that cop that I'm in the last room at the end of the second floor hall! They have to get me to a hospital!

I got out my phone and texted Yumi this information, but I kept walking. *You're safer with me,* I said. *When Yumi finds you, I'm sure she'll let me know.*

Vic moved ahead of me again when I stopped talking to him. I followed his tail across a street, trusting him to get us back to the entrance. *This isn't fair,* Penny complained in my head.

No, I agreed, *it's not. Do you remember what you were doing last night? How this might have happened to you?*

She was quiet for a moment. I looked around and saw that we were a few blocks from the plaza. Vic's tail was a few feet ahead of me now. *Forget the Starbucks,* she said. *I need to see another friend of mine.*

Which friend?

Marta! It's really important!

I have to know how to get you there, I said, *or this isn't going to—*

Hands grabbed me from behind and pulled me off balance. Out of pure instinct, I twisted away and threw an elbow back, catching whoever it was in the midsection. They let go, but I was still disoriented, and when I tried to run, I crashed into them. Then they were behind me and there was a hand at my throat, not grabbing, but patting, like it was looking for a necklace. I reached up to grab at it as I was pulled against a wall, and whoever it was grabbed my hand with theirs. I smelled aftershave and sweat, nothing wolfy, and as I elbowed back at their side with my free arm, their fingers slid up my wrist and then down to the fingers. They found the ring holding Penny.

I jerked my hand away, still trying to wrest free; they grabbed my forearm and slid their hand down to go for the ring again. "Is this where the ghost is?" they demanded in a rough voice.

What's happening? Penny asked. *What's going on?*

They're trying to get you. I tried to throw them off with my body weight, but they were larger and heavier than me, and my breath came with more of an effort. "Give me that fucking ring."

What can I do? Her tone edged more frantic.

I closed my hand into a fist. My attacker had pulled me back to a wall and now tried smashing my hand against it to get me to open it. *Nothing,* I told Penny. *Unless you can manifest and yell for help.*

I don't know how to do that! she wailed.

I tried to keep my fist closed, but my attacker pulled my fingers open. I shook him off again but his fingers returned more determined than ever. The gleam of a knife blade flashed into my eyes. "Take it off," he growled, "or I'll cut it—"

And then a flurry of brown fur burst into my vision, and the pressure around my neck vanished. "Get off him!" Vic yelled.

I fell onto my butt, gasping for air, in time to see a red-haired man in a long-sleeved shirt and slacks running down the street. "You okay?" Vic asked.

"Yeah," I choked out. "Go."

He didn't need to be told twice, but took off after the guy, who'd turned down a side street. In the meantime, I caught my breath and scanned the area to make sure nobody else was going to come after me. There weren't any other humans, just four or five werewolves who'd paused to watch me get assaulted. One of them, a short, slight one in jeans, had his phone up, and another in green running shorts leaned over to offer me a paw. "You okay?" they said in a high voice.

The one in jeans lowered their phone. "Pssht," they said. "That was hardly a fight."

"Thanks for the help," I said sarcastically as the one in shorts helped me to my feet. I wished my legs were steadier, but I didn't want to lean on this stranger.

"You want help, go outside the walls," the phone-holder said, and turned to walk away with a swish of his tail.

"I didn't know what to do," the one who'd helped me said as the others around also dispersed.

You okay? I asked Penny.

That guy was trying to get me, wasn't he? she asked. She sounded on the verge of tears.

Obviously he was; he'd asked where the ghost was. *Yeah*, I told her. *But he didn't.*

The werewolf in shorts was studying me, his ears perked. "You okay?"

"I'm fine," I told him. "And it's okay. I know the laws and stuff."

"It's just," they said, "that other guy had a suit and looked official."

"A suit?" I realized I only had an impression of his red hair and a shirt and slacks. It couldn't have been Zawada, not with that hair, but it had been someone after the ring—and Penny—for sure. And who else could've known but Zawada and the BEA?

"Nah, he didn't have a jacket on," the werewolf's friend, with darker fur and blue running shorts said, stepping up next to them. "Just a shirt and tie."

"That's a suit!"

"Ha. You barely ever wear shirts, how would you know?"

The green-shorts werewolf tossed their head, shaggy fur waving. "Whatever. He looked like he was arresting you, but—but more violently."

"He looked like a cop," Blue-shorts werewolf said, arms folded. "Or acted like one, I guess."

The first one, still sounding apologetic, asked, "Was he a cop? I guess you don't know. If we interfered with him and he was a cop, we could get in trouble."

Even if he wasn't a cop, an extra attacking a human didn't have a good chance of being found justified. I held up a hand. "I know, I know. Don't worry, I'm fine and he didn't get what he was after." I looked around for Vic.

"Oh, good." The werewolf in green shorts sounded relieved, and their ears came up. "I'm glad you're okay. That was so random!"

Vic appeared around the corner, hurrying toward me. "I don't think it was," I said. "Excuse me."

I walked up to meet him, through a street that had largely returned to normal, the brief scuffle between two humans forgotten by nearly everyone. "Hey," he said. "You're still okay?"

"Yeah. Where'd he go?"

Vic shook his head. "I didn't think until I was coming back that I shouldn't have left you. There might've been two of them, one to distract me while the other one attacked you again."

"There weren't." But now I looked around, wondering if Rock himself was waiting somewhere nearby. No; he didn't seem like the type to get his own hands dirty. "So you lost the guy?"

Vic's ears flattened. "Yeah," he said. "He musta had a place to bolt around the corner. Went up and down the street, couldn't sniff where he went, though. Sorry about that."

"It's okay. You got him off me, which was the important part."

"Did he say something about cutting you?" Vic looked worriedly at me.

"Yeah." Now that I'd collected myself, I could review the attack. It felt rather amateurish, hasty and unplanned. Why hadn't the guy knocked me out, dragged me into a place where he could search me at his leisure? Not that it was easy to knock someone out, but there were ways. But no, he'd attacked me on the street, gambling (I guess) that the ghost binding I had would be easy to steal. "But I don't think he planned on me having a ring. Lots of people keep ghost bindings on medallions around their neck or as bracelets."

"Because it has to touch skin, right."

"It doesn't have to, but it's good if it does. It's more because it's harder to lose if you're wearing it than if it's a coin in a pocket you could forget about."

"So he was after the ghost." Vic's ears flattened. "That agent must've called over. That was *fast*."

Penny was still quiet. *You okay?* I asked her.

I was going to have to get used to not getting answers from her, unlike Sergei, who'd taken every opportunity to talk to me. "Yeah," I said. "All right, let's go."

Vic walked at my side the rest of the way to Kennelly Plaza and then to the security checkpoint. "You'll be okay here?" he asked. "I can shift and escort you all the way back, wherever that is."

"If they attack me on 71st," I said, "I think people will get involved." But in the back of my head, I was wondering, should I call someone?

"You sure? I mean...they're just human. No offense."

It made me laugh. "It's okay. I didn't think they would jump me to try to get Penny, but now I'm on my guard, they'll have a harder time sneaking up on me. I was talking to Penny —the ghost—and not paying close attention. That won't happen again."

"All right." He patted me on the shoulder. "Stay safe, okay?"

"Will do. Thanks."

Motherfuckers, Penny said as I went back through the checkpoint, which was not as rigorous when leaving. *It was the BEA for sure.*

Yeah, I said. *I think so too. I haven't dealt with them much.*

They were just going to take me. She paused. *And they could have. If that guy had gotten me, would you have gotten a lawyer to get me back?*

I'd try, I said, *but I don't know if a lawyer could help. I'm supposed to take you to your next of kin "promptly," and the government could take you from me and claim that I wasn't doing it promptly enough.*

It's been twenty minutes!

I know, and you haven't told me who to call or where to go yet.

It's not that easy, she told me. *I don't want to go to my mother, but I don't know how to get in touch with Marta. She always got in touch with me.*

I can't—

I know, Marta isn't my next of kin. I just have to see her. It's really important.

Well, I said, *can we go to a place where she might try to get in touch with you?* When she didn't answer, I asked, *Would it help to go back and get your phone?*

No, she said immediately. *I'm not going to let you look through my phone. I'll figure out another way.*

Security doesn't check for ghosts leaving Wolftown, so I walked through without any trouble. *Can I help?* I asked.

What, by asking your cop friends? Forget it.

Hey, I said. *I told you I'm not a cop.*

Yeah, but I still don't trust you.

Why not?

Because you just grabbed me and bound me without even asking.

You'd rather have waited until the BEA guy showed up to bind you? She didn't respond to that, so I went on, gentler. *What did cops do to you? What do you think I'm going to do? Whatever you're worried about getting in trouble for, it's not a big deal now that you're—a ghost.*

Remained person, she said.

Cops can't arrest you now. But the BEA can take you, and you're safer with your family than with me, legally.

She was quiet as I emerged into the glassine Visitor Center amid a few tour groups getting organized to go inside. Finally, as I walked out onto 71st Street, she said, *Just don't get caught, okay? I'll figure something out.*

I'm gonna try not to.

I can't believe they can just take me if they catch you. That's so fucking unfair!

You said you knew about ghosts, right?

I know about remained persons, but I didn't get—I mean, I knew they didn't have rights, but—

I knew how she felt. Knowing someone has a problem is different from being the person with the problem. That doesn't mean you can't sympathize. *As far as I'm concerned,* I said, *you have rights. I'm going to keep you safe until we find your family. Even if you won't help me find them.*

Like I'm some artifact Lara Croft is trying to get to a museum or whatever.

Like you're a person, a minor, who needs to be returned to her family before evil men can kidnap you, I said.

She stayed silent. *All right,* she said finally, *I like that one better.*

CHAPTER
SIX

Halfway home, I got a terse text from Yumi: *Found body, no ID*. I didn't specifically tell Penny that, but she could easily have seen it through my eyes—ghosts can access their binder's senses, but can also withdraw from them. It didn't seem like it was going to start a good conversation for me to say, "hey, they found your dead body." After all, Yumi hadn't said "found living person in coma." Besides, now I was paranoid that more BEA goons might be waiting for me.

Out here in Chicago proper, I didn't think they'd assault me on the street. They felt like amateurs, but even amateurs would know that humans are less worried about breaking up what looks like an assault, and I kept to large, crowded sidewalks. But Christ, I hadn't been wrong about Rock Zawada thinking he was in a movie. Sending someone to assault me and take the ring by force? I eyed the top of the Wolftown walls, half expecting him to leap over them on a motorcycle or something.

Penny stayed quiet, and it probably wasn't helpful of me to be lost in my own thoughts while she was coping with the existential crisis of being dead, but I figured I was here if she needed me, and if I got attacked by the BEA again, I wouldn't be any help to her.

While I was scanning the streets, I thought about being on the BEA's bad side, and that made me wonder about my FBI job. I didn't know how closely the BEA worked with the FBI, but they were both government agencies, and I knew that as reluctant as the government was to share information when *I* wanted them to, if there were something like, oh, say, "hey, this guy refused to cooperate with an BEA agent," that shit might make its way through the grapevine fast.

Especially if Rock Zawada, who now had my name, decided to run it though a government database to see if anyone else had been talking to me.

You know, when you're working for yourself, you learn pretty quickly that you have to push your card into any open hand. It's an instinct at this point, just like cooperating with authorities. Now I wondered if I wouldn't have been much better served by taking a page from Czoltan's activism manual and refusing to identify myself.

Too late for that now. He knew me, but I could make sure he didn't ruin my future.

Thank God my building is air-conditioned. The cool of the lobby air on my damp shirt felt great. I texted back to Yumi to ask if she'd found a phone, and she replied with a single word: *Locked*. So much for that.

In theory, I could have asked Penny, but I couldn't force her to talk. I might be able to see more of her mind if I pushed, but there'd be no hope of having a good relationship with her after that.

I know, I didn't need to have a good relationship with her because I'd be handing her off to her next of kin soon enough, but look, if I were a ghost and I wanted some privacy to process my own death, I wouldn't want Agent Zawada or whatever suit had bound me to push their way into my mind. Penny might be a ghost, but she still deserved respect.

The urgency I felt around the FBI job drove me to the computer before the door had swung fully shut behind me. All the research I'd been doing remained up on the screen, so I cleared it, swept the papers back into the drawer and locked it, and tried not to look at any of it in case Penny was looking out of my eyes while I did.

This is all classified stuff, I told her. *I'm not supposed to show it to anyone else, but I need to send this email real quick, so don't look at it.*

Ha, she said. *You know how that works. It's like saying 'don't think about an elephant.'*

Boom, I thought of an elephant. I think I kept it from her so she wouldn't feel smug about it, but I wasn't sure. *Yeah, but you don't have to look at things just because I am. You have control over that.*

Do I? I can't look away.

You can, you just don't know how yet. We can work on that. But let me finish this letter.

What's so important about it? Why can't I look?

It's confidential. Like most of my work, I'm not supposed to show it to anyone who doesn't need to know about it.

I think that means more people should see it.

I could get in trouble if more people see this, I said, *and if I get in trouble, that would make it easier for Zawada to take you away from me. So just let me do this please?*

She didn't say anything as I finished the email to Agent Jefferson: *Thanks for the info. I can definitely do this work. Please send a contract over.*

I hoped Penny had respected my wishes, or (because that seemed like pie-in-the-sky wishing) at least hadn't seen the email address with its "fbi dot gov." She already wasn't inclined to trust me, and I was sure that corresponding with the feds would make that worse.

The main job I had right now was finding Penny's next of kin, which would be a lot easier if she would tell me who they were. But, as I often reminded myself, if people would do the sensible thing all the time, I would have to find a different job. Besides, I had some sympathy for someone who might not want to be delivered to their immediate family if there was an alternative available. As for that alternative, Penny had only given me one clue to go on.

Who's Marta? I asked, *besides a friend of yours?*

Penny remained silent, so I set out to do my job. It'd be nice if someone would pay me for it. Maybe Marta, when we found them.

The Unified Society Alliance, who owned the building where Penny had been found, seemed like a good place to start. They had a functional webpage with a few photos, a Donate button, and a mission statement: "Working toward an equitable society for all unimorph, multimorph, and remained persons."

Multimorph was a new term for extranormal, but it hadn't gained a lot of traction (Czoltan still used "extras"); unimorph meant someone like me who only had one form. "Remained persons" was a term I wasn't familiar with, but one more search showed that it was a relatively new term for a ghost. Oh —Penny had said that just before we left Wolftown.

Unimorph and multimorph I get; even though "extranormal" is way better than "creature" or "monster" (the term for extras even into the 19th century), it still implies that a human like me is "normal," which carries with it the feeling of being natural, expected, and good, and implies that anything not normal is abnormal. We use "extranormal" to say that they're normal plus more, but...that's still not normal. Using unimorph and multimorph removes some of the value judgment from it. There are people with one form and people with more than one, end of story.

But "remained person," that just felt clunky. If I thought through it, I guess "ghost" has some baggage with it, mainly because ghosts freaked people out for centuries and nobody understood them, but what else could we call them? Shade? Spirit?

Language aside, it looked like the USA (they had to have picked those initials on purpose) was another one of the respectable faces of the Teardown movement. Their goal was to have unis and multis living together in an atmosphere of mutual understanding, and so they supported legislation protecting extras in workplaces, banning housing discrimination, lots of the same things the Civil Rights movement had done for different races sixty-some years ago. They didn't have a lot of people there—there was one person listed as head of each city branch and that was all.

They're also working for remained persons, Penny said unexpectedly.

I didn't say anything for a moment, worried I'd say the wrong thing and offend her back into silence. But I couldn't help my curiosity. *Is that why you were there? Did you expect to—* don't say "die"—*become a ghost?*

No!

I waited, suppressing the questions while I scrolled through recent news about the USA. They had been scheduled to join today's protest march, which partly explained why the house had been empty. They'd sponsored some legislation in the Chicago city council and the Illinois and U.S. Congress. But the most prominent news item was that the head of their Chicago branch, a vampire named Gina Przybyla, had joined with NOPE and a couple other groups in a roundtable discussion with the BEA and the mayors of several cities with Wolftowns. I remembered hearing about this and watching some of the proceedings, but I hadn't seen Gina's opening remarks. I clicked through and read a bit of her speech, and checked whether Agent Rock Zawada was one of the BEA people there (he wasn't).

She's great, Penny said as I read through her speech.

I like a lot of what she says. 'Everyone deserves the right to live with dignity, whatever form that life takes.' Good stuff.

She means it, too.

How did you meet her?

Silence. Wrong question, I guess, so I tried again. *Were you going to go to the march today?*

Yeah.

Is that where you planned to meet Marta?

I got a strong sense that I was right from her, though she didn't confirm it verbally. So Marta was some kind of activist, and maybe someone associated with the Teardown movement (or some other underground movement), if she initiated contacts and didn't leave people a way to reach her. That gave me an idea or two for ways to find her.

Penny, if she could follow those thoughts, didn't object to them, but I went another route to try to re-engage her. *My boyfriend's there.* I did a web search to find some video and got to a live stream of the protest. I couldn't see Czoltan anywhere, but I did spot Carla in her thunderbird form. Hard to miss the twelve-foot tall bird-faced woman with the twenty-foot wingspan.

You're gay?

Yeah.

Huh.

I let that sit for a moment. *Are you?*

I'm demi and pan, she said. *I'm not seeing anyone. I mean, not —I'm not seeing anyone.*

Can I ask how old you are?

She paused again. *I'm seventeen. So don't get any ideas.* Then immediately she said, *I guess if you're gay, you wouldn't get ideas like that. And anyway it doesn't matter, because I'm a ghost and I don't have rights anymore.*

I know, I said. *I had a ghost for five years.*

What happened to her?

Him. He resolved his business and passed on.

Oh! Did you go to Moving On with him?

No. I scanned the list of people at the roundtable. Gina's biography said that she also worked with a group called NAPR that I hadn't heard of, so I searched for them. *We worked it out on our own.*

No wonder it took five years.

Do you know Agent Zawada? I asked as the page came up. It was the National Association for the Protection of the Remained, an activist group focused on remained persons and their rights. Not very large, which was maybe why I hadn't heard of it before, but also maybe I'd avoided looking up ghost rights groups out of guilt for having a ghost partner. I'd treated Sergei well, but I had no illusion that he had any power in our relationship, and that bothered me (and he knew it did, so he brought it up often).

I told you, no, I never saw him before. But he looked like a creep. And the government totally does sell girl ghosts. There was a big thing about it like ten years ago. There were a couple people in the BEA who were buying ghosts from ghost-chasers and selling them to rich old perverts for donations.

Right, I remember that. But they arrested those guys.

She scoffed. *You think they're not still doing it?*

Seems like people would be watching them more closely. I read through NAPR's main talking points. The first one that jumped out at me was that they didn't approve of people who kept ghosts as partners in their work. They equated it to child labor because ghosts couldn't legally consent to work. Ghosts could "freelance," but according to them, the ghost should have the freedom to leave a job at any time. They were also agitating for legal recognition of ghosts as people in general, and for health insurance to fully cover mental health treatment for people whose relatives ended up remained (to help the remained move on).

They're just more careful is all. Don't you think that Zawada guy looks just like someone who'd sell young girls?

I did, but... *Don't judge only on looks.*

You sound like Marta.

Is Marta with NAPR?

She paused and then dodged my query. *Fine, I'm judging him on the way he strutted up like he owned the place and how he tried so hard to get me.*

If you'd never seen him, how did he know you were a girl?

The ensuing pause stretched on. *I don't know,* she confessed.

I'll see if I can figure that out. It might be that he wanted you to sell as a...

Sex ghost?

I didn't like the way that sounded, even less so in a teenaged girl's voice. *Yeah. But maybe there was something else. Why else might he be interested in you?*

I don't know, she said.

But I felt fairly sure that she did. It wasn't just that she was in my head; it was years of experience in talking to people who wanted to hide something from me. I kept that thought partitioned off, because if she didn't want to tell me, she wasn't going to be convinced by me saying "Yuh-huh, you do so know." But I did think, a little more loudly, that if she wanted me to get her to Marta, it was a little odd that she wasn't telling me how to get in touch with them.

So I asked instead, *Are your parents still alive?*

I don't want to go back to them. I want to go to... She hesitated. *To Marta.*

I had to tread delicately; she'd already shut down when I asked her more about Marta before. *Do you have a number for Marta?*

No, she replied. *I already told you.*

Your phone's back at the house. If I get Yumi to bring it over, will you let me unlock it? Maybe there's a message from Marta on it.

No.

At least this "no" was less vehement than some of the previous ones. *Then how am I supposed to reach her?*

I think Gina knows how. The Unified Society vampire. Before you ask, I don't know her number, but she's out there. People know her.

And what am I supposed to say to her? Does she know you?

Yeah. There was some pain behind that, but it felt true.

All right, I said. *When Czoltan gets back, I'll see if he can hook me up with her. Until then, I guess I'll learn more about the USA.*

You don't have to keep doing that. Don't you have other work to do?

I can't work on my other cases with you in my head. Confidentiality, remember?

Look, I don't like being here either.

Well, I'm not going to hand you over to Zawada, at least not until I understand why he wants you so badly. So I'll just have to try to find someone else who can take responsibility for you. Unless you want to tell me?

Get me to Marta, she said.

By the time Czoltan texted me that he was on his way home, and that he was excited I was coming back to Detroit with him, I had tracked down an email for Gina and sent a message off. It took a while to compose the message, but after a lot of false starts I settled on "Penny is with me, please contact me." There was a phone number for the Unified Society, but it went to a voicemail, so I left a message there too, a more circumspect one. I did a little digging on Agent Zawada, but I didn't find much beyond his LinkedIn stuff—college at Princeton, interned at the New York mayor's Wolftown Liaison office, then joined BEA ten years ago, which would make him, let's see, probably graduated at 22, three years in New York, so pretty close to my age right now. But there wasn't much else on him, except that he'd gone to high school in Chicago, which probably explained why he'd come back here.

I was reading an article he was quoted in from a few years ago about a ghost appearance at the Museum of Arts and Sciences when the door opened and Czoltan came in in his human form.

I jumped up to greet him, and in the space between the door closing and my hug, he'd shifted from human to standing wolf, which allowed me to feel his wagging tail and his fur against my face as we kissed. "How was the march?" I asked.

"It went great!"

Your boyfriend's a werewolf? Penny sounded impressed.

Czoltan went on, ears up, tail still wagging. "The speeches were all so good, and the mayor shook hands with Carla and promised to help extras who want to live outside Wolftown, and he even said, 'Chicago is for all Chicagoans.'"

"That's great!"

"Yeah." He leaned back to smile at me. "I know, I know,

it's just talk, but he said it in public, so maybe......and Senator Birch was there, and he talked about broadening opportunities for all extras, and said he's trying to encourage extras living 'outside the walls.' Anyway, did you see Carla's speech?"

"I only saw a little of the march. I got called into Wolftown on a job."

His ears flicked back and his whiskers went down. "What job?"

"There was a ghost screaming—"

Singing!

"—and Yumi was having trouble, so I went in to help out. And I..." I turned the ring on my finger.

Czoltan's eyes went to it. "You bound it?" I nodded, and his ears flattened. "Seriously? That's so dangerous. Why would you go in with no preparation and try to—"

"I've been trained, and I've bound ghosts before."

"And almost gotten possessed!"

Really?

"This wasn't like with Richard. It's usually pretty safe."

Oh, dammit. I should've possessed you. Then this would all have been easier.

He let me go and stepped back. "'Usually.' You had no idea who she was."

"She was in pain and she was shouting that pain at everyone for like half a mile. I got there first. And listen," I said, before he could find another objection, "a BEA guy showed up and there's something hinky about him. He showed up really fast and he seemed to know who Penny was but he wouldn't say why."

"Penny? Is that her name?"

Tell him he's cool and I like him.

"Yeah. She's seventeen and she says you're cool."

"Seventeen." Czoltan rubbed his face. "What happened to her?"

Penny stayed quiet. "She doesn't remember."

"Is that normal? Or was she, like, drugged?"

"Ghosts don't always remember how they died," I said.

"Can she appear?" He waved at the air next to me. "I want to see her."

"She hasn't done that yet. It's something we can work on." *If you want to talk to him directly*, I added silently to Penny.

She didn't reply. Czoltan waited a moment, then asked, "So is she your new partner?"

That got a *Hah!* from Penny, and a shake of the head from me. "No; she's not trained and she doesn't want to do it. So I need to find her next of kin and hand over custody, only she doesn't seem to want to tell me who that is or where to find them."

"Why not?"

Penny didn't volunteer an answer, so I made my best guess. "She was shouting—sorry, singing loudly—about her mother, and she was living in an activist headquarters, so I assume she's not on good terms with her family."

His ears perked. "What headquarters?"

"Unified Society Alliance."

"Oh yeah. Wait, is she an extra?" I shook my head. "That makes sense, then. The USA has a bunch of humans working with them."

"See, that's cool. I didn't know that. Useful information."

Czoltan snorted, but smiled. "Some detective you are."

"I don't solve all my cases in a day, sheesh." I grinned at him. "Give me a break."

He flicked his ears and his whiskers came up. "So I guess no sex until you get rid of her."

Eww.

"Definitely not," I said. "But don't worry. This case is my top priority now, mainly because I can't work on anything else until I find a place for Penny."

He glanced at my computer and the locked drawer and then met my eyes. "So what about Richard?"

I nodded. "I can't go deal with him until I resolve this situation."

"Jesus, Jae."

"Look," I said, "I didn't do this to put off dealing with Richard."

"It's been months."

"I know how long it's been." My voice rose, getting close to snapping, and I reined it in. "This isn't about that. It was just someone in need."

Czoltan paced back and forth and then sat on the back of the couch. "I guess it's not out of character for you to take a stupid risk like that."

"Thanks?" I pulled out the chair from my desk and sat down. "I promise that's all this was, just something needed to be done."

It was in moments like this that I worried that Czoltan would decide he'd had enough of tying his life to a risk-taking ex-soldier with a savior complex. But then I remembered that that's why I'd met him in the first place, and he'd fallen for me then, so I was probably okay. Still, he was clearly disappointed when he said, "I guess you'd better cancel your flight to Detroit."

"Yeah," I said, "Or maybe we both postpone our flights for a week? Would you be able to stay here longer?"

His ears went up. "I can call work, but it shouldn't be a problem to work remotely. You think you can find a place for Penny in that time?"

"I hope so. If not, this case is more complicated than I thought, or I'm not as good as I think."

Czoltan's whiskers bounced up and down. "And this BEA agent doesn't complicate things?"

"Well," I said, "yeah. That's a problem. But if I act quick, it won't be my problem. Once she's with her legal guardian, the government will have a lot harder time getting hold of her for... whatever they want."

For the record, I don't like being talked about like a piece of luggage you need to dump off somewhere.

I don't think of you that way. I told you.

Yeah, but you're talking to your boyfriend behind—in front of me without talking to me.

You want to learn to manifest so you can be part of the conversation?

She sighed. *I guess.*

Czoltan rested a paw on my shoulder. "So I guess we're not having chicken tagine tonight."

CHAPTER
SEVEN

While I tried to teach Penny about manifesting, I told Czoltan more about the incident and what I knew about Penny. He nodded thoughtfully, and said, "So you've got to take her to her next of kin so that agent can't get her, but she won't tell you who her relatives are?"

"That's about it," I said. "Makes my job a lot harder."

If I had any decent relatives, I'd tell you.

I know, I know. You sure you don't have any who are even half-decent?

Take me to Marta. That's all I care about.

Aloud, so Czoltan could follow the argument, I said, "I'm trying to get you to her, but the BEA knows I have you, so you're not safe with me. If I can get you to your parents, you'll be safer there, and we can work on getting you to Marta after that."

I don't think it'll be that easy. Dad's gone and Mom...doesn't like remained people.

"Well, unless you can give me Marta's phone number, I'm

going to keep trying to find your parents, and I'm a pretty good detective."

You do what you gotta do. I don't have to help you.

"Who's Marta?" Czoltan asked.

"Friend of hers. She won't tell me anything more about her, but she's an activist, I think. Gina from USA knows her."

He rubbed his whiskers. "It can't hurt to talk to her, can it?"

I knew I liked him.

"Sure," I said. "Any lead. But Penny doesn't know how to get in touch with her."

His ears splayed. "She doesn't? But she's a friend?"

"My guess, since she was sleeping at USA headquarters, is that Marta's an underground activist who's deliberately hard to find."

"Then what..." His whiskers fluffed out as he probably thought the same question I'd been wondering, about what Penny had been doing with an underground activist, and he came to the same conclusion I had about asking it. "Uh, what can you do to find her?"

"I left Gina an email. I don't have any other leads. But maybe you can help? Penny had her number, but it's in her phone and a, we don't have it, and b, if we did get it she probably wouldn't let me unlock it because she doesn't trust me not to go snooping around in it for her mom's number."

It's not just that.

"She's probably right," Czoltan said.

"Probably," I agreed, but now I was wondering what else was in her phone that she was worried about. If she'd been working with an underground activist, she might be worried not about herself getting in trouble, but getting other people— still alive—in trouble.

Czoltan paced. "Gina's probably busy with press and stuff

from the march. Come to think of it, she's probably around Carla. I'll text her and see if Gina's there."

And likely Gina wouldn't just give out the contact info of an underground activist over the phone. I'd have to see her in person to let her touch the ring so she could talk to Penny, and then she'd give me the contact. "Would anyone else from USA have her number?"

He looked up from typing on his phone and asked, "Was that to me or Penny?"

"Either."

I don't know everyone who has her number, but Gina's the only one I know contacted her. Marta would just...show up at meetings.

I wanted to ask how Penny would normally get in touch with her, but the phrase "if you were still alive" loomed in the background of that question, and she still felt shaky enough that I didn't feel comfortable saying it. *So other USA people might know her? Or NAPR?*

Yeah. NAPR more likely, but we had meetings together a lot.

"Penny says other USA people might, or people from the National Association for the Protection of the Remained."

"Who?" Czoltan tilted his head. "Who's 'Remained'?"

"Ghosts. 'Remained people.'" I leaned back in my chair. "You know anyone else in USA or NAPR?"

He shook his head. "But I know some guys who work with USA. I was marching with them, so they should be home now. You want me to get in touch?"

"Sure. Any lead will help."

"All right. They won't talk on the phone, but we can go into Wolftown to meet them."

I frowned. "Why won't they talk on the phone?"

"They like to smell the person they're talking to."

Gross.

It's a werewolf thing, I said. *You want to try manifesting again?*

She made a teenager's sound of frustration. *It doesn't work for me.*

You've been trying for all of half an hour, I said. *Sometimes it takes longer than that.*

I'll try later.

I kept my sigh voiceless, but all that did was hide it from Czoltan; Penny caught it. *Hey,* she said, *I just died. Give me a break.*

At least she was starting to process her death. That had to be a good sign, right? I wasn't sure I'd be so casual about it an hour or two after it happened. Aloud I said, "All right, so your werewolf friends can get us in touch with Marta, maybe, and Gina will get back to us when she's free. I'm waiting for Yumi to get me a positive ID on Penny so we can get to her parents. Whichever comes in first, we'll pursue."

"Yup."

"And if we get Penny's parents first and hand her over, we'll keep trying to connect her with Marta. Sounds like a plan. Thanks," I added. "This would be a lot harder without you."

Czoltan gave me a big smile. "I know," he said, and brought his phone up to text again.

Hey, Penny said. *While we're waiting for you to ruin my afterlife, tell me how you two met.*

"She wants to know how I met," I told Czoltan.

He waved a paw. "I was a refugee in the Kosovan War—the second one—and Jae was in the U.S. Army at a Red Cross facility."

You were in the Army? I guess that figures.

"I went into the Army for a lot of reasons," I said. "My dad was gone from an early age—"

Yours too, huh?

"—and I guess, looking back, I wanted to get away from home but I didn't want to be completely on my own yet,

79

because I didn't trust myself. But the Army wasn't great either. It was supposed to be all structure and discipline, and there was a lot of that, but there were also a lot of guys who'd push to see what they could get away with."

"That happens everywhere," Czoltan supplied helpfully.

"Yeah, but it's one thing when it's privates sneaking cigarettes after lights-out; it's another when it's some guy figuring nobody'll miss a refugee carrying a lot of cash, or something."

Fuck.

"I didn't know the guy who got charged for that," I added quickly. "He was in a different unit. But that kind of shit happened. Anyway. Czoltan was one of the people who came into the camp, and I dunno, I ended up talking to him more than any of the other refugees. He seemed like he needed someone."

"You did too," Czoltan said. "The rest of the soldiers would slop my meal on a tray or toss me new clothes and barely say two words. You asked how I was and where I was from and every day you checked on me."

"And then we discovered we're both gay."

"Or at least open to a same-sex relationship."

Yeah, yeah, you flirted and you made out and then it happened, Penny said.

At the same time, Czoltan went on, "But yeah, we started dating there at the camp and then back here."

And you've been together since then?

"We haven't been together since then," I said aloud. "I fucked up five or six years ago and it took us a while to get past that."

Ooh, I want to hear that story.

Czoltan's phone chimed. He checked it, and with some relief I saw him text back and then raise his head. "They'll meet us today, if you want."

"Yeah." I checked my phone. "Nothing from Carla?"

"Nah." He looked again. "She hasn't even read the text, looks like."

"All right. If we go now, we could grab pupusas from La Espuela on the way back."

"Sounds great. I'll tell them we're on our way and they'll give us a location."

He shifted to human form and we rode down to the lobby, where the afternoon sun was throwing crisp shadows and bright golden light onto the old wood and worn carpeting. I put my hand to the door handle and then froze there, arresting the reflexive action of opening the door.

Czoltan, behind me, stopped himself from bumping into me with a hand on my shoulder. "What?"

I stepped to one side and pulled him with me. "That car, the Ford. You see it?"

He peered out. "The brown one?"

"Yeah."

"What about it?"

"There's a person sitting in it."

Czoltan sounded doubtful. "People sit in cars. They're probably smoking weed."

"There's no smoke. And it's in a loading dock space."

"Okay, well." He peered over my shoulder. "There's other reasons to sit in cars. Maybe they're an undercover cop staking out someone else."

"Or maybe they're BEA."

That stopped him. "Seriously?"

"They look like they're staking out. I mean, they're doing it really badly, right in front of the building, but the BEA is just bureaucrats. They don't have surveillance operatives as far as I know. Which isn't very far, but anyway, yeah, they have a suit on and are watching the building. And it's been hours since

Rock Zawada threatened me. They had plenty of time to get here."

Czoltan leaned against the wall outside the glass of the door. "Couldn't the BEA use a ghost to spy on you?"

What if they've tapped into the security cameras in your building?

Possible, I told Penny, *even though this isn't a movie. Our cameras are on a closed circuit, so there's no easy feed they could get. They'd have to physically be in the basement looking at the monitors, or they'd have to install a device that would transmit, which I don't think they've had time to do.*

Good security system.

Thanks, I said. *I helped set it up.* To Czoltan, I said, "The building is ghostproofed, and also, Penny would be able to detect if another ghost was around."

I would?

Sergei could.

Czoltan tilted his head. "But you can bring, like, Penny and Sergei in."

"Yeah, I can carry a ghost in, but they can't come in on their own."

You get ghosts coming after you?

Cheating husbands, mostly, at the time. But the super was putting in cameras because we'd had some damage to the stairwells and he wanted to catch the guys. He asked my advice and I helped him make it better.

She laughed shortly. *Cheating husbands?*

I don't do that kind of work anymore, but I used to have a lot of clients who thought their spouse was cheating on them. If they were right, and the spouse was a man, sometimes he'd look up where I lived after I made the report and would come threaten me. Nothing serious ever happened, though.

My mom didn't hire a private eye to track down my dad, Penny said. *She just threw him out.*

"Right." Czoltan rubbed his chin. "What makes you think they're here for you?"

How long ago was that? I asked Penny, keeping it casual and conversational.

Go ahead and answer him.

In a minute. I didn't really want to have the conversation about being attacked right here, right now, but it looked like I wasn't going to be able to put it off for more than a few more seconds.

You're going to have to tell him about the attack sometime.

I must've thought that really loudly. *I'll tell him in a minute.*

Ugh, fine. It was five or six years ago. Now answer your boyfriend.

I focused on Czoltan again. Couldn't put this moment off any longer. "Well," I said. "I'm pretty sure they're here for me, because a BEA guy kind of tried to grab the ring on my way back."

My boyfriend glared at me. "What?"

Uh-oh! Penny said in a mocking singsong.

"It wasn't a big deal," I said. "One of the peacekeepers was with me and helped fight the guy off."

It felt like a big deal. He threatened to cut the ring off!

He put his paws on his hips. "When were you going to tell me this part?"

"Um...now?"

He shook his head. "Christ, Jae, I told you that was dangerous. Now there's a guy waiting outside for you?"

"Probably." I squinted at the car. "They look like a fed, at least, and they're definitely staking out, and it's hours after I took possession of something the BEA apparently really wants, so my years of detective experience say it's very likely."

He didn't bite on my attempt at humor. "Well, so what now? You going to lead the BEA to my friends?"

"Of course not. If they think the way to stake out my place is to sit in a car outside the door, I'm sure I can lose them, if not before I get to the Visitor Center, then at least in Wolftown. And anyway, they're not interested in where I'm going. They just want to get the ring." To Penny, I said, *You okay if I send you with Czoltan?*

Hell yes.

"So leave the ring in the apartment," Czoltan said.

"Penny's a new ghost and I'd rather not leave her alone."

Don't worry about me, she said, but that sounded like bravado.

"And anyway," I went on, "if I were them and I knew I'd gone out, I'd send someone to check the apartment just in case. I'd rather give you the ring and have you meet me there."

"Me?" The glower was gone; his eyes widened.

"I trust you to keep her safe," I said. "They probably know we're dating and they might even have files on you, but I wager if I come out alone they'll follow me away from the building. When we're gone, you can leave. Just keep an eye out in case there's a second team."

"What am I watching for?" He eyed the brown Ford out front and the person in it.

"That," I said. "Guys in dark suits in summer, or really any kind of suit or just a tie, who seem to be following you. These guys aren't experienced tails so they'll be easy to spot. If you spot one..."

"I'll get back to the apartment." He grinned enough to show me his canine teeth. "Whatever way I can."

"Good." I dropped the ring into his palm and covered it with my own for a moment. *You can trust him,* I told Penny. *And if something goes wrong, you're bound to me. You can still talk to me if you want to.*

Got it, she said.

I let go and couldn't help feeling a little resentful. She trusted Czoltan more than me just because he was a werewolf? Or maybe because he was an activist. Either way, I was used to people not trusting me, and that couldn't affect how I did my job. Right now my job seemed like it was to keep Penny safe until I could get her to her relatives, or Marta. So I was going to do that even if I had to drag the resentful teenager all the way there. Which it seemed like I might. I didn't have time for her to outgrow this rebellious phase, and I didn't even know how long it was going to last. Mine had lasted until I joined the Army.

Czoltan stepped forward; I kissed him and said, "Good luck."

"You need it more than I do." He squeezed my shoulder.

I met his eyes and smiled, then turned, took a breath, and walked out.

The air had not cooled much with the sun still making its way down the afternoon sky, but a breeze had picked up. I walked down the side of the street opposite the brown Ford, taking care not to look directly at it.

At a glance, the driver appeared to be Black with long hair, so it wasn't the red-haired guy who'd assaulted me, nor was it Rock. The amateur nature of the assault and now the stakeout gave me the strong impression that these were not professional investigators or field agents. So maybe they were BEA employees from Rock's office. And if they were trying to get Penny back themselves rather than contact the CPD or the FBI, that meant that my impression of Rock had been accurate, and what they were doing with her was not completely above board.

But it was also possible that I was trying to confirm my first impression of Rock by assuming that one amateur stakeout was representative of the whole operation. It was possible that they'd planted the super-obvious person in front of my building to put me off guard, while the more skilled agents followed me.

When I had Sergei, I could have him watch the person in the car to see if they called someone else. Just as I was thinking that, I heard a car door slam behind me. I turned in time to see the Black agent—a woman, I thought—duck behind some people on the sidewalk. Which was tough because she was about six feet tall, so she had to stoop a little, which was even more of a giveaway.

So I had to figure out if there was someone else following me more expertly, and that would be hard, but not impossible. I took out my phone and used the selfie camera to get a look behind me on the street, then walked briskly down toward busy 71st. I turned left there rather than going right, toward the Visitor Center, turned left again a block later, left at 72nd, and as I was approaching my street, took my phone out again.

The tall woman was still behind me, looking annoyed or frustrated or both. I didn't recognize anyone else from the first time I'd looked. Some of the really good FBI guys will change outfits on a dime, and me making four left turns was a sign to a good tail that I suspected I was being followed, so it was still slightly possible that there was a more expert tail who'd changed their hat or glasses or even a tie (in winter, someone might switch jackets or sweaters, but it was 80 degrees out and nobody was even wearing a suit jacket outside today). But as I turned back down my street, I felt more confident that it was only the woman, and only Rock's team involved.

That made them him, her, and the red-haired guy. Probably there were more, but there couldn't be too many more or they wouldn't have sent the agent here by herself to follow me. So I headed for the Visitor Center, checking every now and then that she was still behind me.

The BEA had a presence inside Wolftown—that red-haired agent who'd attacked me was probably still in there—and now they knew that's where I was headed, it was likely they were going to try to get me there. The woman following me had already probably called ahead to get someone ready in Kennelly Plaza. If I wanted to avoid running from one agent into another, I needed to change my appearance to have any chance of getting past them.

As I walked into the Visitor Center's cool, lightly wolf-smelling lobby, shaded from the sun, another way to do that—at least partly—presented itself. There were two tourist groups gathering, and one of them included a half-dozen Japanese tourists. Currently they were studying the wall mural that depicted the history of Wolftown, so they would likely be going in in about ten minutes. So if I could go with them...and find a way to change my clothes...that'd give me a good chance of getting ahead of the BEA.

The vending machines caught my eye, and a plan formed in my head. All right. I got this. I think.

I heard an echo of Sergei's snort from my memory as I went and bought an orange Fanta. The bottle cold in my hand, I gave it a good shake as unobtrusively as I could, holding it at my side and rotating my hand back and forth as I went through the double doors to get in line for the security checkpoint.

There were a half dozen people ahead of me, and on the other side of the checkpoint, telling people to move along, was Portia, a short uniformed Black woman with emerald earrings and a sharp look unlike a lot of the bored expressions you tended to get at Wolftown security. She and I had been friendly for years, since she took this job, and just seeing her there relaxed me. This might be another case of things aligning in my favor, but I preferred to view it as the result of a lot of work to be nice to the security staff every time I went into Wolftown, which was often, so the chances that I'd meet a guard who was going to be nice to me went way up.

The silver detector went off, but before the guard had time to look at me, Portia turned to stare across the mechanism, and a smile broke out on her face. "Hey, Jae," she said, waving me around.

I stepped to the side, letting the people behind me go through. The next few didn't set the detector off. "Hi, Portia. How's Vanessa?"

"She's good, she's good." She waved the silver detector wand over me; it caught the implant under my collarbone, a precaution against being bitten by werewolves. "Man, I miss Sergei. That old guy always cracked me up."

"Yep. Me too." I picked up my phone, wallet, and the bottle of Fanta from the table where the guard had slid them across after examining them.

"You gonna get another partner?"

"Yeah," I said. "Trying to figure that out."

"Good for you," Portia said. "You know, we had one of them dingbats in here today?" She gestured at the sign that warned about bringing ghosts into Wolftown and shook her head. "Telling everyone that ghosts are a giant conspiracy to trick grieving people out of their money."

"I ran into one of those ghost-deniers once," I said. "Sergei scared the shit out of him."

She laughed and waved me through. "Wish I could've seen that! Go on, you're clear."

"Thanks." I slipped the phone and wallet into my pocket and cracked the top of the bottle of soda.

It gave one warning hiss, but I'd already opened it all the

way, and the next thing that happened was that orange soda foamed all over my hand, pouring over it and down onto my shirt. I tried to keep it angled toward me, but a little got on Portia too. "Hey!" she yelled, jumping back.

"Ah, shit." I held the bubbling, foaming bottle at arm's length as Fanta burbled over my fingers and dripped to the floor. It was too late for the cap to do any good, but I screwed it back on anyway. "Dammit. It must've gotten shaken up in the machine or something."

Portia snorted. "Damn machines," she said.

I made a show of looking down at my shirt. "I'm going to meet a client," I said. "I can't go like this."

Portia kept an eye on the checkpoint. "Get something in the plaza."

"They're meeting me in the plaza. Do you have a lost and found or something?"

She sighed, and then waved at one of the other guards, a short straw-haired white man with a square face. "Brian, take Jae to the lost and found and let him grab a shirt outta there."

"Thanks so much," I said. "I appreciate it."

Brian, a guard I'd seen a few times but hadn't been introduced to, led me off to the side to a door marked, "Authorized Entry Only." "Wait here," he told me, and went inside.

I could see the people going through security, but I was standing in shadow and none of them were looking my way. I stripped off my shirt and used it to wipe off the Fanta. Orange was a nice smell that Czoltan didn't mind.

Brian came out a moment later with a box full of clothing in his arms. He dropped it on the floor. "There you go," he said. "Grab a shirt."

It took me a couple minutes to find one in my size, during which time I kept an eye on the security line to see when the Japanese group would come through. "Thanks," I said as I dropped my old shirt in the lost and found and picked out the other one. It was a reasonable fit, and more importantly, it was black with gold stitching, about as different from my blue-striped white shirt as I could've asked for.

The Japanese group still wasn't in evidence. "Hey," I said to Brian as he picked up the box, "can I grab that Cubs hat out of the box too? My client is a big baseball fan and I forgot mine."

He frowned at me, and then he shrugged and set the box down. "Yeah, sure," he said.

New hat and different shirt plus a different group should be enough to confuse them. The Japanese group had just come through and were waiting in the line. I checked my phone, but Czoltan hadn't sent anything since that text that he was on his way.

The BEA would likely be worrying right now that I hadn't come through. The other agent might even check the security line. But she wasn't in it yet, and now the first of the Japanese tourists was going through.

I stalled until a few of them had gone, and then, with the Cubs hat tucked under my arm so Portia wouldn't notice it, I waved to her and headed for the exit. I kept pace with the tourists, pulled the Cubs hat down over my brow and walked out into Wolftown in the middle of them.

CHAPTER
EIGHT

Kennelly Plaza bustled with more tourists in the afternoon than it had in the early morning. "Keep to the left, please," our tour group leader told us, gesturing around the werewolf posing for tourist pictures and taking us right past the churro cart where Carey was still working. She glanced my way but didn't show any sign of recognition, so that gave me a little hope that my disguise was working well.

The guide gathered us in one spot and launched into a lecture in Japanese and English about how the first Wolftown was built in New York, and then the specific history of this one. Two of the people around me took their phones out, so I did too.

Czoltan had still not messaged me. I texted to tell him I was in Wolftown and to confirm that I was headed for the butcher shop his friends had told us to go to. He didn't respond as I switched to my maps app and committed the route to memory.

The guide wrapped up his talk and asked if there were any questions. The person in front of me asked one, and then we were off to the next stop, the Wolftown Community Center, where there was a small show going on and guides who would talk about life in Wolftown. The Community Center wasn't near the butcher shop where I was headed, but once I got out of the plaza, I was less worried about BEA's eyes on me.

And in fact, as we left the plaza, I caught sight of a man lurking in the shadows, pretending to be looking at his phone while he kept looking up to scan the entrance to Wolftown. His face wasn't terribly familiar, but the red hair left me no doubt that this was the guy who'd attacked me this morning. I kept my cap down low over my face and pretended to be talking to one of the other people in the group as we turned the corner and disappeared from his sight.

Down Grozny, the other main street leading into the plaza, there was a t-shirt store that was still open. I slowed down to the back of the group and scanned the street—no other agents that I could see. I was a little surprised not to find a third person following me, but maybe it really was just Zawada and the other two. Or maybe the fourth person was actually good at surveillance.

Well, I couldn't run away from shadows. I had to rely on what I could see, and what I could see was nothing. So I ducked into the t-shirt store, bought a "Wolftown Guest Pass" hat and a generic hoodie, and tossed the Cubs hat in the trash behind the counter, somewhat to the surprise of the old were-wolf running the store, who said, "Hey, they got a chance this year!" as I hurried out.

"Not until those jagoffs sell the team," I called back to him.

"Ah, ya got a point there," he said as the door closed.

I got up to the next street and turned toward the butcher shop.

Out here, away from the plaza, most of the people on the street were extras in their semi-transformed form. A few with human features also had the pallid complexion and wide-brimmed hats that marked them as vampires. I got a few curious looks, but my new hat marked me as a tourist and my determined gait meant I knew where I was going, so most people left me alone.

I kept scanning the streets around me for any sign of the BEA, but I didn't see anyone. Here in Wolftown there were no cars they could sit in semi-inconspicuously, so they would have to be either out in the open or stationed inside buildings. I had no doubt they had a place with a window looking onto the plaza, but they couldn't very well have an office staffed on every street of Wolftown. And cameras in public spaces were still banned in Wolftown—in all Wolftowns, actually. In the seventies, there were a number of FBI raids on extras-rights groups in Port City, and one famous activist named Hank Markovic was shot, and when the details of the surveillance behind those raids came out in the nineties, all Wolftown governments banned cameras. Understandably.

I reached the butcher shop without any further incident and walked inside, setting off a tiny bell as I did so. The aromas of sausage and raw meat overwhelmed me as a female werewolf behind the counter, with reddish-brown fur and dark brown eyes, looked up and her gaze lingered over my hat before she said, "Can I help you?"

"I'm just going to look around," I said.

"I'll be here." She wiped a paw on her apron and went back to doing whatever she was doing back there with a knife and a pile of meat.

There were no other customers in the store. I walked around looking at the sausages, and while I did, I texted Czoltan that I was here. He didn't respond right away, but a few minutes later, I got a text that he was on his way. It was terse, so he was probably going through security.

A moment later, a tall werewolf with black fur and bright green eyes came in. He waved to the wolf behind the counter, said, "Hi, Lucia," and walked right toward me as Lucia said, "Hey," back to him.

I looked up and into the wolf's unsettlingly direct gaze. "Ey," he said with a light Italian accent. "You Jae?"

"Yeah."

He leaned forward, his nose inches from my collar, and he inhaled with his eyes closed. Then he stayed very still as if sorting through flavors of a wine, and finally leaned back and fixed my eyes with his.

I returned his gaze as confidently as I could, and after a moment he nodded. "Come with me." He turned and waved to Lucia. "We're goin' out the back," he said.

She grunted in acknowledgment. As the werewolf took me out through the Employees Only door at the back of the store, I said, "Hey, so what's your name?"

"Later," he said over his shoulder, holding the door for me.

We stepped into a dimly lit short hallway, at the end of which an emergency door was cracked open. The wolf put his nose to the crack, then an eye to it, and then pushed the door open and beckoned me through.

We walked briskly across the street and up the stairs of an old brownstone-style house. When we got to the top, someone inside opened the door and the werewolf hustled me through with a terse, "Come on."

The person who'd opened the door was a female werewolf with grey and white fur. She closed it and then followed us down the mosaic-tiled hallway to the end, where the first werewolf turned left, under the stairs, and went into apartment #2.

The door opened into a living room, with a kitchen visible through a doorway to my left and a hallway to the right. From a couch in the living room, a third werewolf got up, a short one with grey fur. "You found him?" she said, also with a light Italian accent.

"No," said the black-furred werewolf, "this is some other Korean private detective we found wandering around, thought we'd see if he had anything to say."

"I'm a Korean American," I said.

"Funny," the wolf from the couch said to the other wolf, and then stuck out her paw to me. "Hi, I'm Angela."

"Jae," I said, shaking the paw.

"Zo says you're a good guy," she said.

"I'm Matt," said the black-furred werewolf, "and that's Falda."

"Hey," the werewolf who'd opened the door said, nodding.

"You two didn't introduce yourself to him?" Angela said. "What's wrong with you? I brought you up better than that!" She cuffed Matt on the arm.

"There wasn't time, Ma!" He flinched.

"There's always time. How's he supposed to trust you if he doesn't even know your name?" She turned back to me. "I'm so sorry for my kids, but what are you gonna do, huh? Is Zo coming?"

"He's on his way. We had to split up because," I took a breath, "the BEA was following me."

All three werewolves' ears flattened. "Those sons of bitches," Angela said.

"Ma!" Matt protested, and Falda rolled her eyes theatrically.

"I know, I know, I didn't grow up a werewolf like you two, I'm sorry, I still say that sometimes." She stared at Matt. "Did they follow him here?"

TIM SUSMAN

Matt shook his head, and I said, "I changed clothes twice and they only had a couple guys on the job."

Angela's ears came up. "All right, then," she said. "Come on over to the couch. You want something to eat? We got crackers and cheese. Falda! Get some crackers and cheese."

"I'm good," I said, walking over to the couch, but the short grey werewolf was already on her way to the kitchen.

"So why you looking for Marta?" Angela asked as we sat. "You want some wine or beer?"

"Not while I'm working, thanks." I felt lost in the couch, a huge Teflon-fabric affair that wouldn't let me lean against its back with my feet on the floor. I settled for feet on the floor leaning forward. "I got called to Wolftown this morning—"

"Pepsi? Diet? Water?"

"Water, thanks."

"Falda!" Angela called to the kitchen. "Bring a water and a glass of the rosé on the counter there. So." She turned her muzzle back toward me. "You got called here to Wolftown."

Matt sat on the couch on the other side of Angela. "Zo said there's a ghost."

"They're called 'remained,'" Falda called from the kitchen. "And Zo said it's a girl."

"Let Jae tell the story," Angela told them.

"Nobody calls them 'remained' except you," Matt said.

"'Ghost' has lots of baggage," Falda shot back.

"Go on," Angela urged me. "So there's this girl ghost."

"Yeah," I said. "Anyway, I'm supposed to get her to her next of kin, but she doesn't want to go to them, she only wants to—"

"What's wrong with her next of kin?" Angela asked. "If I was a ghost, I'd want Matty or Falda to have me."

"What are we supposed to do with you, Ma?" Falda came in from the kitchen holding a plate with crackers and cheese

96

and a water glass on it, and a glass of wine in the other paw. "Matt, you want a beer? I'm getting one."

"Sure," Matt said.

Falda plopped the plate down on the coffee table in front of me and then reached across me to give Angela the wine. "Thanks, dear," Angela said. "So what's with her family?"

"She won't tell me," I said. "But she wants to talk to someone named Marta."

All three sets of ears went up. "Marta? You mean Marta Delmonico?"

Meanwhile, Falda, on her way back to the kitchen, had said, "How many other Martas do we know?" and Angela had replied, "It could be a Marta we don't know."

"Is she someone hard to get in touch with?" I asked.

Falda laughed, a sharp bark. "Yeah, you could say that."

"That sounds like the right one, then."

"We can't put you in touch with Marta," Angela said. "But we'll tell Zo how to get a message to her when he gets here, and she can decide if she wants to get in touch with you. Have some cheese. There's a Stella Asiago—a real one, fresh, not the salty dry crap you get in the grocery stores—and a Pecorino Sardo, and some Gorgonzola, and—what's this orange one?"

"It's cheddar, Ma." Matt reached past her to grab one of the cheese knives and slice off a bit of it.

"Cheddar?" Angela looked about to sweep the cheese off the plate.

Matt speared it with a claw and popped it into his muzzle. "I like it," he said while chewing. "It's good."

"Aah." She waved him away and appealed to me. "You see what I get, raising my kids in America? Cheddar. Next he'll be eating Velveeta."

Falda returned with two beers, gave one to Matt, and stuck

out her tongue at her mother. "Gross. Mr. Jae, have some cheese. It's really good."

I took some of the closest one, which was the Pecorino, and laid it on a cracker. "How do you all know Czoltan?"

"Oh, Zo worked with our cousin Gaz in Detroit for a while and they started talking about stuff and when Zo came to Chicago, Gaz hooked him up with us," Matt said. "He's a good guy. But you know that."

"I do." The cheese was great, creamy but not soft, with a nutty flavor and a sharpness that lingered on my tongue. "So you guys and Gaz, you're with NOPE?"

"Course we are," Angela said, but I hadn't missed the glance Falda and Matt shared, and that told me enough about whether they were also part of Teardown.

I didn't need to press further, so I switched tacks. "Why'd you say the BEA are 'sons of'...you know?" I asked. "I thought they worked with NOPE."

"I should've said 'bastards,'" she said, and theatrically spit to one side.

"I'm not saying I disagree with you, just wondering what your experience is."

"Fah. When I came over here, I was entitled to benefits for housing, and I went to the office every day for a month before they gave me the papers, and then it took them a year to process, and *then* I only got five thousand dollars, when they'd said I was going to get eight."

"That was fifty years ago, Ma," Matt said.

"So what? He asked!"

"They done worse stuff than that," he replied. "We've been trying to make our conditions better here, you know, Ma taught us if you want something to change, you gotta go make it change, so me and Falda and Gaz and everyone, we march, we write letters, we organize, we call our politicians. Sometimes we print up information for Wolftown people to let them know why we're doing stuff. Not everyone thinks the same way about a 'better life,' you know?"

"Not just werewolves," Falda jumped in. "We try to make sure everyone has a say. We talk to vampires, kitsune, gumiho, naga, nagual, ravens, coyotes, tigers, everyone."

"Right," Matt said. "Anyway, a couple years ago we noticed stuff happening, like we'd print up a flyer and find other flyers already up warning people our flyer was fake. Or we'd do a town meeting to talk about laws coming out and people would show up with signs and yelling, like they'd been organizing and knew what we were gonna say even though the agenda wasn't public. We couldn't get a meeting together for like a month."

"The BEA put a fucking mole in our local group," Falda burst out.

"There was a guy," Matt said, "this werewolf, he'd joined a few months before this started happening, and he was one of those 'oh I want change but I don't wanna break anything' guys, you know?"

"But he smelled funny." Falda tapped her nose.

"Right, he smelled like he wore suits," Matt said. "Even though he always showed up in a t-shirt."

"And he, like, brought a *luna malvagia*." Falda made a circle with both paws and held it in front of her eyes. "Evil moon."

Evil moon was sort of the werewolf equivalent of evil eye, but less personal. The idea was that if you changed under an evil moon, you'd be cursed and things would go wrong for you. Some people brought an evil moon and made things go wrong around them.

"Yeah," Matt said, cutting some more cheddar. "So after a while of things going wrong, he missed a meeting, and presto, the info session we planned didn't have any problems. We figured it might be him."

"And it was the BEA behind him," Angela said triumphantly.

"How do you know it was the BEA?" I asked, more to be a good detective than because I actually doubted them.

"You think we can't sniff out a fed?" Matt asked.

"We went through his wallet," Angela said.

"Ma!" Matt and Falda chorused.

"What, it was years ago and Jae's not gonna turn us in."

She paused there, so I said, "Absolutely not. Even if someone hired me to, there's no evidence other than you talking about it, and that would never hold up in court."

"Right. See?" Angela went on. "We had a swim party, this was after we thought the guy was funny, and so Matty kept him busy in the lake and I found his wallet and he had an BEA thing in it, not a badge but like an old paper card with phone numbers on it." She held up her right arm, which had a beaded bracelet on it. "I got a *protezione*, so the *luna malvagia* don't work on me. He never knew."

"What happened after that?" I asked.

"We told him to fuck off." Falda munched on a plain cracker. "Hey, look, if you wanna help your friend, Marta's a good one. She's with NAPR."

"Ah, that's why you say 'remained,'" I said.

"Yeah. Marta's good. She'll help you."

"But also," Angela said, "the BEA is lookin' for her. She took some ghosts from them."

"'Remained,'" Falda protested. "Ma, you gotta start saying it, it's respectful."

"I will when everyone else does," Angela said, and then to me, "Don't you go leading BEA to Marta. You meet her, you make sure you're clear."

"I will," I promised, reaching for another cracker and some Gorgonzola. "I lost them on the way here, didn't I?"

"That's true," Matt said. "Hey, Ma, do we have any of that apricot tart left?"

"Wait 'til Zo gets here," she said.

"Oh." Matt checked his phone. "He texted. He's down at the shop."

"Go let him in," Angela ordered. "I'll get the tart."

CHAPTER
NINE

I had a flash of wondering why Czoltan hadn't texted me that he was here, but then, he didn't really need to. I wasn't the one who could let him in, after all. But when he came in behind Matt, I didn't even get a chance to say "Good job getting here without being followed" before I saw the angry expression on his muzzle, unmistakable.

"You're taking money from the *FBI*?" he spat.

My skin went cold. How did he—oh. Penny *had* seen the email I'd sent.

The other three werewolves in the room turned to stare at me, and I had a very good idea of how a rabbit might feel. "Ah," I said, "not yet."

"But you're talking to them?"

I searched for an elegant way out of this, while I told myself that the elegant way out was to not have responded to the FBI when they reached out. Nobody else said anything, and Angela moved the apricot tart away from me. "Hey," I said, standing up to face him. "Let's not do this here."

He looked up and saw the other three werewolves staring

at us. His own ears went from flat to splayed. "What," I said, "you thought I wouldn't tell you before I signed anything? Give me a little credit."

"Sorry." His expression changed to confused. He turned Penny's ring over in his paw.

"Maybe you ought to leave," Angela said.

"Yeah. I'm sorry." I walked out from the couch just as my phone buzzed. Without looking, I hit the off button to ignore the call. "I don't want to have this conversation here."

"Oh," Angela said, "I meant just you. Zo can stay."

"But we're not gonna put Marta in touch with you, normie," Falda said.

"It's not for me," I snapped. "Put her in touch with Czoltan if you want. But that remained person," I pointed to Czoltan's paw where he was holding the ring, "she needs to find Marta and I promised her I'd do whatever I could to get her to someone who can help her. The BEA is after her. They attacked me to steal the ring and they tried to follow me here. And my only other option to keep her safe is her abusive family, so think about that, too."

Matt and Falda still looked like they wanted to shred me, but Angela's ears came up a little. "Is that remained person here?"

Czoltan held out the ring. "Let me talk to her," Angela ordered, and Matt picked up the ring and brought it over to her.

They communed silently for a moment, and then Angela opened her eyes. "She's gonna stay with us, and we'll get her to Marta," she said. "That's what she wants."

That almost made sense. I was two seconds away from saying, "Sure, take her," but then I ran through the conse-quences in my mind. "The BEA's looking for her," I said. "So

TIM SUSMAN

you're putting yourselves in danger by taking her. They can detect ghosts—remained persons."

Penny didn't say anything to me and I didn't say anything to her. "Specific ones?" Angela asked sharply.

"Probably not," I said. "But how many do you think there are in Wolftown that they don't control?"

The werewolves all looked at each other. *You don't have to threaten them*, Penny said.

I'm not threatening them, I told her, still angry. *You are.*

Hey! It's not my fault! She sounded close to tears, and I felt worse. Aloud, I said, "And if they find her with you, they can take her, legally, and you know the BEA can make your life difficult too." Already the three Italian werewolves were looking uneasy, and I added, "And that doesn't even touch what happens when you try to get her to Marta."

Angela closed her eyes again, and then held out the ring. "Sorry," she said aloud. "I think Jae's right. You're probably better off with him."

I took the ring back and slipped it on. *Is that why you told him? To get away from me?* I asked.

She didn't answer, but of course, she didn't want to go back to her parents. "I'll go," I said. "But again: Marta's not for me; Marta's for her." I held up the hand the ring was on. "She's been really insistent that she needs to get in touch with Marta. There's got to be a reason for that and maybe Penny and Marta are the only ones who really know how important it is."

That got a nod from Angela, and even Matt and Falda softened a little. "Second," I said, "this FBI thing has nothing to do with Marta or any of you. It's not about Chicago at all. You can go ahead and tell Marta that I'm considering a job with the FBI and she can take whatever precautions she needs to. I wouldn't trust me either, in your shoes, not unless you knew me better."

I couldn't resist a look at Czoltan. The movie line "I'm

doing this for you" ran briefly through my head before I discarded it, but not before Penny caught it. *Yeah*, she said, *don't say that shit.*

Oh, now you're talking to me? I said to her, and then said aloud to Czoltan, "I'm sorry that you found out before I had a chance to tell you. I got spooked when the BEA attacked me. But I promise I haven't signed anything yet, and I won't until we discuss it. Okay?"

"Then you won't sign anything," he said, but his eyes flicked to the other wolves as he said it, and I thought I understood that that was bravado for the audience.

"We'll discuss it," I said, and met his eyes, and he didn't retort this time. I knew he was trying to look tough in front of his friends, but if I managed to talk him into letting me take the FBI job, he was going to have to defend that decision to them. But that was a problem for future me and future him. "Thanks for the hospitality," I said to Angela. "I hope you'll connect us with Marta, for Penny's sake."

"I hope you don't work for the oppressors," she said.

Neither Matt nor Falda said anything to me as I walked past Czoltan and out the door. "See you at home," I said to him, and then the door closed behind me.

Before you say anything, Penny said, in a hurried tone that sounded like she'd been rehearsing for the past few minutes, *this is on you. You should've been honest with him. If he knew about the FBI job, then me telling him wouldn't have mattered at all.*

It's none of your business, I said, marching down the hall and out into the street. I was still going to have to get past the red-haired guy in the plaza, but now that I knew where he was, I wasn't too worried about that. *That was between me and him. And you spied on me.*

You bound me! This is all your fault, if you think about it.

So you'd rather be in the custody of Agent Zawada now? She fell silent. *I don't think he's going to sell you to a pervy Russian billionaire,* I said, *but I do think there's something pretty fucking weird going on here, and if you don't remember or won't tell me what it is, that's fine, but maybe you should have a little bit of respect for the guy who is doing a lot of work—unpaid work, too—to help you.*

We emerged onto the street. I checked for anyone watching and then took a roundabout way back to the plaza.

Oh, mister private detective, Penny said in a simpering voice, *I am so sorry. You're right. I'm ever so grateful to you for saving my honor. Whatever would I do without you?*

Jesus, I said.

Well, don't ask me to give up my principles just because I'm in danger and you happened to volunteer to save me. If a fireman carried me out of a burning building and he had a "People are people, not extras" bumper sticker on his truck, I'd still read him for filth, right?

I'm not asking you to compromise your principles.

You're mad because I'm right, though.

I reminded myself that she was scared and still processing stuff. Even if she was unreasonable, I owed her some slack. Or at least I had to keep this relationship healthy until I found her mom. *I'm mad,* I said, trying to be reasonable, *because you deliberately got Czoltan upset, and because you told him about something you didn't know anything about. I'm not asking you to compromise your principles, but you could've asked me about it first instead of running to tell him. That was a shitty thing to do.*

She didn't respond to that, but I got a stubbornly petulant vibe from her. Navigating through werewolf crowds, I kept turning my head to see if anyone was following me, and I thought it might be helpful to turn her attention to something else. *Hey,* I said. *Can you see behind us?*

How would I do that? I'm seeing through your eyes.

Try to turn your point of view. Like turning your head.

I got to Alvarez and turned right toward the plaza. This should bring us out opposite the red-haired guy. Hopefully I was right about Zawada not having a very big team. One outside in Chicago following me, one in here watching out for me. And Zawada himself, the only one I hadn't seen in the field.

Is it working? I asked Penny.

No. The sullen voice of a teenager who wanted to surpass limitations and couldn't.

It's fine. I checked behind me and saw only werewolves. Angela had said there was a werewolf who worked for the BEA, but I saw nobody in a suit, nobody who ducked away when I turned or seemed to have an excessive interest in me. *Keep working at it. It's hard to do.*

Oh, how would you know how hard it is to do? You're not a remained person.

I worked with one for years and I've trained with them, I said, slowing as we approached the plaza. *All right, can you look at what I'm seeing and see if you can spot the red-haired guy? Is he still there?*

I see him, she said.

I'd spotted him a minute ago, but I pretended I hadn't. *Where?*

There under the awning. Don't pretend you didn't see him just to make me feel better.

Try to keep your gaze on him, I said, and slowly turned my head toward the entrance.

I can't see him anymore.

I turned back until he was in my field of view. *All right. Keep your focus on him.*

I'm trying! But as soon as my head turned, Penny said, *It didn't work.*

One more time, then.

No. Just go. We need to get out.

She wasn't wrong about that. Last I'd seen, the red-haired guy wasn't looking in my direction but at the entrance, which meant he might see me leaving, but might not ping that it was me. In any case, I'd have to be prepared for the other one to be waiting either at the Visitor Center or outside my apartment.

I do have a way to get back into my apartment building that doesn't involve going in the front. It's a little bit dangerous, but probably less so than getting assaulted by the BEA again.

So I kept my head down and pulled the cap low and followed a little group of tourists—German, by the sound of it—to the exit and back out through security. I wished Penny could watch the red-haired guy behind me to see if he perked up at all, but she couldn't, and that was that.

I heard that, she said miserably.

It's fine, I told her as I went back through the much less stringent security. I waved to Portia as I was leaving. *It's not easy.*

Most remained can do it.

Not right away. Just keep practicing. Don't stress about it.

Hah.

She stayed quiet as I entered the Visitor Center cautiously, scanned the crowd and then the sidewalk outside, standing by the souvenir stand. *I don't see any of them. Do you?*

Who am I looking for?

There was a Black woman in a suit. She was driving a brown Ford.

Penny was silent while I continued to scan the area. *I don't see anyone like that*, she said finally.

Me neither. Okay. Keep an eye out. I'm going to take the tricky way back into the apartment.

I made my way down the crowded Chicago streets. My new

t-shirt, some kind of synthetic fabric, was making me sweat more than I'm used to, but I ignored that, keeping my hat down as best I could while still trying to watch the streets.

Back to the apartment. Once I laid out my reasons for taking the job—*looking into* taking the job, that was all I'd done—then I was sure Czoltan and I could figure out...well, not a compromise exactly. I was either going to take it or I wasn't. And if he felt so strongly about it that there was no way I could take it, which I thought might be a danger now after his reaction, well...I'd figure out something. We'd just keep living in separate cities for five more years until we could save up enough for a place.

I was mad at myself for not having the conversation sooner, but also mad at Penny for precipitating it, because now it would be harder than it had to be. If I'd been able to have the conversation in my own time...but I'd had plenty of time.

I had to double-check to be sure that that hadn't been in Penny's voice. No; she was withdrawn and not paying attention to me very much, and the feeling I got from her was uncertainty and some fear. And then I caught an image of a dark office building, a computer screen, and a feeling of tension and triumph.

Where's that? I asked.

I shouldn't tell you, she said.

That was better than "won't," I guess. *Why not?*

If I committed a crime—hypothetically—you'd have to tell someone about it, wouldn't you? Like one of your cop friends?

Is that why the BEA is after you? Did you steal something from them?

I'm not saying I did, but if I did, I was only trying to help people.

Well, shit. How was I supposed to be mad at her now? Just get home, I told myself, and then we'll deal with the rest of it.

Two more blocks. We made it to the corner of my street,

where I slowed and peered down to see if the brown Ford was there. It was hard to tell from this angle, but there was a brown car that looked like it, and it was right around where the front of my building was.

I turned down the street, but went into the high rise two doors down from mine, which had the advantage of an entry alcove hidden from the street and a door entry code I knew. I slipped into the cool lobby and headed for the elevators.

This was an older building that didn't have key card or code validation on the elevators that mine had, so I rode to the top floor without any problem. From there, it was just a matter of going past a bunch of apartments to the maintenance stairwell, and up a flight to the roof.

I emerged out into the humid heat again with the smell of rooftop tar. The door swung shut behind me with a click that seemed to rouse Penny.

Why didn't you leave the apartment this way? she asked.

I turned around and pulled on the door, which was locked. *Can't get in this way unless I come up and tape the door open.*

But you can get in yours?

I jingled keys in my pocket. *Being a long-time resident has its privileges.*

Handy. You come this way often?

Not if I can help it. I walked to the edge and over to the next roof. *I don't like rooftops.*

Afraid of heights? Don't look down, by the way.

Not so much that. There's usually only one entrance and exit and if people follow you up, you're cornered. That's not good. I navigated around a large vent and to the opposite roof. *And lots of people see movies and think running to the roof is a good idea. There are some places, like here, where they connect and they're not so dangerous, but if the buildings aren't the same height and you're not trained in parkour, you're way more likely to hurt yourself than to get away.*

Makes sense, she said, still sounding a little distant.

I wanted to ask how she was doing, but I was also still mad at her, so I gave myself until I was back in the apartment. A quick step over to the other roof, where I peered down at the street.

Hey! What did I say?

Sorry. I stepped back, having seen the brown Ford. *Just wanted to check. They're there again.*

Now what? Going to stay in your apartment forever?

Once I get back there, there's things I can do. I think there's only a few of them, so they're not going to do round-the-clock surveillance. I walked over to the access door and unlocked it.

So we can get out to see Marta?

If Czoltan's friends still give us her contact info after that shit you pulled.

Me? Her tone got more energized. *This was your decision.*

Yeah. And you picked the time to tell my boyfriend about it.

She didn't say anything as I walked down the maintenance stairwell to my floor, and from there into the apartment. When I'd gotten inside and closed the door, I took a moment to sink into the couch and relax. I pulled out my phone to see if Czoltan had texted, and saw that the call I'd missed had been from Mom.

Shit. I reflexively moved my finger to the "Call Back" link but then stopped it. I didn't want to be talking to Mom when Czoltan came home. I'd just talked to her this morning; she had more wedding plans or questions and they could wait until tomorrow. Still, my chest got tight as I cleared the notification without calling back, and I had to repeat, It's okay, you just talked to her, it's fine.

Penny's voice came tentative again, breaking into my guilt mantra. *Am I gonna lose my mind?*

No. Why do you ask that?

It was something Czoltan said about remained, that they can lose themselves. I know that can happen but I never, like, felt it could happen.

You know being bound protects you from that, right? Having another body linked to yours grounds you. You're used to having a body, and an untethered mind without input from the outside world can lose itself. But binding stabilizes you.

But there are bound remained who lose their minds.

When the people who've bound them also have mental stability problems.

There was a pause, and then she said, *I think I'm in trouble.*

My initial reaction was to reassure her, but before I could formulate the words, I realized that she was being funny, so I said, *Ha ha*, and I got up to go to my police scanner.

I have a list of the allocated bands next to it. The BEA has a few, so I checked each one. Nothing on any of them, but it was a long shot anyway, if Rock and his people were doing something outside of normal protocol. I shut it off and went to get myself a drink from the fridge.

Czoltan hadn't texted me. When I'd drained most of a glass of iced tea, I sent him a text asking when he was coming home, and if he could pick up stuff for the chicken tagine because I didn't want to leave the apartment. Act as though everything's normal, I told myself. Act like you're not worried he's just going to crash with his friends.

He won't, Penny said.

How do you know?

Because he loves you. It's kinda gross. He was really upset about the FBI thing and you don't get that upset if you're gonna dump someone. Like I was sort of seeing this guy, and when I dropped out of school, we just stopped texting. But we weren't in love or anything.

I savored the warmth from knowing that for a moment before my detective instincts kicked in. *What'd you drop out of school for?*

To make a difference in the world, she said.

With the Unified Society people.

A second of hesitation. *Yeah.*

You feel strongly about extras too, huh?

They get a shit deal, she said. *But you know that.*

Yeah. I didn't want to go near the window in case Brown Ford Agent was looking up through binoculars, but I didn't have to get close to see the walls of Wolftown. *You think they should be able to live wherever they want?*

Sure, I guess.

The words, and the lukewarm feeling of assent, rang a little strange to me. Someone who'd left home to agitate for extras rights should feel more passionate about that, and Penny was clearly passionate about some things. *You're more concerned with remained persons?*

There was a pause and then, *Yeah, you got me. Look at you, mister detective. You do a lot of interrogations?*

A lot of what I do is process serving, I said, texting Czoltan to keep an eye out for the brown Ford out front and that I could let him in the back door.

Penny watched that text. *So you know a lot about being followed.*

She didn't seem to want to talk about ghost rights, so I let that go for now. *I have to know all the tricks people use to try to shake me. Going in a back door is a classic one.*

And onto the roof?

I laughed. *Sometimes.*

Hell of a job, she said.

I was trying to move on to other stuff, I said.

Yeah, she replied, *I'm not sure working for the feds is a step up, y'know?*

Money-wise it is. I refilled the iced tea and walked back to the couch.

Money isn't everything.

I remember when I was young enough to think that too, I told her.

Maybe you should try to remember harder, she said, and I didn't have a good reply to that.

CHAPTER

TEN

C zoltan got home at quarter to six and dumped a bag of groceries onto the counter, then pulled his shirt off and shifted from human to wolf. "There wasn't a brown car there," he said.

Do me a favor, I said to Penny as I got up, *and keep quiet for a minute here.*

I wasn't quite able to disguise my irritation with her, the resentment that I'd gone out of my way to help her and she'd rewarded me by fucking around with my relationship. I half-expected her to tell me again that the whole thing was my fault, and we'd go around that whole tangle of guilt and blame one more time, but she said, *Sure*, and went quiet.

"I got the stuff," he said, and headed for the living room.

I put a hand on his shoulder, and he stopped. I breathed through the tightness, feeling all bunched up. "Can I explain?"

He gave a quick nod, and his ears weren't all the way back, so that was a good sign. "All right. First off, like I said, it's true: I haven't taken the job yet. I did tell them I thought I could and to send off a contract, but I haven't gotten the contract yet, let alone signed it. I was going to talk to you before I even did that, but I got spooked after the BEA thing."

His ear flicked. I went on. "Because I bound this ghost and apparently they really want her. Enough to attack me. And I thought that once they knew who I was, they might contact the FBI and I'd lose the chance at the job."

"I told you you shouldn't have bound that ghost," Czoltan said. "And why is this FBI job so important?"

"Because of what they're paying." I told him the number.

That brought his ears back up. "Seriously?"

"Yeah."

"That's like..."

"It's a third of what I usually make in a year."

He recovered from the sticker shock. "It's just money, though. You'd be helping the FBI. You remember about Hank Markovic and the Port City raids, right?"

"It's not the money. Not just the money." I wanted to go on but the words stuck.

"What did you need that much money for?" He tilted his head. "If it was for a big vacation, I don't need it."

"I've been looking at bigger places to live here in Chicago."

His ears came all the way up and he stared at me. The anger at the job wasn't gone, but he understood what it was about now, and he was there with me, which was a huge relief, let me tell you. A lot of the tension went out of my neck and shoulders. "Bigger...for just you, or...?"

"I know we haven't talked about moving in together. But it feels like it's heading that way. Ah, at least to me."

"No, me too," he jumped in. "I was going to say something."

"But everything bigger around here is way more expensive. And I don't think I can move my job to Detroit very easily."

"But Jae," he said. "The FBI? Come on."

"I know. But…it's not the seventies anymore. And this isn't in Chicago or Detroit. It's some East Coast guy. All I have to do is find him. They didn't say they're going to arrest him or anything. Maybe they just want to…yeah, okay," I said under his glare. "I know it's not worth saying 'sometimes the government isn't actively oppressing extras.'"

He shook his head. "Sometimes they're not, but y'know, when they're actively looking for a guy they can't find, it's probably because he doesn't want them to find him."

"Yeah." I looked away, out my living room window, toward the walls of Wolftown.

"But," Czoltan said. "This place really is too small."

"I know. It was a little small just for me, too."

He put an arm around my shoulders. "Find out what they want him for. Don't sign anything until you hear that, and make a judgment. Sound fair?"

"Nah," I said, leaning into him. The relief of being in his embrace overwhelmed everything else. I'd done something stupid and lost him for five years; I didn't want to lose him again. "I mean, yes, it sounds fair, but I don't want you resenting me because of the work I'm doing. I should just turn it down."

"I don't want you resenting me if we're still living in separate cities in a year," Czoltan said. "Let's get more information. If it's really something that's, y'know, really criminal and not just an attempt to oppress activism, then go ahead and do it."

"I'll find out more," I promised.

"And tell me before you do big shit like this." He pushed his cold, damp nose against mine. "I get that your job means you can't always share everything, but…"

"Yeah," I said, a knife blade of guilt cutting through the relief. "I know." And to make myself feel better, I put my hands on his sides, pressing through the fur, and said, "But you do want to move in together?"

He smiled. "Yeah, silly. Course I do."

I pushed aside the thought that he cared more about activism than about our future together and hugged him, pressing my face into his fur. He hugged me back, and then he pushed his lips against mine and kissed me, and his tongue brushed my lips. I kissed back without thinking, felt the wag of his tail, felt his hips press into mine—

Ahem.

"Shit," I said, and pulled away from the kiss.

His ears went back. "I have a ghost," I said. "I mean, Penny, she's still..." I held up the hand with the ring on it.

"Oh," he said. "I forgot about that."

"Yeah, me too."

"Can you...take the ring off?"

"And leave Penny alone in the dark so we can have sex? She can't see except through my eyes yet."

Also I don't want to see your recent memories, thank you.

He kissed my nose. "I love the impulse that made you go bind this ghost, but also your good impulses lead you to really inconvenient places sometimes."

I hugged him one more time and then went to the kitchen to start dinner. "Like with the BEA after me? Yeah, I know. Don't worry, hopefully your friends come through or Yumi does and tomorrow she'll be safe."

"And we can...celebrate." He winked at me.

You guys are so gross.

It's called 'adults navigating a relationship,' I told her, taking the chicken and figs out and getting the rest of the ingredients ready. *I guess you didn't have that kind of model growing up.*

Bingo.

Want to talk about it?

Not really. Maybe I'll tell you later.

So while I made dinner—we decided to do that chicken tagine anyway—I talked over the kitchen bar to Czoltan in the living room, acting like everything was normal and we weren't under surveillance from the BEA and our future wasn't hanging on the moral standards of the FBI. "Penny didn't happen to tell *you* how to get in touch with Marta, did she?"

"No," Czoltan said. "Did you get a reply from Gina?"

Hey, I can hear you.

I figured you might trust him more than me, I said as I got my phone out.

I do, but I also know he'll tell you anything.

Fair. I checked my email and I did have a reply from Gina. "She doesn't have a way to get in touch with Marta. She apologizes for not being more help." I shoved the phone back in my pocket. "I guess she doesn't trust me either."

"Or maybe," Czoltan said, "she really doesn't. If Marta's an activist and people are after her, maybe she doesn't have a phone number or an address."

Do you have a way to get in touch with her that you're not telling me? I asked Penny, and then vocalized it for Czoltan's benefit even though he understood what was happening if I stared into space and didn't answer.

There was a long pause. *No,* Penny confessed. *She always contacted me. If it was by phone it was always a different number. I thought Gina would know because Marta shows up to Gina's meetings, but maybe she doesn't.*

I looked at Czoltan and shook my head. *Why do you want to go to her so badly?*

I have to—I have to give her something. I can't trust anyone else with it. And she took care of me these last few months.

Something you took from the BEA. Something Rock wants back.

She didn't answer, and I moved on. *Does this have something to do with how you died?*

There was a longer pause. *Maybe,* she said. *I don't really know how I died. I just went to sleep. When I woke up, everything was different. I really thought I was dreaming until—until after you bound me.*

All right, I said. *I promise we'll try to get you to Marta.*

Before you take that FBI job, thank you.

All right, all right.

"Penny says she doesn't know how to reach Marta," I told Czoltan, "but she has something really important to give her."

"You think that's why the BEA is after her?" he asked.

I nodded. "It would make sense. Also that would explain why Zawada showed up so quickly to the scene."

"What does she say about that?" he asked.

I waited. "Nothing," I said when she stayed silent. "Hey, did you know the BEA did, like, counter-terrorism drills against extras?"

"Kind of?" Czoltan sighed. "People talk about it but they never got proof. Gaz said they found an BEA guy snooping on their meetings."

"They found a card in his wallet," I said as I chopped the chicken into manageable pieces. "That's what Angela said."

"Really? Shit. The thing is..." He made a low growl. "In Detroit, at least, they do good stuff too. You know? There's one guy, he comes into Wolftown and gives talks on laws and how they affect extras and all that. He's really nice and approachable and it feels like he wants us to do well."

"Yeah?" I moved on to chopping the eggplant and carrots.

"So I don't want people to stop trusting him because the Chicago branch is a bunch of Eliot Ness wanna-bes." He growled and then leaned back and stared up at the ceiling. "And

I know what I said before about the FBI maybe doing things for the right reasons. I guess the first BEA people I met really did help me, but I've only heard of the FBI as the guys who, y'know, killed Markovic. And Fred Hampton, here in Chicago."

Ooh, I really like him, Penny said. *But the BEA are just as bad as the FBI, if not worse.*

I started to say, "Allegedly," but I believed it as much as he did, so instead I said, "Ness was Treasury. And I'm not sure it's the whole branch here, not that that matters."

He snorted. "The point is, we know they watch us, we know they don't like the activism, but they feel like they're trying to help us the way they know how. And if we fuck around with them, they could make things so much worse."

I asked Penny, *Do you think there's a chance the FBI wants me to find this guy for regular crimes? Seriously, not a smartass answer. They said it's for smuggling wolfsbane, and that happens.*

Seriously? There's a chance, sure. I don't think it's a good one.

To Czoltan I said, "Why don't they like the activism, though? If the point is to make life better for extras, and that's their job, shouldn't they support the activism?"

He nodded. "Some of them do. Dave, that's the guy I was talking about, he won't come to meetings because sometimes it's anti-government activity, and he's part of the government, so he says he shouldn't do it because of his job, but also it's like the cops showing up and he wouldn't want that. Some of the others are like that too. I guess some of them want to know what's going on?"

"Maybe." I sighed. "Maybe I'm making it more complicated than it needs to be. Why is a government agency interesting in stopping people who are trying to upset the power structure? When you put the question that way, there's not much mystery to it."

"I guess." Czoltan scratched behind one ear. "The question is more: Why are there people like Dave?"

"Any government agency is going to be like that," I said. "There's going to be people who care about the work, and people who care about the politics."

"It sucks," Czoltan said.

"Sure." I tossed the chicken into the pan to sauté and went to get the spices. "But if the government was on board with what you want to do, you wouldn't have to be an activist. So it sorta happens by definition."

He grumbled. "No more politics."

"No," I agreed. "Hey, see what's on TV." Things felt normal, if a shaky kind of normal, and the chicken tagine ended up being good. Even Penny said so.

CHAPTER
ELEVEN

In the morning, a call from Yumi woke me up. "We got an ID on the body," she said. "I'm going to notify the next of kin. Want to come along?"

I blinked and rubbed my eyes. "Yeah," I said. "When?"

"I'll come by and collect you. Forty-five minutes?"

When I pulled my phone away from my ear to look at it, the time said 8:07. "I've got BEA agents watching the apartment," I said. "I'll be ready, but check for a stakeout before you show up."

"Ugh," Yumi said. She didn't sound surprised. "You want to meet me somewhere else? Flower shop on 71st?"

"Sure," I said. "I'll be there in forty."

Beside me, Czoltan rolled over and threw a large paw over my stomach. I put the phone back on the nightstand. "Where you goin'?" he murmured.

I rubbed the ring on my finger. "You hear back from Angela yet?"

He checked. "No."

"Then I'm going to see Penny's relatives and, hopefully, turn custody of her over to them."

Hey! I didn't agree to this! You haven't even heard back from Marta yet.

I'm sorry, I really am, but keeping you safe from the BEA is more important. If Marta contacts us, we can get her in touch with your next of kin.

It's hard enough to get Marta to talk to you, what makes you think she'll talk to my mom?

I'm available as a go-between. I can't keep custody of you but that doesn't mean I'll just go away.

This just makes it more complicated.

All right, I told her as I got up and got dressed. *We have to go report your death. I'll tell them that you're a ghost, but if you can convince me there's a good reason not to turn over your custody, I'll stall and say we need to do some paperwork. Deal?*

Deal. She said it quickly enough that I suspected I'd tripped up somehow, but I couldn't see how.

I risked a peek out the bedroom window, and didn't see the brown Ford out front, or anywhere on the block. That didn't mean they weren't watching from somewhere, but I gambled that they either thought I was still in Wolftown or that they'd given up. Still, I went out the back door and kept an eye out for any surveillance.

I'd expected Yumi to be in the beige Toyota Camry that the Wolftown peacekeepers kept for use out in the city proper, but she was standing on the sidewalk in front of the flower shop in a black full-length overcoat. When I walked up, she looked up from her phone. "Hey," she said. "It's this way."

I looked around for the brown Ford, or for any people suspiciously sitting in their car on the street, but didn't see any. That didn't mean they had given up. But it didn't matter, because we were on our way to hand over custody of Penny to her mom, and with Yumi at my side I was less worried about being attacked.

I ignored the nagging thought of "what if Penny's mom was more deferential to the government than I was," and Penny didn't say anything about that either. I sensed her apprehension, but it wasn't all that strong, so either her mom wasn't as bad as she was making out, or...she was confident this day wouldn't end with her in her mom's custody.

While I was looking at the windows of buildings across the way for, I dunno, glints of binoculars or something, Yumi walked away, nodding for me to follow. I hurried to keep up. "It's a walk?"

"Half a mile." She pointed in the direction of the Wolftown walls, but to one side. "We're going to her office."

"Her office?"

"She's in today," Yumi said. "I just called to check. Didn't want to give her the news over the phone."

"Okay." There were a lot of small business offices around that part of town: lawyers, chiropractors, shops that sold polished geodes as home decoration, that sort of thing. "What's she do?"

"First of all," Yumi said, "tell me why the BEA is following you. Is it that guy Rock?"

"Pretty sure it's him and a few of his colleagues, but not much more than that." I filled her in on what had happened since I'd left her at the house: the attack by the red-haired BEA agent, the surveillance, the pursuit, Penny's insistence on meeting Marta, whom I suspected was an activist.

When I was done, Yumi shook her head, then looked around, checking our surroundings. I admired her cool. "Stepped in it this time, didn't we? Why do they want her so bad?"

"She's mixed up with activists, so it might be that. She

125

says..." I paused, not wanting to implicate Penny in anything criminal. "She knows something they don't want to get out."

"I know something else it might be," Yumi said, looking down the street.

"You do?" Penny, who had been radiating mild appreciation for my restraint in talking to Yumi about her, was also startled.

Yumi gave me a sidelong look and then said, "Her mom is the Alderman."

"For the 13th?"

"Yep. So...when you have two strange things on the same case, chances are they're related."

Well, shit. Everyone associated with Wolftown Chicago knew Sylvia Louderman, the Alderman for the 13th Ward, which included mostly Wolftown and just enough other property to allow the Alderman to live outside its walls. Which they always had, because every Alderman who had ever represented Wolftown to the Chicago City Council had been human.

An Alderman presided over each of Chicago's fifty wards, and the fifty together made up the City Council. Each Alderman's office represented their constituents in Chicago as a whole, and made sure their concerns would be heard and addressed by the city. The Alderman for the 13th held a lot of power over Wolftown, not only what improvements were slated to be made to buildings and roads, but how much went to the annual budget every year.

As with many of the Alderman offices, the 13th was a family business. Sylvia had taken over from her father, Roger Louderman, who'd represented the 13th for forty years. He'd passed away five years ago, and was remembered as a fair man who'd kept the streets in good repair, built lots of new housing, and kept his corruption to levels that never attracted too much attention. Just like most local politicians, in other words.

Sylvia I hadn't heard too much about. But that Penny was her daughter? That gave the BEA's pursuit of her a whole other angle I hadn't even considered. Did they want her as leverage to get some concessions from Sylvia? It was hard to imagine that Penny could have information about her mother's office that the government couldn't get through regular channels.

Yep, Penny said. *That's my mom. She's a bitch, by the way.*

I figured you had to be if you were a woman in politics.

Right, but she's like, super-bitch.

How so?

Penny laughed. *You'll see. But I don't think that's why the feds are after me.*

I considered whether to tell Yumi about this, but decided it wasn't worth coloring her impression of Ms. Louderman before we arrived. *How long ago did you run away from her?* I asked.

I got a wave of surprise from Penny. *How did you know that?*

I didn't, but I guessed, I said. *She's a public figure, and if she'd been expecting to see you back, she would've been worried and called the police. Plus you dropped out of school and were in a house full of activists, so she probably didn't know where you were. It's summer, so you could possibly have been away at camp or something—*

I used to go to camp.

—But you're a little old for that. And your whole attitude about going back to her has been kind of "don't send me back there." So I made a guess.

Good guess, she said grudgingly. *It's been almost a year.*

I did not press as to the cause of the running away. In a few moments I would be able to ask the mother herself.

"You talking to the ghost or just staring off into space?" Yumi asked at my silence.

"Talking to her."

"She saying anything interesting?"

"She hasn't seen her mother in almost a year."

I ran away a year ago. I saw her—once or twice after that.

That didn't seem worth correcting, so I let Yumi reflect on that. "That explains why her mother hasn't filed a missing person report. I know if I hadn't heard from my kid in 24 hours, I'd be freaking out. But then, we have check-in times in the morning and afternoon."

Then she asked what had happened to drive Penny away, and I said I didn't know. The streets grew more crowded as we approached the Alderman's office, with people going to work or getting errands done before the heat of the day really took hold. Already I felt like even the light jacket I had on over my shirt had been a mistake.

Yumi's bone-white skin didn't show any flush despite her long overcoat. "Does the heat even bother you?" I asked.

"I feel like I'm melting," she snapped back. "But the coat helps."

It was definitely drawing some curious looks, but she knew her body better than I did, or the people staring did, so I didn't question it. After a moment, Yumi glanced over at me. "I can go snow inside the coat a little bit when I get too warm, and that helps."

We walked a little longer, and I kept glancing at the coat, until Yumi said, "If you want to see, I can show you."

"Ah," I said, "maybe some other time."

"I didn't mean right now." She scowled. "I know where we are."

I looked around at all the humans. "Right," I said. "Some other time, then."

Ms. Louderman's office, at about 65th and Pulaski, was a three-story building with a slick rose marble facade that stood out from the limestone buildings around it. A semi-cylindrical red awning sheltered us from the sun as we approached the glass doors, and a blast of air conditioned air cooled us as we entered.

The Alderman's office was on the third floor, so we took the elevator up. A young man in a white pinstriped shirt with a bright orange tie greeted us from behind a receptionist desk without any of the surprise the people on the street had shown at Yumi's pallid features and long black coat. "Do you have an appointment?" he asked.

"We have to see the Alderman about an urgent family matter," Yumi said, and produced a badge. "I'm with the Wolftown peacekeepers."

The young man looked at the badge, and now his features creased with anxiety. "What's happened to Penny?" he asked.

You know him? I asked Penny.

Yeah, she said, sounding miserable.

"Why do you assume it's Penny?" Yumi asked.

"Penny was the one who—she always cared about the extras," he said. "She was supposed to call me this morning and she hasn't, and now a Wolftown peacekeeper is here. It's about her, isn't it?"

"I really should talk to Ms. Louderman," Yumi said gently.

His face fell. "She's on a call right now, but she should be off in ten minutes. Can you wait?"

Yumi nodded. "We can wait."

There were three threadbare cloth chairs that looked like Ms. Louderman's father had originally bought them—second-hand—so Yumi and I took two of them. As I sat, my vision blurred and split, and I seemed to have remained standing from one perspective, while my body definitely sat in the chair.

I realized that this was Penny experimenting just as she said, *That sort of worked*, and my vision snapped back to normal.

Yumi said something to me, but I missed it, and she

seemed to understand I was preoccupied with Penny because she stopped trying to talk to me. *You were trying to leave the ring?* I asked Penny. *That was a good first try.*

That was my fourth try. She sounded discouraged. *I worked on it while you were asleep.*

Still good, I told her. *Sergei—he was my old partner—he said it took him a week to learn to manifest.*

I can't even imagine how to manifest, she said. *But I don't want to go in there.*

I might have to leave the ring outside if the office is ghost-proofed, I said. *A lot of politicians' offices are. If I do, it'll only be for a short time. Will you be okay?*

She laughed. *The office isn't ghost-proofed,* she said. *I just don't want to go in.*

Again my vision split, and this time my reflexive memory of how it had worked with Sergei clicked in. *That lasted longer,* I told her.

Yeah. I think I get how to do it, she said. *It's just tiring.*

The more you do it, the easier it is.

You sound so old, she said, and left the ring again, this time drifting through the floor to the offices below. *Hey, I like going through walls, though. What would happen if a place was...ghost-proofed?* She said that last word contemptuously.

You wouldn't be able to go into it, I told her. *Like walking into a wall when you were corporeal.*

That doesn't seem fair. Through her eyes I saw a series of cubicles, and then office doors with signs that read "A. Zemaitis, Senior Partner," and "B. Laukaitis, Senior Partner." A law firm, then; there had been one listed in the lobby. Penny zoomed in to look at the papers one of the clerks in a cubicle was working on.

Hey, I said. *No spying.*

If they didn't want remained looking at their papers, she retorted, *they should've ghost-proofed the office.*

Regardless, I said as she examined a paper full of incomprehensible (to me) legalese, *you wouldn't just walk into an office and start looking at papers.*

If they left the door unlocked, I absolutely would.

I sighed. *Well, can you hold off for another,* I checked my phone, *five minutes? Please?*

Penny snorted. *I can tell you're anxious to get rid of me, but trust me, you're not gonna.*

Fine, I said, *but can you stay out of the law offices until we finish with your mom?*

Ugh. I'll go outside, how about that? Is that permissible?

I had no idea how to answer a sarcastic teenager, so I said, *That's fine, thank you.*

My point of view swept sickeningly through walls and floors until it came to rest outside the building on the sidewalk, just as the receptionist said, "She's off the call."

I partitioned that sidewalk view out of my mind to focus on the present, following Yumi over to the reception desk as the receptionist told Ms. Louderman that there were some Wolftown peacekeepers to see her on an urgent matter.

To the right of the desk, there were an array of pamphlets, the usual kinds of things that politicians had up in their office: photocopied "How the System Works" and "Know Your Rights" and so on, but a few at the end caught my eye. The first was a color pamphlet on shiny paper that said, "Extra-Human Relations," and had a human and a werewolf shaking hand and paw over a small replica of the Wolftown wall, both with big smiles. The second was a less well-produced pamphlet for NOPE with the headline "Protecting Extranormal People Since 1968," and a color picture of a werewolf, a vampire, and a kitsune holding protest signs.

The third was a simple photocopied page with the footer "NAPR." It wasn't in the rack with the other pamphlets, but half-hidden under the end of the rack, so all that was visible was some text, the NAPR logo, and the slogan, "People Remain People." It felt odd to see their flyer here, but if Ms. Louderman was in charge of Wolftown, maybe she was also active in ghost rights. Was that why she wouldn't take custody of Penny?

"She'll see you," the receptionist said. He met my eyes as Yumi headed for the door, and I was surprised by the gleam of tears.

Sylvia Louderman sat behind a large desk, but despite her small stature, she presided over the desk and the room with an air of authority that made me think she'd be a tough opponent in any debate. Her blond shoulder-length hair gleamed over a pair of sharp eyes that assessed us warily as we walked in.

She stood, straightening her beige suit jacket, and waved us to the chairs in front of her desk. "Come in," she said. "What's the urgent matter? It's Penny, isn't it?"

"It is," Yumi said.

Before she could continue, Ms. Louderman sat. "I knew it. That girl has been nothing but trouble. Well, I'll bail her out if I have to." But she didn't reach for a checkbook or anything, her eyes on Yumi. I felt that she was pleading for the trouble to only be that Penny had been arrested.

"It's not that," Yumi said. "I'm sorry—"

"Please sit down," Ms. Louderman said with some desperation. I got it: now she knew the news was bad, and the longer she stalled, the longer before she would have to hear it, even if it were just a second or two.

"I'd rather stand," Yumi said, and then, probably sensing that Ms. Louderman was going to interrupt again, she hurried out the rest of it. "I'm sorry to tell you that Penny died a day ago."

Ms. Louderman stared at her for several seconds, showing no reaction except to swallow visibly, twice. "What happened?" she asked in a strained voice.

"We don't know yet. We're investigating."

"Was it drugs?" Now her voice had acquired a harsh, emotional edge. Before Yumi could answer, she went on. "I knew those friends of hers were into drugs. I warned her—" Here, finally, her voice broke. She caught a sob in her throat.

Yumi waited, but the Alderman didn't continue even when she'd composed herself, tears running down her cheeks. "We don't know," Yumi said gently. "There were no signs of violence."

"When are you going to know?" Her tone got harsher; she wiped her tears away with brusque swats of her fingers.

"Now that we've identified her, we'll be in touch with you as soon as we know," Yumi said. "I'm so sorry. I can give you the number of our grief counselor—"

"I know you're sorry," Ms. Louderman said. "You said that. It won't bring my daughter back, will it? Who's this?" She jerked her head toward me.

"This is Jae Kim. He's a private investigator—"

"Looking into Penny's death?" She narrowed her eyes. "Who hired you?"

"In a sense," I said. "But nobody's hired me yet."

"How dare you come looking for work, you ambulance-chaser. Get out!"

"No, no." I held up my hands. "What I mean is, your daughter remained behind as a ghost, and I've got experience—"

That was as far as I got before she let out a scream that raised the hackles on the back of my neck. She stood up and glared at me as though I'd murdered her daughter right there that moment. "Get *out!*" she yelled.

I took a step back. Yumi did too, but recovered quicker. "Maybe you don't understand, Ms. Louderman," she said. "This is good news."

"Oh, I understand," said Ms. Louderman, stepping out from behind her desk. "I understand perfectly well." She advanced on me and I took another step back. "I know how people like you prey on the recently bereaved, how you use mimics and tricks to make people think their loved ones haven't really died." I'd backed up to the door, and she was barely two feet from me now, her face flushed, her hair already ruffled.

"I don't do any of that," I protested.

"Nooooo, of course not," she said. "You really believe that people's spirits remain behind, somehow don't move on to the afterlife."

"Ghosts are real." I couldn't think of a counterargument better than that.

"Out!" she screamed again. "How dare you! How *dare* you!"

Yumi moved toward the door and I retreated into the doorway. But I couldn't look away from Penny's mother's grief, and I couldn't stop thinking that Penny was just outside the building. "I'm just trying to do what's best for her," I said. "I'm not trying to take advantage of you."

She raised an arm, anger and grief blazing out of her eyes. I backpedaled out of the office. "I'll leave a card with your receptionist," I called through the door. "Please contact me."

Yumi hurried out of the office to stand beside me. The door slammed in our faces.

"Well." Yumi gathered her topcoat around herself. "I didn't expect that."

Told you she's a bitch, Penny said smugly.

The young man behind the desk cleared his throat to get our attention. "I wish you'd told me Penny remained behind," he said in almost a whisper. "Ms. Louderman doesn't believe in remained persons."

"I gathered that," I said. "I guess she follows Mike Warden, huh?"

He nodded. "She's even talked to him on the phone."

"Who's Mike Warden?" Yumi asked.

"This YouTube guy," I told her. "Says that ghosts—remained—are fake and that people who try to get you to believe in them are—well, basically what she said in there, like charlatans preying on the bereaved. But I don't get why she's got NAPR fliers out." I gestured to the rack.

The young man smiled guiltily. "They're mine," he said. "When she sees them, she throws them out. That's why I keep them around this side of the desk. Let me take your card," he said.

At that moment, Penny spoke. *There's people out front*, she told me with some alarm.

I fished out a card to give the receptionist. *What kind of people?*

"Thanks," he said, taking it. "I'm Jake, by the way." He pushed a card across the desk that had Sylvia Louderman's name on it and tapped the phone number. "This number rings here, if you ever need to talk to me."

Can't you see? Penny asked impatiently.

I could, I realized. I turned my attention to what she was seeing, and there were three people in dark suits, which already raised alarms on a Chicago summer day. But one of them was Rock Zawada and the other two were the Black woman and the red-haired man. That was worse. "Thanks, Jake," I said. "Hey, are there back stairs?"

"There's a fire exit," he said. "Out the main office there and to the left, you'll see it."

"Great," I said. "Thanks. I'll be in touch. Yumi, we should go."

"Yeah," she agreed, and left the office with me.

Once we were outside, she reached for the elevator button, but I stopped her. She gave me a curious look. "What's this about the stairs?"

"BEA is downstairs." I was looking through Penny's point of view to make sure all three of the agents got in the elevator. As they stood outside the doors waiting, the woman checked a handheld device and startled, then looked around. "Code 45," she said sharply.

What's that thing she's holding? Penny asked.

Probably a ghost detector, I replied grimly. *Sorry—remained person detector. They can't tell exactly where you are, but they know when you're within fifty feet or so.*

My view spun and shifted, making me clap one hand to my head. *No*, I told her, *stay down there.*

But they can see me!

They can't see you. They know you're around, but they have a code specifically so they don't alert the remained person that they know she's there. If you disappear, they'll start to wonder if you know their codes. And I need to know if they all get into the elevator.

Penny's view spun back and stabilized again, out in the street. *Are you sure they can't get me?*

They could trap you, but they need to cast a spell to do that, and as long as I have the ring, I can break it if that happens. They can't take you away from here or break the binding without the ring.

"What's going on?" Yumi asked.

"We're going to take the stairs as soon as I see them get into the elevator," I said.

What if they get the ring?

Then they could put it in a ghost-proofed case and I wouldn't be able to talk to you or sense you.

And they could break the binding?

Maybe, yeah. I closed my hand into a fist. *But they're not going to get the ring.*

All right. Penny moved slowly back inside, where the three agents still waited in front of the elevator. Zawada murmured to the agent with the detector, both of them looking at it.

"I'd just gotten used to you being able to give your full attention to a conversation," Yumi grumbled. "How did the BEA track you here? Or have they been watching us the whole time?"

"That's what I'm hoping to find out." The elevator in the lobby opened. Zawada took the detector and got in; the other two remained in the lobby. "Shit. He's coming up, the other two are still there. Let's hit the stairs." To Penny I said, *Come back up here. I want to hear what he says.*

I'm not your partner, she said.

I followed Yumi toward the green EXIT sign and the door beneath it. *I'm sorry*, I said. *But he's got the detector and he's going to expect you to be around. He thinks I gave you to your mother and he's coming to get you from her.*

Fuck, Penny said. *She'd give me up too, I know she would.*

The door led to a bare concrete stairwell. "I'm gonna snow down to the lobby," Yumi said. "I'll let you know what I find." And before I could say the second word of "Sounds good," she was a flurry of cold white powder spiraling down the staircase.

Your mom can't give you up, I told her, *because she didn't take you. But it'll help if—*I broke off and changed tactics. *Don't you want to know how Zawada found you?*

I don't care. I just want to get away from him.

All right, I said reasonably. *I'm going downstairs right now, and anytime you want, you can come back to the ring. You're perfectly safe.*

She came back to the ring as soon as I said that, and I staggered as my double vision resolved. I grabbed the handrail beside the stairs and started down again. *See?*

All right, she said. *I'll try.*

And her point of view floated out through the stairs, arriving at her mother's office just as the elevator doors opened and Zawada walked out by himself.

At the sight of him, Penny fled back to the ring again. But before I could say anything, she floated free and returned to the office in time to see Zawada showing his badge to Jake.

I hurried down to the landing that let onto the lobby, where a flurry of snow resolved itself into Yumi. "There's no way out without those guys seeing you," she said as the black coat billowed out and settled around her.

"All right," I said. "But they think I handed over Penny already, so...why shouldn't we just walk past them?" I was trying to convince myself as well as her. I really didn't want to get that close to them again.

"Because they might be able to detect that you still have the ring? And they'd chase you down and take it away?"

"Rock's got the detector," I said. "Hold on a second."

I was getting Penny's view of the office, with Zawada walking through her mother's office door. Her mother said, "I don't want to talk to anyone else about her!"

"I know how hard it can be to deal with a child's death," Zawada said. "Especially when she's also trying to adjust to a new life. The BEA is experienced in these sorts of transitions, and so if you want, we can take her for a short period of time to allow you and she to adjust in your own ways."

"What the fuck are you talking about?" Sylvia Louderman's tone made even Penny recoil.

I nodded to Yumi. "Can you call a rideshare to get us to Wolftown?"

"Why would I have that app?"

"Christ." I got my phone out. "If I call one, can you go out and meet it? I'll run out when it's there."

"Sure." She watched my phone with interest as I requested the ride.

Two floors up, Zawada had slipped into a conciliatory, slightly patronizing tone. "Hey, I understand if you're a bit hysterical," he said. "It's a horrible thing. But we're here to help. We can make this whole situation less stressful for you."

Penny's mom said, "Less stressful? Less stressful? I've just lost my daughter, you condescending asshole."

"I know," Zawada said. "That's why I'm offering to help."

The ride came in available and asked me to confirm. I hit the button.

"Help?" Penny's mom shrieked above me. "Get out!"

How much longer do I have to stay? Penny sounded miserable.

"Listen," Zawada said, his tone hardening. "I get that you're upset, but your daughter has information about terrorist activity, and we need to talk to her."

I stared down at the rideshare app. It said the car would be here in three minutes. Was going to be close. "What?" Yumi asked me.

"It's on the way. Silver Camry." To Penny, I said, *Terrorist activity?*

"Talk to her?" Ms. Louderman's tone rose. "Talk to her? Call a seance, then! You're as crazy as those other people!"

Yumi pushed open the door and strode through the lobby. I caught a glimpse of the two BEA agents as the door swung shut, but their eyes were on Yumi, not me. When she walked out to the street, they turned back to face the elevators, their backs to the door. I slid my foot forward to stop the door from latching shut.

For the first time, Zawada seemed flustered. "What do you mean, crazy?"

Everything's terrorism to the suits, Penny said, and my view of her mother's office vanished.

I watched the car get closer on the little map. Two minutes. *So it's not a sex trade thing*, I said to Penny.

They do sell teenage girls to perverts. Look it up.

What terrorist activity is he talking about?

How should I know?

Because you broke into his office, didn't you?

At that moment my phone rang. I thought it might be the driver. "This is Jae," I said, picking up.

A hushed whisper rasped, "Mr. Kim, it's Jake from Sheila Louderman's office, there was a guy here from the BEA after Penny and he just left after Ms. Louderman told him she didn't have Penny, I think he's coming after you."

One minute to go. I stared at the map. The driver would just be turning onto Pulaski now. I couldn't wait for Rock to get back to the lobby; I had to gamble he wouldn't radio his agents right away. "Got it, thanks," I said. "I appreciate it."

"No problem," he said, and then he kept talking as I pushed the door open as quietly as I could. I held it out as I walked into the lobby, and gave it a little push further open as I let go.

The two agents were still standing in front of the elevator facing it, talking to each other. I hurried between them and the security desk, striding quietly, thankful for the sounds of traffic outside that hid my light footsteps. They might not have been expecting to have to apprehend anyone in the lobby, but they were still standing way too casually to be professional field agents.

I made it most of the way to the exit before the door I'd come out of slammed closed. The BEA agents turned, and then whirled around to see me at the door.

"Hey," the red-haired man called. "Hey, hold on a minute."

I suppressed a shiver, realizing how close the distance between us was and how easy it would be for him to jump me like he had in Wolftown. "Sorry," I said with as much of a smile as I could muster, and waved to the security desk guard, then grabbed the lobby door and ran out. "You have a nice day now."

"What's going on?" Jake asked on the phone in my ear.

"Give me a minute," I said, joining Yumi onto the street. The silver Camry pulled up to the curb next to Yumi just as I reached her. I ran around the back and got in the passenger-side back door as Yumi jumped in the driver side.

CHAPTER
TWELVE

"Jae?" the driver asked . Her smile shone in the rear view mirror.

"Yeah." The suits had come out of the building and started running toward the car. "We're in a bit of a hurry."

"Sure thing." She spotted an opening in the traffic and screeched into it, throwing Yumi and I back against the seat. "I tell all my passengers, I don't just ask for five stars, I'm gonna earn 'em. You in a hurry, we go in a hurry. There's water bottles if you want 'em, and I can change the music to whatever you want."

"Music's fine," I said, "thanks." Behind us on the street, Zawada was staring down at his phone while the other two were squinting after us. Even if they wrote down the car's make and license plate number, it'd only lead them to the rideshare. I didn't care if they figured out we were in Wolftown once we were there. I didn't see the brown Ford anywhere nearby; thank goodness for shitty parking situations.

Jake was still talking. "—you there?"

"I'm here," I said. "Sorry. Thanks for the heads up."

"No problem," he repeated in that whisper. "I was just saying, I know the BEA isn't always on our side."

"Right," I said. "Do you know that agent?"

"I don't, but I can ask around."

"Sure, if you'd do that, that'd be great. Thanks, Jake."

"Anything to help Penny," he said.

I saved his number as a contact. *You know Jake pretty well, huh?*

He's a good guy. He also thinks my mom is a bitch, bee tee dub.

I left that aside. *Did he get you into NAPR?* When she didn't answer, I said, *Come on. Even if I wasn't a detective, it's not that hard to figure out.*

No, she said. *He's not involved in any of this.*

The idea wasn't to get her to tell on him, because I figured she wouldn't, but to admit that she was part of—or at least working with—NAPR.

She caught my satisfaction. *Dang*, she said, *you don't have to investigate me like that.*

Right, I said, *because you've been so straightforward with me. Why not tell me your mom was a ghost-denier?*

Because then you'd have started looking for another relative instead of giving your boyfriend a whole morning to find Marta.

My phone buzzed again, and I checked in case it was Jake, but it was Desiree, Richard's widow. We talked frequently, but right now I didn't feel like reassuring her again that I really was going to come out there and take charge of Richard. When this situation with Penny was over, I'd fly right out to Detroit as soon as I could.

Yumi glanced over. "You can take that if you want."

I hit Ignore. "Thanks, but it can wait until tomorrow. Just another ghost I have to take care of."

She looked at me sideways. "*Another* ghost? Jae. I think you might have a problem."

"Ha ha."

"Okay," she said, "So where are we going?"

"Wolftown," I said. "I'll figure out more when we're inside. But we have to get her to see Marta, I think."

Like I was telling you.

If you'd told me your mom didn't believe in ghosts, I wouldn't have wasted my time, I snapped back. And then, to Yumi, "And that meeting will probably be in Wolftown."

"Marta's the activist friend?"

"Yeah."

Yumi turned to look back along the street. "Why don't you come to the peacekeepers' station first? Until you figure out where you're going next."

"Sure," I said.

I texted Czoltan while we pulled up outside the Visitor Center, and he said he'd meet us in Wolftown. He hadn't heard from Marta yet, so meeting at the peacekeepers' station seemed like the best option for now.

In the meantime, I said to Penny as we walked into the Visitor Center, *you want to tell me any more about what you've got on Zawada?*

No, she said. *What I know wouldn't be useful to you anyway. It's just for Marta. And I didn't know it was him specifically. I wasn't lying when I said I didn't know him.*

I don't want details, I said, *but things are different now. These guys are amateurs at surveillance, but you've got something important to them that they're willing to assault me for.*

Be glad you're not an extra, she said. *I know someone who got deported because he was sniffing around the BEA too much.*

If someone got deported— I stopped myself before I could say that there must be a good reason, but Penny picked up on it.

They can deport anyone for stupid small reasons. There's so many laws that immigrants have to follow, and more for extras, and so if you like fucked up a line on your taxes, they can spin that into something where oops, got to send you back to a war zone.

Czoltan had told me about the BEA helping in the deportation of terrorists, though he hadn't said he knew anyone that had happened to. Mostly when he talked about them, though, it was to complain about paperwork and bureaucracy. They hadn't seemed like a threat, but I was starting to see them more that way. *Guess it's good you didn't lead them to Angela and her family then, huh?*

She was quiet for a moment and then said, *I didn't think about that.*

All right. Well, luckily your family is human. If your mom won't take custody of you, is there someone else who will? Who else could legally be your guardian? Is your dad still alive?

He's not an option, she said with finality. *I think he moved to Shenzen. I haven't talked to him in years.*

Aunts? Uncles? Grandmother?

Grammy's in a nursing home. My mom's uncle has two kids I've met, but...

But what?

She sighed. *They're not as bad as Mom about remained persons, but they're worse about everything else.*

What happened with your mom and remained? I knew there were people who didn't believe, but I thought they were all tin-foil hat types.

We had to stop then for the ghost check at Wolftown security, which took a minute or two. Portia smiled as I went through and I said hi to her, distracted talking to Penny. That reminded me of talking to Sergei while walking through security. Don't get used to it, I reminded myself. She's not sticking around.

We got through security and into Kennelly Plaza, where a few tourists milled about in the growing heat of the morning. Out of habit, I looked around for any of our BEA friends—or anyone else who might be watching me, since I'd be surprised if they'd gotten back to Wolftown before us—but nobody pinged my radar, so I relaxed. "Over here," Yumi told me, waving me to Alvarez. "You've been all spacey. She talking about her mom?"

"A little. I'm trying to figure out what to do if we can't get in touch with this other person she wants to go to. I can't keep her, her mom doesn't want her. Someone has to be designated as legal guardian or the BEA's going to get her eventually. I can't hold them off forever."

You better try! Penny said.

I'm being real with you. They know where I live, and if I'm not actively trying to get you back to your legal guardian, I don't have any right to keep you.

People keep remained persons all the time.

Not when the government knows about and actively wants them, I retorted. *Agent Zawada might be an asshole, but he's got the law on his side.*

Assholes often do.

You're not wrong. But I have to have some kind of plan, or the next time Zawada comes around, I'm going to have to hand you over.

Collaborator.

Hey, I said sharply as I followed Yumi down Alvarez, *when he catches up to me, the options are, one, hand you over and they get you, or two, don't hand you over, then they arrest me and they still get you. I'm gonna put that off as long as I can, but I can't save you by going to jail.*

Better to be a virtuous man in prison than a guilty man and free, she said.

Who said that?

I dunno, she said. *I'm probably quoting it wrong. But it sounds good.*

I shook my head. *I know better than to ask you to give up your friends to save yourself, but if you can tell them anything, or if you can find one relative, I can maybe put together some logical reason to keep you.*

She didn't answer for a minute, and then she said, *You asked what happened with my mom and remained.*

"How much longer?" I asked Yumi.

"It's about five more minutes," she said.

All right, I said to Penny. *Tell me about your mom.*

As we walked down among extras along the sidewalk, Penny launched into the story. *Mom loved Grandpa, like, more than anything. When he died, she flew the flag on her office at half mast for a month. I looked it up. You're only supposed to fly it that long for presidents. Governors only get a few days. People, like, called us about it.*

This was what, about five years ago?

Yeah. So she spent a lot of time on the Internet and hanging around the place where he died, but she didn't really talk to me at all. I only found out later that she was trying to talk to his spirit, and when she couldn't find it, she decided that remained persons couldn't be real because if they were and Grandpa didn't stay behind, it meant he didn't love her. That's messed up, huh? I told her that if he felt at peace, he'd just go. Most people do.

You told her then?

No, later. I didn't know what was going on then or I wouldn't have told her about Cindy's dad.

Who's Cindy?

Cindy was my tenth grade best friend. Her dad was mowing the lawn and had a heart attack but he remained. It was really fucked up. She slept at our house a lot because even though he wasn't both-

ering her, she knew he was around and she couldn't sleep, she couldn't eat, she cried all the time. Anyway, that was when I found out that her dad was still considered dead even though he was still around. How fucked up is that?

Yeah, it's—troubling.

"Troubling," Jesus. It's wrong. But people are scared of "ghosts." So I was trying to help Cindy with her dad, and then he started to get violent, so someone from the BEA came and took him away. I didn't know what they did. I guess they bound him like you did for me. But then he was gone, and it was like he was dead—which he was—but he wasn't properly. Where was he? Where is he? Cindy went to therapy, she was really messed up.

I'm sorry about that. I knew that these kinds of things happened with ghosts and their families, that there were resources out there, but because it was uncommon for someone to remain, a lot of people didn't know how to access remained persons or even that they existed. Having been in a war and worked with remained, it was easy to forget that many people hadn't ever so much as seen one. *So what happened with your mom?*

Oh, right. Mom kept trying to comfort Cindy over her dad's death, and Cindy tried to explain that her dad was a ghost, and Mom would get really weird. She'd be like, I know you think you heard things, but there's an explanation for it, it's called post-separation psychosis and you can get help for it.

Post-separation psychosis? I knew about ghost deniers, but this term was a new one on me.

Yeah, there's all these YouTubes of gross sketchy guys talking about how post-separation psychosis makes you think you hear your dead dad or whatever when really they're not there. Cindy kept telling her that no, her dad really did remain behind, and Mom would get really worked up and try to make us watch her stupid videos. I had to take Cindy and run back to my room.

"We're here," Yumi said.

The Wolftown peacekeepers' headquarters in Chicago had been newly built four years ago, with energy-efficient construction and solar panels on the roof. The spare concrete design still had some nice flourishes around the windows and the roof, and even though the building was mostly anonymous (you had to squint to see the peacekeepers' logo on the glass doors), someone had spray-painted "ACAB" on the corner facing the street.

"We used to wash it off, but it came back every time," Yumi said, following my gaze to the graffiti. "You would think that someone would've come up with a security camera that can track a vampire by now, but..." She spread her arms.

That sounds like it sucks, I told Penny, and I couldn't think of how to start talking about the fact that her mom wouldn't acknowledge her existence now, which might hurt but might not because they'd been fighting. Even if my mom and I had been fighting that badly, if I died and remained, I'd want her to acknowledge me.

It super sucks, she said. *Cindy just wanted to get away from all that and Mom kept bringing it up. We had a big fight about it after.*

I followed Yumi into the building and the cool air-conditioned disinfectant smell with the undertone of wolf that was in almost every building in Wolftown. *So that was why you ran away.*

Kind of.

And found some people to try to make the world a better place for remained persons.

She sounded pleased. *I mean, if I didn't do it, who would? And now...it's ironic, or something.*

I checked my phone to see where Czoltan was; he was in the Visitor Center so he should be with us shortly. He hadn't gotten any more news about Marta, at least none he'd communicated to me. *Or something,* I agreed with her. *I admire that, you know?*

"If her friends are terrorists," Yumi said to me, quietly, "or even just antagonizing the BEA, we can't meet them here. We need to keep up at least the appearance of a good relationship with them." We were not alone in the lobby, but nobody else stood on this side of the reception desk, some ten feet away. On the front of the desk, against the light wood veneer, the peacekeeper logo showed prominently: a gold-edged blue circle with a white hand in the middle. Behind the desk, a Coyote watched us with bright yellow eyes.

Penny snorted. *You admire it but you're bringing me to a place where we have to play nice with the bad guys.*

"That mean you'll give us up if Zawada asks?" I asked Yumi.

Yumi shook her head. "But if it gets too official, we might have to get creative."

I scuffed my foot against the carpet and waited a moment to see whether Penny would chime in, but she didn't. "That's fine," I said. "I think we'll be safe here until we can figure out where to go next. When Czoltan gets here, we'll know better."

She nodded. "I figured. Just wanted to be clear that we can't meet here."

"I know."

The Coyote behind the desk cleared her throat. "Sorry," she said. "Are you Mr. Kim?"

Yumi and I both turned sharply. "Yes," I said. "Why?"

"There's a message for you."

I looked at Yumi, who shook her head. "I didn't tell anyone."

"I only told Czoltan, and..." I checked the phone again. "He'd just text me. He's walking here. Who is it?"

That was to the Coyote. She checked her pad. "He said his name was Rock Zawada. Is that a real name?"

My skin prickled. "Unfortunately." I walked over to the desk. "What was the message?"

She held out a piece of paper in tan-furred fingers. "He said to call him at this number when you arrived here."

Yumi followed me. "How did he know where we were going?"

"Maybe he saw me with you. Maybe he asked Louderman who else had been with me." I took the paper. "Maybe he called a bunch of places so wherever I ended up, I'd think he knew in advance."

"Are you going to call him?"

"I don't think I'd better." I stared down at the number on the paper. "I'm pretty sure he wants Penny because she has some information he wants. If I talk to him and he tells me that, then if I don't hand her over, I become an accessory to whatever she's involved in."

And here you've been asking me to tell you, Penny said dryly.

Not details. Anyway, it's not as bad if he doesn't know I know. If he tells me—

Then he knows you know.

Bingo.

"Not to mention that if she actually tells me what she's involved in, or the information he wants, *I* could be in trouble. So I don't think I want to give him the chance to tell me what he thinks she knows."

"So what now?" Yumi asked. "Wait for Czoltan, take her to the meeting?"

Yes.

I scuffled a shoe on the carpet. "Yeah," I said. "Of course. But there's another problem."

Yumi raised an eyebrow. "What?"

"The problem is," I said, talking it out for myself as well as Yumi, "where does she go when all this is over? Her mom won't take her and she doesn't have any other living relative. I can't keep her now because I'm on the BEA's radar, and I don't have a legal right to her." Again, the idea that someone had a "legal right" or not to Penny, a sentient being, was fucked up. I'd known that with Sergei, but thinking that this poor girl had been alive yesterday and now was the same person, just in a different state, and yet her legal rights were gone—that was wrong. On top of which, the government agency that was supposed to look out for her was doing pretty much exactly the opposite. "I can't let her to go to the BEA now. Not with all this shit that's been happening."

"Yeah." Yumi rubbed her face. "Tcheh. Can the activists keep her?"

"Maybe. They are remained persons activists, I think, so... they might have experience at that."

Yumi raised an eyebrow. "Oh, that's what they are? That makes a lot of sense. For the BEA to be after them, I mean."

I nodded. "But maybe having her would lead the BEA to them as well."

They're good at hiding.

What if Zawada is using you as bait to draw them out into the open? What if them taking possession of you is the one illegal act that lets him arrest them? What if he arrests me while we're waiting for Marta to contact us?

Penny didn't respond. Yumi said, "I don't see that we have a lot of options here."

"No good ones," I said, running through the possibilities in my head. If only her mom would take her, I wouldn't have to worry about her giving up Penny to Rock; she'd kicked him out of her office and would do it again, I was sure. But I couldn't trick her into taking Penny.

Could I?

I called up my phone's history and looked at Jake's call. "But maybe a less worse one."

The way my mom thought about extras wasn't quite the same as what Ms. Louderman believed—or didn't believe—about ghosts, even if the end result felt similar. Ms. Louderman reminded me more of a conspiracy theorist, someone whose beliefs, grounded in emotion rather than fact, were in the minority. They were painfully aware of that. They got loud and desperate when confronted, just like Ms. Louderman had done.

But I didn't need her to believe in ghosts. I just needed her to take the ring and not give it up to the government. And I had an idea of how to do that. See, my mother wouldn't care so much if other people didn't share her dislike of extras (immediate family excepted), but a conspiracy theorist lived to convince other people of their truth. So I just needed to tell Penny's mom a good story.

I took a breath and tapped Jake's number to call him back.

THIRTEEN

H*ey! What are you doing?*

I'm going to try to talk your mom into taking charge of you.

NO!

I don't feel safe here, I don't feel safe in my home—safe for you, I mean. I—

You're just trying to ditch me. You promised you'd get me in touch with Marta!

The phone rang. *I will,* I said. *I promise I'll come back once we reach her. It's just the safest place for you until Zawada goes away.*

AAAAAAAAAAH! AAAAAAAAAAH!

Stop that, I told Penny, *or I'll take the ring off.*

Do it! You don't care what I want anyway. You think I want to be trapped with my mom or just dropped in a drawer somewhere?

That clutched at my heart. But it was either that or give her to Rock, and I had seen enough of him to think that a little terrifying isolation was preferable to his custody. It felt depressingly like a decision a parent would have to make for their kid. I didn't want to think about that too much, so I took the ring off and slipped it into my pocket just as Jake's voice came on the line. "Mr. Kim?"

"Yeah," I said.

"What can I do for you?" He kept his voice low.

"How did Ms. Louderman leave things with the government guy, Zawada?"

"Whoof." He let out a nervous chuckle. "She was madder at him than she was at you. Accused him of wasting tax money and, uh, what did she say, 'legitimizing charlatans and fakery,' and being the worst parts of government...you get the idea. Um, why?"

"Good," I said. "Listen, I don't...I don't need her to believe in—ghosts. I just need her to take possession of Penny's ring for a while. Maybe you can hold onto it and keep Penny company, something like that. I don't want to burden you—"

"It's no burden," he said quickly. "I'd do anything to help Penny."

"Great. But I can't just show up and give her the ring. Ms. Louderman, I mean. She doesn't trust me or Yumi now."

"I could take the ring from you."

"You could," I said, "but Zawada is looking for her, and whoever takes possession has to be Penny's relative. It has to be her mom. But listen. I have an idea. How do you think she'd react if I told her I was having doubts about ghosts and I needed someone to talk to about it?"

"Oh! She'd eat that up," he said. "She's always trying to tell me about the latest videos. Do you think that will work?"

"Unless you have another suggestion, it's got to." I looked at Yumi, who was watching the door nervously. "I don't know how much time we have. Zawada might know where we are."

"I'll put her on the phone. I'll tell her that you're having doubts about ghosts and need to talk to someone. If that doesn't work, I'll find something that does. I'll get her on the phone for you."

"Thanks, Jake," I said.

Yumi had called over someone to the desk and was hunched over talking in low, urgent tones while they looked at their phones. I turned my gaze to the front door as it opened, but it wasn't Czoltan; it was a vampire in a long trenchcoat and wide-brimmed sun hat. She walked up to the counter and barged in on the conversation between Yumi and the Coyote.

Jake came back on the phone, hurried. "I'm putting you through," he said.

As I was thanking him, there were clicks and then the clatter of a receiver being picked up. Ms. Louderman's voice came on the phone, quick and urgent. "Mr. Kim."

"Yes. Hi—"

"Did that government agent come after you? He thinks you have Penny. I know you think you do too, and I yelled at you for it. I was in shock."

"I understand," I said.

"I thought you were trying to scam me. But Jake says you have doubts?"

I turned my gaze to Yumi and said a soft apology in my head to her. "That watch officer I was with, she was the one who found your daughter, and she told me that Penny was a ghost in that ring."

"She did a voice for you, probably," Ms. Louderman said, confidently. "Did anything in the room move, and she said it was the spirit?"

"The ring moved," I said, improvising. "Look—"

"I'll text you some videos. They'll help you argue with him. I don't know if they can stop you from being arrested, though."

"Arrested?"

"The government agent who came to my office after you, I told you. He was looking for Penny too, or I suppose the ring or whatever it is. He had the same stories about ghosts, but he was a lot more angry about it. You know that there's a whole division of the BEA that scams people out of their property by claiming ghosts exist? I have a video about that too. I'll send it."

"Actually," I said, "would it be too much trouble for you to come into Wolftown and show me yourself?"

"Oh. I—I can't. I am so busy today."

I had to get her to come down here. Think, Jae. "Ms. Louderman...that government agent, Zawada, he's also sent me a message. He wants to come take the ring to do something with Penny's—her memory. It was found with her body and he thinks it's important."

There was a long pause. "I don't see..." she started, and then said, "I don't know any rings Penny had."

"I don't understand why it's important," I lied. "Maybe it's got like a little microchip in it or something. But he doesn't want you to have it. When he thought you had it, he came trying to get you to give it to him, making up that story about a ghost because he thought that would work on you. But now he knows you don't have it, he's after me. Because you're her next of kin, if you have it, he can't do anything. But he can arrest me and take it, and then..."

I let that hang, but she was sharp. "Then what?" she asked. "What can he do? Why should I care if he has a ring?"

"Because it was important to her for some reason," I said. I thought about the years I'd been away from Czoltan, missing him, and how I'd feel if I'd heard that he'd died. What if someone had come to me asking me to take something of his? I'd have been reluctant too, at first. "I don't know about you, but if my daughter died and some government guy was trying

157

so hard to get something of hers, I'd be a little curious about it."

She was quiet for a moment, and when she spoke again her voice was cracking. "I don't understand what happened. I haven't gotten any information about Penny and now you're talking about a ring..."

"Okay," I said. "Okay. I'm sorry. This is a really difficult time. But you saw the government agent. I'm only trying to do what your daughter would have wanted."

"How do you know what she would have wanted?" Her voice cracked again, sharper this time. "How would I even know?"

The front door stayed closed. I gauged how much time I might have. "When was the last time you talked to her?" I said gently.

She sniffed. "Months ago. Toward the end of last year."

"What did you talk about?"

"Oh, we fought. She told me she was going to make a difference, I told her that teenagers can't make a difference, that she should come home and get her education and then we could make a difference together. She didn't agree, as you can guess. Do you have any children, Mr. Kim?"

"I don't."

"Then you can't understand what it's like to have your child turn against you."

I couldn't respond to that, so I kept quiet, and after a moment she went on. "She suffered a trauma, and I tried to be there for her, but...she was at that age where children don't want to listen to their parents. I tried too hard. I drove her away. She found other people who would tell her what she wanted to hear, and she closed herself off to the truth, and to me."

"I'm sorry," I said.

"So I don't know what she wanted, and I don't know what importance this ring has. As far as I'm concerned, the government can have it as long as they leave me alone."

Yumi had returned to my side and was trying to get my attention with her phone. I waved her away, searching desperately for another play, and came up with one last card. "I went into the Army," I said.

"What?" Her voice regained some strength.

"When I fought with my mother," I said. "I went into the Army. We fought about extras. I thought they should be treated like people, and she thought they should be treated like monsters. I couldn't figure out a way to live with her while that fight was going on, so I joined the Army to escape."

She didn't say anything. I pared down the story to its details. Yumi watched me attentively. "There were things that happened to me in Kosovo, things that were important to me. I didn't talk to her much while I was in the Army, but if anything had happened to me—and some of my friends were killed there—then I would've wanted her to know about them."

This time I let the silence drag on. Finally, Ms. Louderman said, "You think the ring was that important to Penny?"

"I'm certain of it," I said. Now I nodded to Yumi, who held her phone out to me. It had a Maps app up with a pin in a location marked, "151 Glozny St." The app said it was twelve minutes walk from where we were.

"You're in Wolftown?" Ms. Louderman asked.

"Yes. Can you come meet me?"

"When? I have space at three..."

"As soon as possible. I told you, Agent Zawada knows where I am. I can get to another place, a safe place, but I don't know how long it'll be safe."

She made a small, uncertain noise. "Hold on a moment." There was a click.

"What's this address?" I asked Yumi.

"A place we use to meet with people sometimes if it's not a hundred percent official and above board," she said. "It's empty but it's not on our records anywhere so that should slow him down."

"Great," I said.

"Is she coming?"

"I think so. She put me on hold."

"That was quite a story." Yumi eyed me. "How much was true?"

"All of it," I said, trying to calm my heart down. "It has to be true or else it doesn't work."

Ms. Louderman came back on the line. "Hello? Mr. Kim?"

"Hi, I'm here."

"I moved some meetings around. I can come into Wolftown now."

"Great." I read the address off to her. "We'll be there. Come find us."

"I'll be there as soon as I can."

Yumi had some kind of look in her eyes when I hung up the phone. "What?" I said. "I had to tell her something to get her here. The only way out of this problem is for her to take the ring. I don't care what pretext she takes it under as long as she takes it and keeps it."

"When she takes it, she's going to hear Penny and freak out."

"Yes." I felt the weight of the ring in my pocket. "Unless. Unless I can talk to Penny and get her to see that this is the best way to keep her safe."

Yumi's snow-white face crinkled into a frown. "What I was going to say is that it was impressive how you got through to Ms. Louderman. So I think you can get through to Penny, too."

"A teenager is a lot different than a mom. I have a few

decades of experience with moms, and none with teenagers." I rubbed the ring through my jacket pocket. "But I hope so. Hey, why is Czoltan taking so long? He should be here by now, right?"

"I don't know where he was," Yumi said as I took my phone out to check.

The last time he'd texted had been twenty minutes ago, from the Visitor Center. It didn't take twenty minutes to walk here unless he'd been held up at the Center, which was possible. Sometimes you got behind tour groups and that was an extra ten minutes you couldn't do anything about. *You almost here?* I texted him.

"If we're going to go, we should go," Yumi said.

"Just a sec." I stared at the phone, but not even the three dots that indicated he was typing showed up. There was nothing.

"We can wait another few minutes, if you want."

I put the phone in my pocket. "Leave a note for him to call me when he gets here," I said. "Let's go."

CHAPTER

FOURTEEN

As we left the air-conditioned lobby of the peacekeepers' building, the heat of the day and the smells of Wolftown assaulted us, dusty and musky and aided by breezes off the hot concrete that were somehow warmer than the surrounding air. "This is the shortest way," Yumi said, and grimaced. "There's probably not air-con at the house."

"Maybe a fan at least?"

She shook her head. "Doubtful. But I can cool off the place when we get there."

I let her guide us, keeping an eye out in the crowd for either Czoltan or Zawada. In the meantime, I put Penny's ring back on.

About time!

Your mom's coming to get you, I said.

NOOOOOOO.

I talked over her wail. *Jake's going to help.*

Yumi guided me down a street and then around a sharp corner into a more residential area, a little run down: paint peeling, stains on the sidewalk, the hint of mildew from the open basement windows as we passed them. Penny stopped her wailing. *How?* she asked suspiciously.

He knows what we're doing. He helped me talk your mom into taking the ring.

I don't waaaaaaaaant her to take it!

It's the only way you're legally protected.

My friends can protect me!

Listen, I said, angry at her and then at myself for how much I sounded like a movie parent in that moment, *your friends have stayed one step ahead of the BEA by keeping under the radar. You have a big blinking neon sign on you that Agent Zawada can find, and I'm out of places to go. If I don't get you to someone today, he's going to have a warrant to take you from me.*

Then go into hiding! People do it all the time.

I took a breath. *I know you feel safest with your friends, but trust me, if you insist on going to them, all you're going to do is get them arrested and then you'll be in custody anyway.*

She didn't reply. I took a breath. *I'm sorry about this,* I said as I followed Yumi across a street past a corner where three aswang (Filipino ghouls, bluish-black complexions with fangs and jet-black hair and, in this case, tattoo sleeves) spared us a bored glance before looking back at their phones. *I wish there were another way, but your mother is the only legal protection. She hates Agent Zawada as much as you do, so I'm sure she won't give you up.*

Still Penny stayed silent. At least with a living teenager you could read body language when they refused to talk. *And you don't have to talk to her. In fact, it might be better if you don't. Because then she'll just think this is a valuable ring you picked up that the government wants for some reason. I told her maybe there was a microchip in it.*

Fiiiiine, she said. *How is Jake going to help?*

My phone rang then. I grabbed it, hoping it was Czoltan, but it was Mom.

Shame burned the back of my neck. I hadn't called her back after yesterday. *It's okay,* my mantra began, *it's fine, she knows you get busy, remember when you didn't call her back two weeks ago? Nothing happened.*

That didn't put out the fire under my skin. I stared at her name while the phone rang. I couldn't talk to her now, but I'd also never intentionally avoided a call from her (turning my phone's ringer off when I'm on a job does not count, nor does declining a call I don't know is her and not calling her back, nor does leaving my phone in another room for hours when I think she might call).

Go ahead and talk to your mom. What's the problem? Oh, right, she's also a bitch.

Hey! I said sharply. *That is out of line.*

Sorry. She sounded genuinely contrite.

I love my mom. I'm...just not sure this is the best time to talk to her about her visit next month.

Keep staring at it then. It'll go to voicemail.

I ignored a call from her yesterday. If I skip this one, she'll think something is wrong.

Something is *wrong. You're on the run from the BEA with a "terrorist ghost."*

No, that's just how my life is. I hit the green Accept button and put the phone to my ear. *Keep an eye out around us for any agents,* I told Penny as I said, "Hi, Mom."

"Jae, how are you doing?" She sounded chipper enough, but it was the kind of chipper that meant she had something to say once she'd finished with the requisite small talk.

"I'm actually on a job now, Mom. Can we—"

"Oh, since you missed my call yesterday I thought I would

catch you before your day started. Not running across any roofs, are you?"

"No, just—" I looked around the street. "I'm going to a meeting."

Can't tell her you're in Wolftown, huh?

No.

"Well, this won't take long. I just wanted to check with you about my flight. There's one that comes in the 28th and goes back on the 3rd. That should give us enough time together, don't you think?"

It didn't matter what I thought. I couldn't even make the math work in my head to figure out how many days that was right now. Six? Seven? "Mom, I don't have a calendar here. I'm out on the street."

"It's just the wedding weekend with a couple days on either side," she said. "You don't need to look at a calendar, do you?"

"Can we talk about this later?"

"And I'll be staying at your place, right? Judy was asking again."

"Mom. I really gotta go."

"I know you're working," she said, "but can't you answer a simple question?"

"It's fine, Mom," I said.

And you want me to go stay with my mom. Hypocrite.

"What's this job you're doing? Are you back in Detroit yet?"

"Mom, I really have to go." I followed Yumi around another corner, starting to feel that the day was unraveling on me. I was already cobbling together a solution out of string and Scotch tape, and Mom was coming in to tug on parts of my life I'd thought I could leave alone.

She gave a small "hmph" and then said, "Fine. I'll call you tomorrow. Go do your job. Love you."

"I love you, too."

After I hung up, Yumi turned around. "I'm fine," I said. "She's not going to call back."

"Better put your phone on silent," she said.

"Right." I did that before sliding it back into my pocket. *If I were in your position*, I told Penny, *I'd want to go with my mom.*

Even though she hates extras?

She—just doesn't understand them. But yeah. I know that down at the center of everything, she loves me. She'll take care of me.

She probably believes in ghosts, Penny said.

Yeah, she knows I had a remained partner and have to go deal with my former captain's—my remained former captain.

I thought you were in the Army, not the Navy.

There's captains in both. He commanded a unit, not a ship.

And what do you have to go do with him?

Never mind that. Let's just get you to your mom and Jake.

She sighed. *Did Czoltan hear from Marta?*

He hasn't texted me. I took my phone out. Still nothing. My skin prickled, but I reminded myself not to catastrophize. He could take care of himself.

If he's dead, then you can put him in this ring when you get rid of me, Penny said, which didn't make me feel better and I'm sure wasn't intended to.

You're staying in the ring, I told her as Yumi stopped at a corner in a residential neighborhood, 70s stone townhouses along all four streets, and then walked around to the back of the row of houses in front of us. Ahead of us loomed the Wolftown wall, fifty feet of cement. At this distance I could see the graffiti on it, the familiar oversized letters, some angular, some balloony. Someone had spray-painted an outline of a human figure with exaggerated wolf ears and tail, and then black bars over it, like it was in jail. I paused for a moment to look at it and remind myself where we were, despite the townhouses that looked like they could be from any forty-year-old Chicago neighborhood and the slightly doggy werewolf smell that made me think about my boyfriend all the time. The wall reminded me of how vulnerable he was, how he was regarded in our society. Penny was even more so. *And if Czoltan's dead, he might not remain. He might just be…gone.*

I know, Penny said, and her anxiety matched mine in that moment.

I followed Yumi around behind the houses. She walked down three of them and then checked that nobody was peering around from the street before taking out a key and unlocking the back door of the fourth house.

She ushered me into a dusty kitchen with a faint smell of age and decay. Apart from the smell, the room only felt disused, not neglected; the refrigerator hummed and the open cupboard door revealed a stack of cans whose labels hadn't faded. The tile floor felt cool even through my shoes, and yellow-checked curtains gave the room a splash of color that made the dust stand out more. If I hadn't known this was a safe house, I would've felt sad for the family who'd decorated it and then had to abandon it.

Yumi put her finger to her lips and we stood for several seconds listening to the small creaks and rustles of the house. "What are we listening for?" I whispered.

"Anyone who might be moving around after they heard the back door," Yumi whispered back.

I don't have Czoltan's wolf ears, but my hearing's pretty good, and I didn't hear anything unusual. I also didn't have his sense of smell, but I'd learned to be more attuned to what I did have, and I didn't catch any scent fresher than mouse droppings. My eyes, which were better than Czoltan's, didn't see any disturbance in the dust on the counters nor on the floor.

"I think it's well deserted," I said.

Yumi nodded. "I think so, too. All right."

I texted Czoltan: *Hey where are you?* The words sat right below my other words, with no answer. "Shit," I said aloud. "Something's happened."

I could go look for him, Penny said.

What?

I can leave the ring, like I did before. He was supposed to be coming through the Visitor Center, right?

He was in the Visitor Center.

And going to the peacekeeper building?

Right.

All right. I'll go see if I can find out anything. And without another word, I saw through Penny's point of view as she wrenched herself free of the ring and floated through the house and out into the street.

Be careful! I called after her.

You're not my dad, she replied, and drifted on through Wolftown.

"Penny's going to look for Czoltan," I told Yumi.

"By herself?" She looked around the kitchen.

"Yes. She can't manifest yet, but she can leave the ring and show me what she's seeing."

"Useful," Yumi said.

You wouldn't want me to manifest, Penny said. *Then I wouldn't be able to spy.*

There's ghost-detecting equipment that can spot you, I said. *Don't think you're invisible because you can't manifest.*

How would I manifest? she asked.

Sergei said it was a matter of confidence. Being able to see yourself so that others could see you.

That sounds like some bullshit my mom would listen to, like if some affirmation-spewing grifter was a remained person.

Maybe, I said. *I only know what he told me.*

Maybe I can get Jake to take me to a remained persons group.
You know about those groups?

There was a pause, and then she said, *Course I do. I tried to get Cindy's dad into one, but it didn't work out.* She was coming up to the peacekeepers' building. *I don't see him anywhere.*

I didn't either. *You know which way the Visitor Center is?*

Yeah, back here. She sped back along Alvarez toward Kennelly Plaza, going faster as I assumed she gained confidence in being outside the ring.

Wait! I called. *Go back to that street.*

She'd just passed the street where the red-haired agent had vanished after assaulting me. At least, I thought it was that one, but from the other end. *Which street?* she asked.

You remember where the guy jumped me?

Yeah, sort of.

I think he turned this corner and that's where Vic lost him. Can you check the buildings along here?

You think that guy got him? She turned and drifted down the short street of office buildings, empty of people, just as it had been yesterday. *You know which building it is?* she asked. *Want me to just check them all out?*

Go, but be careful. If it is Zawada, he'll have ghost detectors, and there aren't that many remained persons in Wolftown. It could be a trap. Or they could detect you coming and maybe trap you.

I'm already bound, she said dismissively.

"They can still trap you." I said it aloud too because it felt so urgent.

Then you can come break the trap, right? You still have the ring.

"What? Is she okay?" Yumi looked up, alarmed.

"She's okay," I said. "She's looking for Czoltan around the place where the guy attacked me yesterday."

"She shouldn't go there. They'll catch her."

"They'll detect her, but I'll keep an eye out." I watched the buildings of the street go by slowly. "I can't think of anything else that might've happened to Czoltan."

"Maybe he was hit by a car," Yumi said helpfully.

I pushed away that thought, but the tightness in my chest remained. "No; he got to the Visitor Center."

"She's not going to see him through a window or anything." Yumi looked at me, worried. "Tell her to get back here the moment anything doesn't feel right, anything at all."

I relayed this as the brass number 28 swam into my view. *I will,* Penny promised. The number stayed fixed in place. *Ugh. I can't get in there.*

Why are you looking at that place?

I got a flash again of that dark office. *No reason,* Penny said. *It seems sketchy. But I can't get inside.*

It's ghost-proofed, I said. *Makes sense.*

I'm just going to check the windows.

Penny, I said sharply, my heart speeding up, *stay away from the windows. What you want to do is park yourself across the street and watch them from there, or wait until they open a door.*

My view wavered near one of the windows. *I mean it,* I said. *You might not detect a trap until it's too late, but across the street you're almost certainly out of range, and I can watch with you.*

Fine. That word and her tone were becoming quite familiar.

The building receded so I could see the whole thing, an unimpressive townhouse with no indication of its inhabitants except for perhaps a brass plaque beside the door that we were now too far away to read.

Nothing happened for several minutes, during which Yumi kept telling me that Penny shouldn't be there on her own, and Penny refused to come back because nothing was happening at the house. Finally she said, *They won't have him looking out windows at the front. I'm going to go around back.*

Wait, I said, but she was already floating up and over the building, skirting the ghost-proofing to come down around the back. *There's less room for you to hide there*, I said pointlessly.

But these buildings aren't ghost-proofed, Penny said triumphantly, drifting through the window of an office building that faced the one she was investigating—the BEA office, if that's what it was. *So I can hide inside here and watch them this way.*

I bit my tongue. It wasn't actually a bad idea, even if I knew that it wasn't likely the BEA would show anything through the back windows. The blinds were drawn on all the ones in view, anyway, at least as far as I could see through her eyes—

Hey, I said, *that window on the second floor, far right.*

Her gaze shifted to focus on it. *It's just a shadow.*

Someone's holding that blind open and looking out of it.

Oh shit! I see it now.

Keep watching. I hadn't felt this in a while: the ability to surveil a remote location through an invisible ghost. Penny was good at it, too, keeping the window in sight. I'd had to train Sergei for a while, because he'd get bored and start looking around.

There! She said it a second before I did. The blind had moved aside and a wolf's muzzle poked out. *Is that him?*

My heart sank. *Yeah. I think so.* Scenarios flashed through my mind: Czoltan being interrogated, being tortured. And then I remembered what Penny'd said about immigrant extras being deported. All my plans for us to live together, gone. Ice seized my stomach.

At that moment, my phone buzzed. I glanced down, but it wasn't Czoltan's number. Probably Zawada, but I didn't want to talk to him until I was a little more secure in my footing. "He's got Czoltan," I said. "Penny saw him. The BEA can't do that, can they? Take someone into custody?"

Yumi's brow lowered. "No, they cannot. But they do it

anyway. We've fought that battle several times. Unless we have an equal authority on our side, it doesn't go well."

"And what could they do to him?"

"Hold him indefinitely. Deport him maybe."

The ice moved up to my chest. I hadn't wanted Yumi to make my fears more real by verbalizing them. "They—they can't deport him. He's been here seven years. He's a refugee with status and—and—"

Her eyes creased with sympathy. "Yeah," she said. "But there are a lot of ticky-tack little laws that someone could unintentionally break over seven years. Oh, they could plant drugs on him too. That's probably the easiest way to do it."

"Fuck." I weighed my phone in my hand, hating the feeling of helplessness. There had to be something I could do. "You don't know anyone at the DOJ, do you?"

Yumi shook her head. "Do you know a lot of people who do?"

"No, I was just asking. It's better than the FBI, which is the only place I have a contact more influential than the CPD." I scrolled through my phone with a sigh, keeping an eye on the window through Penny's eyes. I knew I was going to make Czoltan mad, talking to the feds without consulting him, but if it was a matter of keeping him free and in the country, I'd take money from fucking Rock Zawada himself if I had to. Nothing was worth losing him.

"You know someone at the FBI?" Yumi's eyes widened.

I waited for Penny to weigh in on this, but apparently she was busy finding a place to hide where she could watch Czoltan. "I wouldn't say I 'know' them. They, ah, approached me about a job," I said.

She folded her arms. "Really. The feds."

"Yeah. I haven't...I mean..." She was staring at me, and I

couldn't complete the lie. "It was a lot of money. I haven't gotten started on the job yet."

"But you think they'll fight the BEA for you."

I hesitated. "I think they really want me to do this job."

She gave me a long, measured look. "It's a slippery slope, taking fed money," she said.

"I know," I told her, pulling up the contact and ignoring the flush of shame. It was keeping the dread at bay and that's what was important. "But it's coming in handy right now, isn't it?"

"Just because you manage to pit Godzilla against King Kong doesn't mean you won't get stepped on," she said.

"Godzilla liked people. Usually." I dialed the number and put the phone on speaker.

"Hey, Jae," Agent Jefferson said when she picked up. "Got your email. I haven't had a chance to get things together for you."

"Jae?" Yumi mouthed at me.

"Hey, you're on speaker," I said. "I'm here with one of the Wolftown peacekeepers."

"Oh." Her tone stiffened. "What's going on?"

"You might not be the right person," I said, "but you might know the right person. My boyfriend's being illegally detained by the BEA and I am looking for a way to, you know, get them to stop."

"Look, Jae, I'd love to help, but I'm not sure there's a lot I can do. Why don't you call CPD? They should be able to handle that."

I met Yumi's eyes. "The thing is," I said, "I don't know how much I'm going to be able to work on your case with my partner detained. I'm sure you understand that that's going to take all my attention until his situation is resolved."

Yumi raised her eyebrows and gave me a short nod. The phone stayed silent while the call time ticked up, second after second. "You haven't even signed the contract yet. And why are you discussing this work in front of another party?"

"I'm not discussing the work itself. But she's here helping with my partner's case and—she can leave if she has to. She doesn't know anything about what you asked me to do."

"She'd better not. Peacekeeper, what's your name, please?"

Yumi looked daggers at me. "Yumi Hachimura," she said in a voice colder than snow.

"Anything Mr. Kim told you about his work with us is covered by an NDA. If he's found in violation of that, anyone who passes on or makes use of information he gave them is also liable. Do you understand?"

"I understand."

Sorry, I mouthed, but Yumi just shook her head.

"At any rate, Jae, I'm sure the work can wait until your partner's legal troubles are sorted out. Sorry, I'm just not sure what you'd like me to do here."

Yumi shrugged, as if to say, *told you so*. But there had to be something else I could do. Zawada couldn't get away with—ah. "What if I told you I might have evidence that someone in the BEA is trafficking ghosts?"

There was a long pause, and then I caught the faintest click on the line. Jefferson was interested enough to record this. "What kind of evidence?"

"I don't know yet. But I was called to Wolftown yesterday to pick up a newly released remained person, and the BEA—this one agent in particular, Rock Zawada—turned up suspiciously quickly, and I believe they have been assaulting and following me to try to get her back. They showed up at her mother's office this morning right after we did, trying to get her."

"So the mother has custody now?"

"No, I still do. The mother...doesn't believe in ghosts."

"Jesus Christ."

"Yeah. Anyway, I think the remained person knows about something illegal Zawada's been doing. She hasn't told me specifically but she's trying to get information to some activist friends."

Jefferson sighed. "You mean terrorists."

"Freedom fighters."

"Touché."

"So look, there's something hinky going on and I don't know what it is, but Zawada is detaining my partner to get me to release the remained person to him."

Her voice got sharper. "He said that?"

"Hasn't yet."

"You can record calls from your phone, right?"

"Yeah."

"Record your conversation. If that's what he's asking, then...I can help you. What's his name again? Spell it."

I did. There was the click of typing. "And," I added, "I convinced the remained's mom to come meet us in Wolftown and hopefully she'll take custody after this, so he won't have a legal avenue to kidnap her."

"The ghost, you mean, not the mom."

"Right."

"How are you going to convince the mom to—you know what, never mind." More typing. "All right, Jae, I don't know what I can do, but I'll make a call. Send me the recording if you get it, and I might be able to do something more."

"Thanks so much, Mrs. Jefferson," I said, and hung up.

"Thanks so much, Mrs. Jefferson," Yumi mocked me. "You're gonna be the FBI's lap dog in no time."

"Don't say that in front of Czoltan," I said. "He'd be insulted. And I don't really care as long as it gets him away from Zawada. I'll worry about that some other time."

"Kicking trouble down the road just means you run into it later."

"And maybe I can kick it down again, or I'll deal with it then." I stared at the phone. I didn't want to wait fifteen minutes. The bad part of calling someone else to help you was that it was out of your hands.

Hey, Penny said.

What's going on?

What would it feel like if another ghost was around?

FIFTEEN

I snapped back to Penny's point of view. She was in a dark office looking through a window across the street to where Czoltan's muzzle had shown. There were desks and laptop docks around her, and a poster on the wall of a kitten hanging from a rope with the caption HANG IN THERE. *What do you feel?*

There's just a sense that someone's near me, but it's—I can tell it's like, there. Her point of view shifted away from the window and toward the poster where the kitten looked desperately out, frozen in time. *Right there.*

Yeah, I said, though I couldn't see anything, *that's probably another ghost. But don't worry, it can't do anything to you except tell Zawada where you are.*

Can I do anything to it?

You can talk to it. But I wouldn't recommend—

Hey! Who are you?

I pressed my fingers to the bridge of my nose. "What?" Yumi asked. "Is it Penny? What's she doing now?"

"She's trying to talk to a ghost near her."

"Agh," Yumi said. "Kids. What's it saying?"

I listened. "Nothing so far that I can hear." To Penny, I said, *Move away from there. Go up a floor or something. You're in danger right now.*

If I can't do anything to it, can it do anything to me?

I drew in a breath and exhaled, working to keep my tone even. *It can tell Zawada where you are.*

But won't I see them coming?

Maybe not. You think they won't have a way into that building?

She didn't say anything for a moment, and then her viewpoint floated up two floors and to the right. *There,* she said, *I can't sense it anymore.*

If you sense it again, move again. They can trap you.

I know, but they can't bind me, right? I'm bound to you. You know where I am, you can come break the trap.

I sighed. *If I can't get there in time....they can break the binding and retake you. It's not the best way, but they can do it.*

You told me they couldn't do that!

Not when I was in the same building and could run down two floors to get to you. I'm at least fifteen minutes away from where you are now. That might be enough time.

What else haven't you told me about ghost binding?

I pressed hands to my forehead. *Penny...*

Seriously! I'm sick of adults not telling me stuff because they're trying to protect me. Marta always told me the truth even when it wasn't nice. I didn't respond to that, and she calmed down, at least a little. *Well, what if I don't let them bind me?*

Then they can keep you in there and refuse to let me in until you tell them whatever they want to know. And if they think I'm a security risk because I can hear everything they tell you, they can kill me. I wasn't sure they'd kill me, but I wasn't sure they wouldn't. It was a lot easier than undoing a binding, and wasn't too far beyond what they were doing now. The thought made me queasy. *Then you'd be a trapped unbound remained person slowly losing your reason. That's the whole truth. That sound better to you?*

She didn't answer, so I pressed on. *Are there people in that building?*

No, she said quietly.

They could have a satellite office there. Look, come back now—

Through Penny's perceptions, I heard a deep male voice say, *Identify yourself.*

It's back, Penny said.

Yeah, I got that. Get out. Come back here.

I can handle this. Who are you?

That last was to the other remained, of course. *I'm not the trespasser*, he replied.

How do I know that when you won't tell me who you are?

Because you know you don't belong here.

In one sense, I admired her bravery. But I also felt responsible for her and there was no point to her bravery, nothing to be gained by it. *Penny, come back! Please!*

She ignored me and kept talking to the other remained. *I belong here as much as you do. Who are you, anyway?*

I'm an employee of the BEA.

To her credit, Penny kept scanning the room they were in, which was a supply room lit only by the one window. *Oh yeah? You got a contract? Didn't know remained persons could sign contracts.*

I'm bound by an employee.

That's not the same thing, is it?

It is legally the same thing. I'm bound to obey an employee of the BEA.

Hey, she said to me. *Do I have to obey you?*

There are ways to compel bound remained persons, but Penny, he's stalling, I said urgently. *They've got someone on the way.*

She spun around to watch the door. *That's slavery*, she said. *You got a name, mister bound employee?*

Identify yourself, the other ghost repeated.

Or what? Penny asked. *What you gonna do?* There was no reply, and after a minute she went on. *I know about you*, she said. *I mean, not you, but you, your situation. I know you're bound, but you don't have to do the stuff they're telling you to do. You deserve the chance to resolve your business and move on. There's groups that can help you with that. They can get you out of there.*

Identify yourself, please, the other ghost said, but its tone was less stern.

Look, I know your master is listening to this, Penny said. *It doesn't matter. There's places you can go and they can help you. They're fighting for rights for remained persons. I'm fighting for rights for remained persons—for us.*

There was a long pause, and then the other said, quickly, *They're coming to trap you. They'll be here in three minutes.* Following that, he said, more loudly, *I don't need to resolve any business. I enjoy my work and my associate is kind to me.*

And then, in the dark supply room, a figure manifested, flickering into being, a tall white man with an unkempt mop of white hair, a flannel shirt over a "one tequila, two tequila, three tequila, floor" t-shirt, jeans with holes in the knees, and a dazed, hopeless expression. "Russell," he whispered. "Russell Jacoby." And then he flickered out again.

Right, Penny said. *I'll remember.*

And then my vision lurched and her point of view disappeared. *I'm back*, she told me.

I figured, I said.

You get all that?

Yeah. That was a hell of a speech.

I was trying to unsettle him, she said smugly.

Uh-huh. I meant the remained persons rights stuff.

"What happened?" Yumi asked urgently. "Did they get her?"

I blinked back to the dusty kitchen. "No," I said. "She's back."

That guy—Russell—is suffering because of the way the laws are now, she said. *It's cruel and unfair what the BEA is doing to them, and sometimes they don't even know it could be better.*

"So what do we do now?" Yumi asked.

What the BEA is doing to them, Penny had said, but I was more focused on something else she'd said, about getting remained persons out of there. I got the recording app ready on my phone. "I'm waiting for Agent Zawada to call me back," I said. "But in the meantime, what do you know about the remained persons rights movement?"

Yumi tilted a head at me. "Penny can tell you more than I can, probably. I don't know any of them personally. They're a smaller group than the Teardown, and there's a public-facing group that's out in L.A. We have some here in Chicago but they never make trouble that surfaces to me. I just hear about them from time to time. National Association for the Protection of Ghosts—no, Protection of the Remained, that's it."

The word "trouble" jarred loose a memory. "NAPR, yeah. Ms. Louderman's assistant belongs to them. Wasn't there something last year, or two years ago? They tried to free some ghosts—some remained persons—from somewhere, or tried to teach them to resolve their unfinished business or something?"

"Oh yeah." Yumi pulled up her phone. "In D.C., right?"

"Something like that."

You won't find my name in that, Penny said.

"She says she wasn't associated with it," I said. "But her friends might be."

Yumi kept searching for records of the incident. "Oh look,

TIM SUSMAN

here's a thing from last year, the Halloween march. NAPR had brought some ghosts to speak, and the BEA confiscated them."

Kidnapped them, Penny said acidly. *But they got released.*

"She says they got released." I asked Penny, *Were you at that one, if not the other?*

Yeah.

Yumi checked. "Yeah, the lawyers ordered their release a few months later. But that's how they operate. They're like cops. They like having authority over ghosts. If the ghost rights people had their way, ghosts would all go to the Moving On groups, stuff like that."

"Aren't you like a cop?" I asked.

Yumi snorted. "If someone told me they wanted to take a whole segment of Wolftown off my plate, I'd be glad. This job pays shit and is nothing but headaches." Anticipating my question, she added, "but it's got to be done, doesn't it? Who else is gonna do this shit if not me?" She thrust her phone at me. "Here's the incident. The L.A. group took credit for it. No names, nobody got caught. It wasn't NAPR, for what it's worth, but that doesn't mean they don't work together."

I scanned the article. I wasn't interested in the names so much as I was interested in the target, and there it was: The BEA offices had been broken into and six remained persons unbound. "They unbound remained," I said. "Must have rebound them right away, because it says nobody knows what happened to them, and if they were unbound—"

"People would know," Yumi said. "They'd be screeching."

It was singing! Penny objected.

"Or something, yeah." I gave the phone back. "But suppose the BEA has footage of the break-in and they didn't release it to the public. If Penny was there—"

I wasn't!

"All right, she says she wasn't, and I believe her, but she

182

knows people who were. Maybe they're trying to round up the rest of the remained rights people? And she stole their footage."

"And then they found out she'd died," Yumi said. "And they knew if she was a remained person, they could make her tell them everything about the movement."

It troubled me that Penny had died right after breaking into their offices, if that's what she'd done (by this point, I assumed it was). Coincidences happened, but that was a huge one. Seventeen-year-old girls don't just have heart attacks. "That would explain why they're so desperate to bind her," I said. "But then will she even be safe with her mother?"

"Legally, she should be."

I've been telling you not to give me back to her.

So is that true?

She paused for only a second. *I thought you didn't want to know anything about what I did.*

If Zawada tells me, then he knows I know. If you tell me, I can always claim you didn't.

Well, I wasn't in D.C., she said.

But you did break into the BEA offices to help NAPR? When she didn't answer, I said, *I know the last times I guessed what your deal was you let me make assumptions. If you tell me, though, I might be able to help you.*

You? The sneer was obvious. *Former ghost master?*

I tried to help Sergei figure out his unfinished business! I said. *He was also my friend, though. When it came time for him to go, I let him go.*

How noble of you. Did you take him to Moving On?

He didn't want to go.

She scoffed. *Just let me see Marta so I can tell her what I need to,* she said, *and then I'll go with my mom.*

That was a change from her previous stance, and felt like

she'd negotiated down to her most essential duty, maybe the thing that had kept her behind. She had some information about the BEA that she absolutely had to tell Marta, and the BEA absolutely did not want Marta to have that information. It was getting much harder to avoid the conclusion that they'd killed her.

It was a weird hypothesis to entertain. For one thing, if they had, they'd botched it by showing up very late to the scene of her death after she had already been causing a fuss. For another, Zawada might be a prick, but was he a murderer?

Not that hard a leap to make, actually. I'd already told Penny they might kill me, and maybe I only half-believed that, but if I thought back to Kosovo and what people in governments thought they could get away with when nobody was looking...certainly our government wasn't above that, either.

Is Marta your unfinished business? I asked.

I'm not sure. She sounded sincere and uncertain. *How would I even know?*

You're the remained persons expert, I said. *You tell me.*

I heard it's like with therapy, she said, *where you might think there's one important thing but there's actually something else underlying it. Did your—Sergei, did he know what his business was?*

No, but I could've guessed it was about his wife. He talked about her all the time.

So what did he do to release?

He, uh...it was when he got me together with Czoltan. I rubbed my eyes. *He was always trying to set me up on dates. So maybe he did know.*

"Hey." Yumi pointed to my phone, which was buzzing.

I picked it up and remembered to start the recording app. "Kim."

"Mr. Kim." It wasn't Jefferson's voice. "This is Agent Zawada of the BEA."

"Oh, hi," I said. "I've been trying to avoid talking to you." I turned the volume up and held the phone a little away from my ear so Yumi could listen as well.

"I—should I be offended?" He put on a joking tone.

"Probably," I said. "But I think I'm the one who should be offended, since you've kidnapped my boyfriend and are holding him illegally."

"Ah," he said, unruffled, "so it was Miss Louderman's ghost that was spying on us. I suspected as much."

"It was her idea," I said. "I was against it, for the record. I thought she should wait for her mom to come pick her up."

"I don't believe for a moment that Sylvia Louderman is going to come pick up her ghost daughter. I visited her shortly after you did and was treated to no doubt the same harangue you were about ghosts."

"I appealed to her sense of family," I said. "Now are you going to let Czoltan go?"

"Well, that's rather up to you, isn't it?"

"What's that supposed to mean?"

"By now," he had his smooth purring voice on again, "you've surely found out that Miss Louderman has information that she wants to pass on to a terrorist group. I somehow doubt that even that information would impel you to turn her over to us on your own, even though you know it's the right thing to do, morally and legally. So I thought I would take a perfectly legal examination of your boyfriend's background, and allow you the chance to give us Miss Louderman in exchange for his release and a promise not to look too closely at him."

I checked that the recording software was working and

gave Yumi a tight-lipped smile. She frowned and typed something on her phone.

"Nobody could blame you for that," Zawada went on. "What do you say?"

Yumi held up her phone. She'd typed, *Illegal but they can find stuff.* I nodded at her. "You can go ahead and look," I said. "His background's clean."

"Oh, maybe of directly illegal activity," he said. "But you'd be surprised how many people forgot to file a form on time, or have associated with people on our list of terrorists, or just missed a deadline they didn't know about. Most of that we let slide, but I promise you, every time we look into a case, we find something. It may ultimately amount to nothing more than a few thousand dollars in fines, but it could be years of paperwork and distraction. And if he did associate with known terrorists, well, we can't let those people remain in the country."

I met Yumi's eyes, looking for confirmation. She creased her brow and her mouth pursed. What I read was that there was substance behind this threat, if not a certainty. "That feels like an abuse of power," I said. "You sure you want to cop to that in front of witnesses? Penny's ghost is listening to this, too."

"I don't care what she hears," he said. "You have something we want, and we have someone you want. It seems like a very easy situation to navigate."

"Maybe for an amoral shithead," I said before I remembered I was recording. "I mean, I'm going to turn over Miss Louderman to her mother, and you need to let Czoltan go."

Zawada exhaled. "Mr. Kim, Miss Louderman is in possession of critical information that the BEA needs. Your failure to turn her over could be considered a breach of national security."

"Could be," I said. "But her mother's already on her way, and I can't be legally enjoined from turning Penny over to her. You can work with her if you want after that."

He paused, and then his voice went back to that silky smooth fake-friendly voice. "That's fine," he said. "I'll be sure to make an appointment with Mrs. Louderman."

"So you'll let Czoltan go?"

"Oh, maybe I'll see what his background turns up first. After all, you're going to make me chase after Mrs. Louderman." There was a pause. "I'm sorry, I have to go."

"You do what you have to," I said. "Just let him go."

"We'll see," he said.

"Bye." I hung up.

Yeah! Penny said. *You got him!*

I think so, I told her. *I hope Jefferson can do something with it.* I sent the recording to her with a note to please call me as soon as she could.

"What now?" Yumi said. "Just wait?"

"Penny's mom should be here...pretty soon now. Even if she walked to the Visitor Center, that would only be twenty minutes and then twenty more to come here, and it's been half an hour already."

"But now Zawada knows she's coming, he'll have one of his agents follow her."

"Or a remained person, yeah. But they would've been following Czoltan anyway. I don't think there's any way the BEA doesn't show up here, but—"

So you hope to hand me over before the BEA gets here. Penny's jubilant tone was gone, just like that.

"I hope we can get you to your mother's custody before Zawada gets here, yes." I spoke aloud so Yumi could hear. "She doesn't like him and she has more political power than I do."

And what about Marta?

"If Czoltan got in touch with Marta, then we can get a message to her. It's probably too dangerous for her to come here, though."

"Definitely," Yumi said.

I can't write down the message and I can't tell you about it, so how am I going to get it to her?

Eventually you can learn to use a tablet, I said. *Sergei could do that. You can influence electronics.*

But not today!

No, but—maybe Jake can help.

Ugh, she scoffed. *Jake's a good guy but he's not going to risk his job.*

Would you trust Czoltan? I asked.

There was a long pause. *More than you.*

That came with more than a touch of bravado and the sense that it wasn't strictly true, but I let it go because my phone rang again, and this time it was Agent Jefferson. I didn't put her on speaker this time.

"Mr. Kim, I want to thank you for bringing this to my attention."

That sounded good. "Did you get my boyfriend released?"

She cleared her throat. "Someone from our Chicago field office contacted Zawada. It turns out they've had their eye on him for a little while. A whistleblower alerted us to some suspicious activity, but we couldn't find any evidence or corroboration."

"Of trafficking remained persons?" I said.

Duh.

"I don't have particulars."

Which probably meant that she did, but couldn't share them with me. "My observation is that it's just him and two associates. He doesn't seem to want to involve the rest of the BEA in this, at least in this office."

"That sounds right," she said, and I heard the clicks of typing.

"So is my boyfriend going to be released?"

"That's my understanding. And Zawada promised to not pursue any retaliation against him."

"For what that's worth," I muttered.

"Jae," she said. "Agent Zawada also said that there's a person of interest involved in this case, a Marta Delmonico."

Oh shit, Penny said.

My skin crawled. "Uh-huh?"

"She's also someone we've had an eye out for. I know the BEA wants to speak with her, but we'd like to have first crack at it."

Don't say anything! You can't give them Marta!

"Uh," I said, and looked at Yumi, who must have read the anxiety in my expression, because her frown deepened. "I don't think I can detain her."

"You don't have to. Just text me when you're in a room with her."

"You can..." I stared back at Yumi so that she mouthed, *What?*

"Our capabilities in Wolftown are confidential, although I imagine your peacekeeper friend knows or suspects them. Don't worry, this isn't covered by your NDA. Sometimes it's helpful for people to know that, especially when there aren't any specifics to know."

Fuck, Penny contributed.

She recited that last part as though it were written down in front of her. "All right," I said. "Just text you the location or..."

"Just text that she's with you. We'll be there shortly."

Fuck me. The creepy feeling of being watched danced along my skin, but there wasn't another room I could go hide in or a camera or bug I could disable. It was just my phone, and I had a feeling that even if I disabled all the location services and whatever else, it wouldn't matter to Agent Jefferson. "All right," I said, instead of one of the ten other things I wanted to say, like "this feels like a violation of my rights" or "Jesus Christ, you people are the fucking worst" or, simply, "Fuck off."

Because this was my own damn fault. Penny and Yumi and Czoltan had been right.

"Great," Agent Jefferson said. "I understand there's a meeting today. I'll wait for your text."

"What?" Yumi asked when I hung up.

"You have to promise not to say 'I told you so,'" I told her, "not because it's not true, but because I've already heard it in my head, loud and clear."

She glared. "What?" she repeated, only slower and deeper. So I told her.

"Jae," Yumi said. "Jae. I—" She stopped, and white flakes blew in a chill breeze off her skin before she regained control. "So you're telling me the BEA *and* the FBI now are coming to this house?"

"I'm sorry. It was the only way I could save Czoltan." I made puppy dog eyes as best I could.

"Whom you also got into this mess."

"All right," I said, "but who invited me to come help them with a remained person yesterday?"

She clamped her mouth shut and gave off a little more snow. "Fine," she said. "I accept partial responsibility for this. So what are we going to do?"

I took a breath. "The FBI..." My phone was still in my hand. I looked down at it and then shoved it in my pants pocket and pressed my hand over the mic. Still, I whispered. "We're going to do the best we can. At least if I fuck up now, I'm the only one who gets arrested. I can handle that."

She fixed me with a level stare. "I don't think Czoltan can, though."

"No," I agreed. "So I'll try my best not to let that happen."

SIXTEEN

I n my pocket, my phone buzzed. Czoltan had texted me: *omw, zawada caught me but let me go,* then, *dunno why,* and then, *carla knew marta, sent addy along to her.*

"Shit," I said aloud, and texted back, *Tell Marta not to come, Zawada trap.*

He didn't respond for a couple minutes, while Yumi and Penny and I looked anxiously at my phone, but it turned out he'd just been texting Carla. *Told carla,* he wrote. *She's going to try to reach marta but might already be on way.*

"God dammit!" I met Yumi's worried eyes. "Maybe you shouldn't be here," I said.

"My job is to protect Wolftown residents," she replied, but her brow creased.

"Yeah, but if there's a terrorist coming—"

Marta's not a terrorist! Penny objected.

"—and the BEA *and* the FBI, you don't want to get in the middle of that."

"I wouldn't mind witnessing more of the BEA's behavior,

though." Yumi looked up to the ceiling, where cobwebs occluded a rusty vent. "They might behave differently if they think you're alone."

"Maybe," I said. "I'm honestly not sure it matters at all to him."

"Still." A knock came at the front door. Yumi smiled at me and then fragmented into a spiral of crystalline white flakes that wafted cold air onto me and then rose into the vent, blowing the cobwebs aside.

Right, I said to Penny. *I have no idea who that is, but are you ready?*

I hope it's Marta, she said. *Then I can—say goodbye to her and she can go.*

I know you have some information to give her, I said, walking into the front room and coughing from the dust my shoes kicked up. *I'm not an idiot. Also, you and Zawada both told me.*

She didn't say anything. The curtains drawn across the front windows and the opaque wooden door offered no clue as to who was outside, but there was a peephole. When I saw Czoltan's muzzle through the fisheye lens, my heart jumped and fingers fumbled with excitement and I couldn't open the door fast enough.

He jumped inside at the same moment I tried to jump forward and hug him, but he's bigger than me, so he pushed me inside and wrapped his arms around me, the soft fur of his muzzle pressed to my cheek. I buried my fingers in the fur of his shoulder and breathed in his warmth and wolfy smell.

"I should—" he said after a moment.

"Yeah, let's get inside."

He reached back to close the door. "Who else is here?"

I started to tell him, and then realized that the BEA's remained might still be watching him. "Nobody," I said. "Yumi didn't want to get into this whole thing. We're just waiting for Penny's mom to show up so we can hand her over."

And for Marta, Penny added with a touch of defiant hope.

We looked at the two threadbare couches, both of them sporting cobwebs as well as dust, and opted to stand on the carpet. A small table held a lamp, and above that table, cobwebs fluttered from a vent in the ceiling, like the one in the kitchen. I felt a little better knowing that Yumi was watching us, even if I wasn't sure who else might be, so I guided Czoltan over to stand by the couches, under the vent.

"They didn't hurt you, did they?" I put a hand on his arm.

He smiled down. "No. Just scared me a bit. I mean..." He hesitated. "I didn't know if they could hold me forever. They took my phone. Who would know that they had me? There were rumors that the BEA could do that, but...I never believed them."

"Penny found you," I said. "She went around back and watched the windows until you looked out of them."

He splayed his ears. "Thank her for me," he said. "Wasn't it dangerous? I was actually looking out the window because I thought Sergei might find me, and then I remembered that he's gone."

It had been five months, but I remembered that feeling well from the first few, and even now, if I wasn't focusing, I would think I heard the old bear's voice. I missed him, and every time I thought I was over that, it would come back in unexpected moments. "It was dangerous. They had another remained person there. But she navigated it really well."

Thanks, Penny said.

"Maybe she'd be a good assistant for you." Czoltan grinned.

"No," I said as Penny said the same thing. "She's underage, for one thing, and for another, she needs to go to her mother."

Czoltan cocked his head. "How does age work with ghosts? Will she be seventeen forever?"

"They're not legally people, so it doesn't matter," I said.

"That's a sucky way to look at it."

"Yeah. But it's the reality. Remained persons don't have rights. They're not really considered people."

Yet.

"That doesn't mean they shouldn't be," I added. "It's just the way it is."

Czoltan grumbled. "We should change that."

"A lot of people are trying. Well, some are. But to your question, Sergei said he was a hundred-plus years old, so I assume Penny will turn eighteen next year."

Later this year!

"Or later this year," I amended, and caught movement outside the front. "There. Look."

Several people passed by the front window, shadows on the curtains, and then there was a knock at the door. Czoltan and I looked at each other and then I walked forward.

Through the peephole, Ms. Louderman looked back at me, in a tan blazer over a white blouse, and beside her was Jake and one other man I didn't recognize, both with short-sleeved shirts and ties. None of them was Zawada, though, so I opened the door and let them in—at least, I let in Ms. Louderman and Jake. "Craig," Ms. Louderman said crisply, "you can wait outside."

The other guy stationed himself beside the door with the stiff, attentive demeanor of a security guard. I closed the door and locked it after them, then turned.

Ms. Louderman had stationed herself in the center of the room, near the arm of one of the couches, and Jake remained at her side. She looked around and waved her hand in front of her

195

nose. "It smells in here," she said. "Why are we meeting in this disgusting old house, of all places?"

I took Penny's ring off. "It was the safest place we could find," I said, and held the ring out. To Penny, I said, *Good-bye and good luck*, and aloud I said, "Please take this."

Penny didn't respond. Her mother eyed the ring and stretched out her hand, then stopped. "Where did you find this?"

"It was—in her hand. She was holding it." I hadn't thought to make up a story, and now I had to improvise.

"And why did you take just that ring? Where are the rest of her effects?"

"With the peacekeepers, I think."

This isn't going well, Penny observed.

I know. Help me convince her!

Jake said, "If she was holding the ring, it must be important. That's probably why Mr. Kim took that and nothing else."

"But then why did that government man want it?" Ms. Louderman's sharp eyes held mine. "If it's evidence of some kind, you know I'm compelled to hand it over to him."

"It's...but it's something of Penny's," I said, without conviction.

"So you said." She stepped back and folded her arms. "And I was convinced on the phone. But on the way over here, I had time to think. Largely because we had to walk so long. I can't believe we still can't have cars in Wolftown. The people here seem determined to reject every convenience—but that's not relevant." Her eyes flicked to Czoltan, still standing near the vent, and back to me. "On the walk, I thought about how strange this all was, and how odd Jake was acting."

"Me?" Jake's eyes widened.

"Jake's a dupe, and that's fine. He's an excellent assistant."

She didn't look away from me. "But he was so eager to come along, and he didn't say any of his usual spiel about keeping an open mind. It got me to thinking. Of course he talked to you on the phone before you talked to me. He could've told you that I'd be excited to come help you see the truth. You put on a nice little charade of that, too, very convincing until I thought back to your first visit."

Your plan didn't work so well, Penny said with some smugness. *See, she's a bitch.*

Never give a mark time to think about the con, I said back. *But it's not over yet.*

"So I asked myself, why would it be so important to you that I take possession of this ring?"

She paused there, searching my eyes. I kept my cool and said, "And what did you come up with?"

Her frown deepened. "Nothing. Nothing! I can't imagine why it would be important to you that I have this ring, whether or not it belonged to Penny. I can't imagine why this government agent would want it. That's why I didn't just turn around and go back to the office. I want to know what's so important about this that you would pull a very busy public servant from her office to take it."

I know that one of the tells that someone is lying is when their eyes flick away from you as they talk, and I couldn't help it; I glanced away as I tried to compose an answer. I couldn't think of anything that would be convincing enough. *Penny, you're going to have to manifest,* I said desperately.

She won't believe it!

I don't think we have a choice.

"The truth is," I said, and gestured to a space beside myself and Czoltan. "The truth is...this."

Everyone in the room stared at the empty space. A heartbeat, then another. "The truth is what?" Ms. Louderman snapped.

Penny!

I'm trying! I can't.

Are you really trying?

Yes!

Her voice was anguished enough that I believed her. "Ah," I said. "The truth is..."

"The truth is," a voice said, "that this ring contains valuable information pertinent to a government investigation of terrorism."

Startled, I looked up at the ceiling, but it wasn't Yumi's voice. Everyone else looked around as well, and then a tall man —taller than Czoltan's six foot three, white-haired and pale-skinned, in a funereal suit and tie—appeared in the space I'd been hoping Penny would manifest in. "It is legally your property," the man continued, and now I recognized the voice as the ghost Penny had been talking to, even though his clothing was different, "but we hope you will turn it over to the government for our investigation."

Ms. Louderman, like the rest of us, had been startled, but now her eyes turned steely and she folded her arms. "So that's why you brought me here," she told me. "Holographic machines hidden in the walls, projecting this nonsense." She waved a hand through the remained's body.

The remained person paused, staring through us, and then said, "Yes, I am a projection. The government agent will be here momentarily to take possession of the ring."

Ms. Louderman stared at it and then peered more closely at the ring. "How does it contain information?" she asked. "I don't see any connectors to it. Is it a tiny USB drive?"

Czoltan walked around the figure, coming to stand next to me by the front windows. I didn't think he could protect me from the remained person, but I appreciated the gesture. "It's a magical artifact," I said to Ms. Louderman.

"Well, what was Penny doing with it, then?"

"If only we could ask her."

She'd been acting so emotionless that I didn't realize how cruel this statement came across until her eyes welled up and she had to turn away from me. She searched her pockets for a tissue, but Jake held one out for her, which she used to wipe her eyes and then blow her nose. "I can't believe she's gone," she said, her voice wavering now. "I mean, she left months ago, but I always knew she was out there. I still feel her there. I don't know how I'm supposed to act now."

Jake, standing beside her, sniffled and wiped his nose with the back of his hand. Ms. Louderman turned to him. "I know you cared for her too."

"I did, very much," he said. "She was a special girl." He eyed the ring. "May I just hold that for a moment?"

Is that okay? I asked Penny, keeping an eye on the door for when Rock showed up.

I guess. Her voice was small. *I don't know what I'm going to say to him.*

It's okay. You can still talk to me, but you can keep it private if you don't want to.

So I held the ring out, and Jake took it. His face froze and then got a faraway look.

"What?" Ms. Louderman stared at him. "What's he hearing?"

"You'd think it was a trick," I told her. "You wouldn't believe it."

Her frown deepened again. "You presume a lot."

I caught a flicker of movement at the kitchen door, and turned that way. Czoltan and Ms. Louderman followed my gaze. The remained person and Jake did not, lost in their own worlds.

In the doorway stood a kushtaka, an otter shifter, wearing a necklace of plain wooden beads and a pleated skirt swirled with patterns in sea foam and sea green. She smiled at our gaze. "I believe I can answer your questions, Ms. Louderman."

At that, Jake turned and stared at her. "Marta?" he said.

CHAPTER
SEVENTEEN

arta! Penny called out, and then I caught through her perceptions a dull roaring noise, as if she were standing next to a waterfall. *Agh! I can't talk to her! He's so loud!*

The otter inclined her head. "I assume that's Penny's ring?"

"Yeah," I said, "but look, you can't be here." My hand moved reflexively to my phone and then I yanked it away. To Penny, I asked, *The other ghost?*

I tried to leave the ring but he's right on top of me and so loud!

"Let me worry about that." Marta had a calm, assured voice, and then I noticed the touches of grey around her muzzle. "Young man, can you bring that ring over here?"

"Jake," snapped Ms. Louderman, "don't you dare. If that ring is needed for a government investigation, you can't hand it over."

The BEA's remained person—Russell, that was his name—nodded his head ponderously. "You cannot give the ring to this person."

"I don't need to take it," Marta said. "I just need to touch it for a moment."

"She probably has a chip reader or something," Ms. Louderman said. "Jake, you stay away from her."

I heard Penny cry, *Please let her touch the ring!*

"I can't!" The struggle twisted Jake's face. "I could be arrested."

Russell moved to stand between Jake and Marta. "Do not try to leave the ring," it warned. "I can hear everything you say if you do, and I can stop you."

Czoltan leaned over to me. "Can he do that?" he whispered.

"The remained can interfere with each other," I whispered back. "She said he's making too much noise for her to communicate if she leaves the ring."

"Who on Earth is he talking to?" Ms. Louderman demanded of nobody in particular. "What's 'in' the ring?"

Jake didn't answer, staring at me with the ring in his fingers. "I can't," he said to Penny. "Don't. Don't tell me, please." And then. "I do! But I can't—my life—"

We all stared at him. I held out my hand. "Jake, give me the ring back."

"Don't give it to him," Russell ordered. "My—agent will be here soon."

"Penny," I said. "You have to manifest."

He'll stop me, Penny said.

Jake turned his frightened eyes on me. "She says he'll stop her," he said.

"He can't," I said, though I didn't know if that was true. "Leave the ring but with confidence. Picture yourself the way you used to be."

I don't know how—

Marta spoke gently. "Imagine I am a mirror," she said.

Russell turned to her and gestured. "Quiet," he said.

She dismissed him with a wave and continued speaking. "Look into my eyes and see yourself reflected there," she continued, in the calming tones of a schoolteacher. She raised her right paw. "Mimic my movements."

I'm trying! Penny wailed.

"Do not listen to her," Russell ordered. "Remain in the ring."

Ms. Louderman laughed shortly. "You are all being ridiculous, keeping up this façade. If it's for my benefit, you can stop."

Jake held the ring out. "She's trying."

Russell floated right in front of Jake, focusing a menacing stare on the ring, but did not speak. "I believe in you," Marta said, gently, from behind him.

For a moment the whole room stood silent. I glanced at the front windows where Ms. Louderman's security stood, and thought there might be movement outside. But no sounds came from the door.

Russell would've told his boss that Marta was here (*like you're supposed to be telling the FBI*), and then what would they do? Make sure they had all exits secure before breaking into the house, in case she ran. It was possible that Penny was just bait to catch Marta—although Penny apparently did have information for Marta, and Zawada seemed pretty intent on not letting her receive it. "Marta," I said. "Maybe you should leave while you can."

"Don't worry about me, young man," she said without taking her eyes from the ring. "This'd be a lot easier without the big fella there, but Penny can do this."

"She's only been remained for a day," I said.

"She's not a ghost!" Ms. Louderman raised her voice. "She's—gone! And I'm not going to give any of you any money, or favors, or—or whatever you're trying to get out of me." She turned and walked toward the door, but before she got there, Marta interrupted.

"You raised a smart girl, Sylvia. She's so talented. She can do this."

"How do you know she was talented?" snapped Ms. Louderman, turning. "I knew her better than any of you did. She was smart, but she wasted her talents. She could have gone to law school."

What a bitch, Penny said. *She wanted me to go to law school. I didn't want to go.*

"She didn't want to go to law school," Jake said.

"Nobody *wants* to go to law school," Ms. Louderman replied. "You do it because it's the path to a career."

"She wanted to help people." He wasn't looking at any of us, clearly still listening to Penny.

"She could have helped people!" She glared at Jake. "You weren't her mother. You didn't know her like I did."

Marta broke in with her calm voice. "Penny, why don't you come speak for yourself?"

"Stop acting like she's alive!" Ms. Louderman turned on her heel. "Jake, drop the ring. Whoever wants it can take it."

NO, JAKE, DON'T, Penny screamed.

He winced. "No, I won't," he said.

"What do you mean, you won't?"

"Sorry," he said to her. "Penny—" He broke off. "This ring means—meant a lot to her, and I can't—"

Maybe it was the imminent dropping of the ring that decided Zawada, or maybe his perimeter of the house was complete, but he chose that moment to make his entrance.

Or try to make his entrance. Czoltan perked his ears, and a moment later I heard the voices outside as well, Ms. Louderman's security guard arguing with at least one other person. A moment later the front door rattled as someone turned the knob, but the lock held.

We all stared at the door as a fist pounded on it and Zawada yelled, "Open this door right now!"

I was closest, Czoltan right beside me, but it was Ms. Louderman who strode to the door and threw the lock.

She barely had time to step backwards toward Jake before the front door burst open, slamming against the wall with a crash that made everyone jump, and Zawada fairly leapt through, flanked by the Black woman. "Everyone stay where you are," he said, unnecessarily, because we'd all turned to stare at the door, and then he started coughing as the dust he'd kicked up filled the air. "Kate," he managed, and then through fits of coughs, "Get the ring."

Russell vanished. Jake turned to run toward Marta, but he'd hesitated long enough for Ms. Louderman to grab his arm. "Don't be an idiot," she said as the woman, Kate, caught up to him and grabbed the hand he'd closed around the ring.

"No!" Jake yelled as they wrestled for it, echoing Penny, who was screaming, *NO!*

Czoltan looked at me, but Zawada saw the look. "Don't interfere," he warned both of us as he brought a small silver box the size of a deck of cards out of his jacket pocket. "I can arrest you for interfering with a government agent, and believe me, the FBI won't stick their nose in to save you this time if I do."

I shook my head at Czoltan, trying desperately to think of a way to salvage the situation. My hand crept toward my phone again. If I texted the FBI, they would—what, interfere with Zawada's attempt to take a remained person into custody? How had I gotten into the middle of this, anyway?

I remembered, and that was my only idea. "Penny!" I yelled. "Sing your song!"

The words burst into my head: *YOU SHOW THE WORLD YOUR PLASTIC FACE BUT UNDERNEATH IT'S ROTTEN. YOU HANG ON TIGHT TO THAT BRIEFCASE BUT WHAT HAVE YOU FORGOTTEN.*

Jake and Kate both winced, staggering back, and Jake dropped the ring onto the floor. Everyone froze for a second, and then Zawada lunged for the ring, dropping the silver box and knocking Ms. Louderman to the ground as he did. Before he could reach it, the air around the ring shimmered, and a skinny white girl in distressed jeans and a faded white t-shirt with Kurt Cobain's face on it appeared in the room, her form shimmering like a heat mirage. She faced the wall, mouth open, and now her song sounded throughout the room.

"YOU CLIMB THE FUCKIN LADDER WHILE THE ONES BENEATH YOU SMOTHER," she screamed. "AND I'M SO FUCKIN' MADDER I'LL NEVER CALL YOU MOTHER."

Zawada lurched, but kept moving forward and grabbed the ring. The rest of us stared at the apparition, and Ms. Louderman said, in a cracked voice, "Penny?"

"YOU THINK LAW SCHOOL IS—" Penny stopped, turned, and faced the room. Her words rang in our ears. "Hi, Mom."

Zawada looked wildly around him and spotted the silver box on the floor. I caught Penny's eye and gestured to Marta. "Right," Penny said, and turned to the otter. "The BEA is keeping your friends in the D.C. facility. They're definitely there."

"Stop talking!" Zawada yelled, grabbing the box and flipping it open.

Penny ignored him. "The other info is in the backup place. Number 34, 1-2-1-9."

"I'm so proud of you," Marta said.

"You're in big trouble," Zawada snarled. He dropped the

ring into the box and snapped it closed. The moment he did, Penny vanished.

"Listen!" Ms. Louderman shouted, staring at the space where Penny had been. Marta and Zawada both turned their attention to her. "Mr. Kim, Mr. Zawada, if you've staged this whole scenario as a way to get me to believe some tripe about ghosts—"

"It's not about you," Marta said gently. "Believe me."

"And you." Ms. Louderman whirled. "I don't even know who you are."

"I'm a friend of your daughter's. She still loved you, you know, even after all that."

"No she didn't. She hated me. You heard that screaming."

Marta smiled sadly. "Love and hate are so close, Sylvia."

The alderman rubbed the lapel of her blazer with nervous fingers. "You can't know—it was so complicated between us."

"I know that you made her take down a Slipknot poster because you said it was too violent, but you let her listen to their music; that you had a cook but her favorite meals were the ones you made on the cook's night off; that your last phone call hurt her more than she would ever admit to you or me; that—"

"Stop!" Ms. Louderman pressed fingers to her eyes.

And then behind Marta, I saw the red-haired agent. Just a glimpse of him, but he was there in the kitchen. He'd snuck through the back door, and carried a gun, which he hadn't raised yet.

"Marta!" I called. "Behind you!" At the same time, I slipped my phone out of my pocket. Being arrested by the FBI seemed preferable to being in this room alone with Rock and his dangerous team any longer.

The otter turned to me and smiled. "I know there's someone behind me," she said.

TIM SUSMAN

Zawada had been studying the silver box in his hand and now looked up, meeting my eyes with a venomous stare. "I'm pretty sick of your interference," he said, and I felt that at last I was getting a glimpse of the true person under the slick plastic exterior.

"That's too bad," I said roughly, fingers fumbling for the Recent Calls menu on my phone. "I don't intend to stop anytime soon."

I expected him to reply, but he kept staring at me, as though I were still talking and he was listening.

No—he *was* listening, and talking. That's the expression I had when I was talking to Sergei, or Penny.

The red-haired agent had lifted his gun now, and he called to Rock, "Ready."

Still, Marta didn't turn. But Rock kept staring at me, and he said, "Stand down."

There was a choking noise behind me. I turned and saw Czoltan clutching his head, and then his arms dropped and his eyes lowered to me. But they weren't his eyes anymore.

My hand with the phone in it dropped to my side. I searched my boyfriend's eyes for any glimmer of recognition, but they were cold and hard, barely registering my presence. "Czoltan?" I said. "What's...what's going on?"

But I knew. Russell was surely experienced enough to possess someone, even though doing so was illegal. Rock hadn't been staring *at* me. He'd been staring past me, at Czoltan, ordering Russell to possess him, the only werewolf in the room.

At the moment I had that realization, Rock took a long step to the door and threw the lock, then stood in front of the door with his arms folded. "Virgil," he said, "nobody leaves the living room."

"Yes, sir," the red-haired agent said.

"What is going on?" Ms. Louderman demanded. "You can't keep us here."

Rock ignored her, his attention on Czoltan. I knew what was coming and I tried to stop it. "Hey," I said. "Czoltan, you're still in there. You can stop this. You can fight against it."

I believed that, and I had to, because if he couldn't, then I knew what was going to come next. Behind me, Rock gave a harsh laugh. "Russell's very good," he said. "There won't be much of a fight."

"What is going on?" Fear crept into Ms. Louderman's voice.

"We are being silenced," Marta said in a tone more sad than afraid.

"Do it!" Rock yelled at Russell/Czoltan.

I reached for Czoltan's paw. "Don't!" I pleaded. "Fight it!"

For a moment, I held his paw and I thought I saw a flicker in his eyes. Hope bloomed in my chest that together we could overcome the possession. But it lasted only a few seconds before he jerked his paw away from me. And as I watched, he began to transform.

His body dropped to the floor as his legs shrank. Lying on his side, he arched his back, his torso compressing and flattening, arms and legs twisting and shrinking.

Ms. Louderman let out a cry, and Jake scrambled bravely to stand in front of her. "Do something!" he yelled, though I didn't know if that was at me or at one of the other agents. He was sweating now, his face glossy and eyes panicked.

I only caught their movement out of the corner of my eye, unable as I was to look away from Czoltan, still gasping and struggling with the change being forced on him. He'd be fully feral in seconds, and then it would be too late.

I reached out both hands, not sure what I would do, and thank goodness I did, because that reminded me that I had my phone in the hand I hadn't extended to Czoltan. I stabbed at the call in the list and turned to face Rock.

"Hey, Agent Zawada," I said, my voice almost a snarl from worry, my heart thumping in fear. I held the phone up in his line of sight so he could see the active call I'd initiated." Maybe you want to explain to the FBI why you had your ghost possess my boyfriend and turn him feral?"

His smile vanished and he stared at the phone. Not-Czoltan's movements slowed, and he let out a low growl that triggered an ancient fear to clutch at my bowels and chill my skin. Jake, Ms. Louderman, and Kate had all turned at my words, and while Kate just stared from the middle of the room, the other two took several hurried steps back, bumping into one of the couches and sending up a cloud of dust. Jake let out a small cry.

Ms. Louderman, to her credit, kept her composure. "You're his boyfriend," she said softly to me. "You can talk him back."

"He's possessed by a ghost," I said, still staring at Rock. "Whose orders, I believe, were to murder all of us so that Rock could 'discover' this horrific crime and kill my boyfriend for it."

Rock forced a laugh, but it was unconvincing even to him and he broke it off halfway through. "That's preposterous," he said. "Your boyfriend has clearly lost control of himself."

"I have a lot of experience of ghosts and of my boyfriend," I said, speaking into the phone, "and I know when someone's possessed. Besides which, Rock just placed himself here in the room with us all, so if we're murdered and he claims to have 'discovered the scene' later, you'll know he's lying."

He glared at me. "I'm prepared to defend myself."

"Then you're to blame if any of the rest of us get killed, aren't you? If you could stop him, and you didn't." My mouth was so dry, my face so cold. I swallowed. "In any case, you won't have to worry about it. The FBI has agents nearby. They'll be here in a few minutes."

I glanced over toward Marta, but she kept smiling that serene smile, watching Rock, and she didn't move at all.

Rock weighed his options in his head and then growled out, "Russell. Return to me."

The growling beside me stopped, and Czoltan's lupine form flopped to the ground. The tension didn't leave me yet; I had to make sure he was all right and could come back to human. But that meant I had to get out of here first, and I needed to make sure Penny was safe before I did that. But how to do that while Rock still had her in the case?

And then I realized what I should have minutes ago, that the coldness on my skin wasn't going away. It was coming from the vent. I looked up toward it, to where a few flakes of white drifted down, barely noticeable unless you were looking for them. "Hey," I said, "why don't we all cool down?"

Rock had turned his attention to Marta. "You're under arrest," he said.

"Oh, I don't think so, dear," she replied, and dodged to one side as the red-haired agent charged. He stumbled past her through the kitchen doorway and barreled into Kate's side. She pushed him away, annoyed.

He ended up in the center of the room as a swirl of snow poured out of the vent, sweeping through the air and forming little eddies around each person. Rock, distracted, was pointing at Marta and said, "Don't let her get a-away!" But the last few words came out in a puff of white breath, and he stared at the swirling snowstorm. "G-get out!" he gasped.

Ice crystals formed on his lips as he said it. He clapped a hand to his face. Kate had already sunk to her knees and the red-haired agent staggered back, ice forming on his lips and skin. Zawada dropped to his knees, his eyes filming over with white.

I felt colder, but not quite so chilled as to be frozen. Penny's mother made an "O" with her mouth as a cloud of breath escaped her, and then she sat down quite hard on the couch, a puff of dust rising to mix with the snow. "Everything is... white..." she murmured, her eyes glazing over as well. Jake was already down on the floor.

Only Marta and I appeared unaffected—and Czoltan, beside me, panting and unfrozen on the floor, though his breath came in quick pants. I knelt beside him and stroked his fur, but he didn't respond.

The eddies of snowflakes left the frozen people to gather in the center of the room. The whirlwind of snow thickened, and then Yumi stepped out of them. She arched an eyebrow as she knelt next to me and Czoltan. "You owe me a very large favor," she said, and cast an eye to Marta, still watching us. "I thought I froze her," she said with a frown.

"She's a remained person," I said, and rested my hand on Czoltan's chest. I had to get him out of this shape as quickly as I could; a werewolf who stayed feral too long might lose his way back entirely. Not for hours, maybe days, but my nerves jangled and I wanted him back now.

Marta laughed softly and drifted over to us. "How did you know?" she asked.

"You didn't kick up any dust." I rubbed the chest of the wolf on the floor, and said, "Come on, Czoltan. It's me. I'm here."

"Before the FBI arrives," Marta said, but I cut her off.

"They're not."

Yumi and Marta both looked confused. "You called them," the yuki-onna said.

"No, I called your phone. You were snow, so it went right to voicemail. Glad you let people record as long as they want." I shook Czoltan a little more roughly, and now his ears flicked and his head lifted.

Yumi sat back on her heels. "Damn."

Even Marta looked impressed. "Quick thinking," she said.

Now Czoltan struggled to sit up. He'd kicked the pants free, but his underwear still stretched across his wolfy hips as he got up to a dog-like sit and stared into my face.

"Yumi," I said softly, returning the wolf's gaze.

"Yeah?"

"Ask Russell what his binding token is."

She got up, and I leaned forward, speaking softly. "Come on back to human," I said. "You're still you, you're still Czoltan. Remember me?"

Some part of him did; he wasn't aggressive, just curious. I hoped that was only disorientation from the possession. "Come on back," I said as he tilted his head. "You're Czoltan."

He leaned his head forward, and knowing how important scent is, I brought my neck to his nose. I closed my eyes as he snuffled, and then he breathed in deeply. I put my hands on either side of his chest as he breathed and recited his name over and over next to his ears.

And then I felt a shift, as he took in a breath. His chest expanded and then kept growing, and his weight grew against me. Then there were paws on my chest, then arms around my torso, and I hugged him back as his body changed.

His breath came ragged, and then he said, in a rough voice, "Jae?"

"Yeah. I'm here." I slid my arms around him.

"What...happened? I don't remember changing." There was a note of panic in his voice and his body trembled. "I—that never happened."

"Rock had a remained possess you," I said. "He forced the change."

"What?" The panic was gone, replaced by cold fury. "What the *fuck*?"

"Yeah," I said. "We gotta get out of here. When you're ready."

"Okay. Okay." But he didn't let go of me. "You brought me back."

"You found the way back," I said. I let him hold on another moment, and then said, "But we really gotta go."

He let go. "I know," he said. "I'm ready."

"Maybe you should put your pants on," Marta said gently.

"Oh, shit." He grabbed them off the floor and shoved one leg into them, and only then looked around at the frozen people in the room. He stopped with one pants leg still hanging free, and then saw Yumi. "Oh."

Behind her floated Russell, now in the outfit Penny had seen him in. He followed Yumi as she walked over to me and held out the small silver box and a pendant. "This is what binds him," she said. "Warm it up before you touch it with bare skin."

"I'll take it." Czoltan stretched out a furred paw and took the case and pendant, then breathed on them. His breath condensed into crystals on its surface, which melted under another breath.

"Can you really help me?" Russell asked in a low voice. He kept flickering, his image switching between one looking at me and one looking back at Rock.

I looked at Marta. "I assume you know some people who can help?"

"Of course," she said. "But I can't take his pendant."

"No." I held out my hand to Czoltan. He dropped the cold case and pendant into it, then finished getting his pants on. I weighed the case, but didn't open it yet. Instead I lifted my gaze to Marta. There was a question I had to ask her before I let Penny out, one that was gnawing at my gut. "You knew the BEA was killing people to capture their spirits. Did you send Penny on that mission knowing that she might die?"

The soft smile that had stayed on the otter's face throughout slid away. "Why would I do that?" she asked. "I loved Penny."

"Because you needed proof."

Marta shook her head. "If anything," she said, "I hoped Penny would be spared. A young human girl? But..."

"But she wasn't."

"If that had been my plan," Marta said, looking steadily back at me, "don't you think I would have been there for her the moment her spirit separated?"

I nodded slowly. "I suppose. But you knew there was danger, and you sent her anyway."

The otter bowed her head. Yumi looked back and forth between us. "You mean the BEA killed her and then tried to capture her ghost?"

Marta nodded slowly. "Penny was looking for evidence that some friends of ours, ghost activists, were being held by the BEA. They had kidnapped other ghosts and we'd gotten them freed, but they denied having these. I suspected—I knew —they were lying." Marta's thick tail swung back and forth behind her, passing through the dust without leaving a trace. "I thought that their practice of killing to keep their secret safe was one they only took in extremes, but..."

Russell cleared his throat. "If you are truly going to help me, I can tell you more." He looked down at Czoltan. "I was not the one who possessed the girl, but I know who did and how it was done."

"How?" Yumi demanded.

The ghost flickered back to looking at Rock, then to us again. He shook his head fearfully. "When I am free of the binding," he said.

"All right." I wasn't sure I trusted Marta. I've known activists to sacrifice more than one life for a cause. But she truly seemed to love Penny, so I gave her the benefit of the doubt. "Russell, I'm going to put your pendant in this box, so you're going to be cut off for a while. When we let you out, there'll be someone to set you free."

"I welcome it," he intoned.

"And you," I said to Marta, "say what you've got to say to Penny and then you should go, too."

She nodded. "I will."

I looked at the small circle of people around me: Yumi, Russell, Marta, Czoltan. Then I opened the case and took out Penny's ring.

Oh my GOD are you okay is Marta okay what's going on it went all dark!

Everything's fine, I told her. *You're fine. Yumi froze the BEA and your mom. Marta's got something to say to you and then she's gotta go.*

Okay. Okay. Oh my fucking god.

Can you manifest?

By way of answer, an image flickered in the center of the circle of people and then Penny was there, facing Marta. "Oh god," she said. "I wish I could hug you."

"You never could." Marta smiled. "You were so brave, dear."

"I guess I can't stay with you." Penny sounded resigned. "I'll have to stay with my mom or Jake or something."

"That may be so. But you will see me again, I promise. And before too long, we might be able to continue our work together, if you'd like that."

"Sure!" Penny brightened. "I mean...what worse can happen to me now?"

Marta's brow lowered. "There are things—"

"I know, I know." Penny gave a half-laugh. "But I mean—you know what I mean."

"I do indeed." Marta smiled past her to me. "I have your information and have passed it on already. Someone is retrieving the documents, and we will work on freeing our friends. Thanks to you."

Unexpectedly, Penny looked over her shoulder. "And to Mr. Kim," she said. "He took care of me."

"He cares about you a great deal," Marta said.

"Gross." But Penny smiled as she stuck her tongue out at me.

"All right," I said. "Marta's got to go and so does Yumi." I dropped the pendant into the case. "Bye, Russell."

He said a quick goodbye. I closed the case over his pendant and then held it out to Yumi. "What?" she said. "Me?"

"Got to be you," I said. "Marta can't take it, and they might search me and Czoltan. I don't think Penny's mom will let them search her, but she'd give them the case if she felt it on her."

She shook her head at me and took the case. "You owe me another big one."

"I'm happy to pay it," I said, walking over to slip Penny's ring into her mother's jacket pocket.

You'll be safest here, I said even though she didn't say anything.

No, I got that, Penny said.

You did really well, I told her. *Manifesting is hard.*

Thanks for remembering my song.

You'll always be able to talk to me. I dropped the ring and stepped back. *See?*

I know, you dork, she said back. *Marta's got the info now and that's what matters.*

I turned to Yumi and my boyfriend, and I took Czoltan's paw in my hand. "Can you freeze me and Czoltan before you go? It'll look better that way."

Yumi nodded, swirls of snow starting to drift out from her long coat. "Wait," Czoltan said. "I changed back and his ghost is gone. Won't that be suspicious?"

"Remained person," I said, "not 'ghost,' and yeah, but it's the best we can do for now."

"Right," Yumi said. "Get on the floor so you don't hurt yourselves. I'll see you soon."

Czoltan and I knelt on the ground, his paw still holding my hand. Snow joined the dust clouds puffing up around us, and whiteness blanketed the world.

CHAPTER
EIGHTEEN

The first thing I heard through the haze of chill as I recovered was Zawada's pinched, aggrieved voice. "—happening?" he croaked. "What—?" He stared around and then scrambled to his feet, lurching awkwardly as his muscles warmed up.

I met Czoltan's eyes and saw him as alert as I was. We'd been frozen less time, and I only felt a little stiff, but still I didn't get up. On the couch and on the floor in front of it, Ms. Louderman and Jake blinked and reached slowly for their faces, and the other two BEA agents, Kate and Virgil, were getting to their feet as Rock yelled at them to get up.

I noticed that Rock had left the front door, so I got to my feet and hurried over there. He saw me and said, "Hey! Hey!" as I reached for the lock, but I'd already thrown the bolt by the time he came over and pulled my arm away. I kicked the door a couple times as he dragged me away, and that had the intended effect: Ms. Louderman's security guard opened the door a moment later.

He looked around the room and put a hand to his holstered

weapon (probably a taser, not a gun), but didn't draw it. "What's going on in here?" he asked. "Ma'am, are you okay? I only let in those BEA agents. Did they attack you?"

"I believe we were bespelled somehow," she said. "I'm fine now."

The guard hurried to her side anyway, apologizing for letting her down while she reassured him. I watched her and Jake get to their feet, then wrenched free of Rock. "I felt all cold, and then everything went white," I told him. "Probably a *yuki-onna*."

Rock glared at me and only then seemed to notice that his hands were empty. "Where is it?" he demanded, spinning to check the floor. "Find it!" he screamed at his agents.

"What?" Virgil asked, looking around.

"The box!" Rock yelled. "Search everyone in the room if you have to."

"You'll do nothing of the sort." Ms. Louderman fixed him with a glare. "We are private citizens and you have no authority to search our persons here."

"It's a little something called the Fourth Amendment," I said helpfully.

"Boss," Kate said. "Shouldn't we go? The Feds..."

Rock swung his gaze around the room. "I don't think he actually called them," he said. "They'd be here by now."

"A *yuki-onna* freeze doesn't last more than a minute after the *yuki-onna* leaves," I said helpfully. "They could still be on their way."

"Boss," Kate said, more urgently. "It's over. We need to go."

"Hey," Virgil said, looking up from the floor. "The otter's gone."

"Of course she is," Rock snapped. "She arranged this whole thing, probably coordinated the attack." He glared at me. "And you were in on it with her."

"I called the FBI," I said. "I don't think she'd have been down with that. But we can wait and ask them, huh?"

That got Rock's attention. He snapped upright, breathing heavily, and then stared into space. Talking to Russell—or trying to, anyway. His brow furrowed, and then darkened, and his face reddened, so angry that I took a step back because he looked like he might take a swing at someone. "Where the fuck is Russell?!" he yelled to nobody in particular, and then his hand went to his neck and all the red drained out of his face.

"Ooh," I said. "That's your remained person, right? The tall white-haired guy? Well, you should be grateful he won't be here to testify for the FBI."

For a long moment, he stared malevolently at me, and then he whirled on his feet. "Come on," he said briskly to the two agents, and they followed him into the kitchen and out the back door.

"Phew," I said when they were gone, turning to Ms. Louderman. "What an asshole, eh?"

"Indeed," she said. "Mr. Kim, wasn't the officer who accompanied you to my office earlier today a *yuki-onna*?"

"Yes, she was," I said. "But Yumi's been at the peacekeeper station since we got back from your office. There are lots of *yuki-onna* in Wolftown."

"A little over a hundred, as I recall." She exhaled. "Can you answer the FBI's questions, or do you feel I should wait as well?"

"Oh, right," I said, and pulled my phone out. "I ought to actually text them."

Jake's eyes widened. "That was a *bluff*?"

Czoltan's ears were splayed, so I explained quickly that I'd pretended to call the FBI to scare Rock. "But, uh, it wasn't exactly a bluff, because I did call them when he took Czoltan prisoner."

"Oh," my boyfriend said, and his ears flicked back as his expression went from reflexively mad to thoughtful.

"Anyway, the agent was interested in what Rock was doing, and that was before he illegally possessed an extra and forced him to change with probable intent of at least harming most of us, so...I should probably update them." I waited to see Czoltan's reaction.

His eyes met mine, and to my relief I saw understanding there. "Call them," he advised. "This isn't all going to fit in a text."

"We'll wait outside." Ms. Louderman swept past me with Jake and her guard. "In case they want to talk to us."

Czoltan paused for a moment, gave me an approving—or at least understanding—nod, and then went with Ms. Louderman, leaving me alone with two dusty couches in the empty house.

I took a moment to figure out my story and then called Jefferson back. I told her most of what had happened more or less as it did, leaving out only that I knew the *yuki-onna* who'd frozen us and that I knew where Penny was. "I would've texted you as soon as Marta showed up," I said, "except for the whole 'Agent Zawada trying to kill me' thing."

"I understand," she said. "I'd like to bring you and Czoltan in for a debriefing in the next few days, and I'll reach out to Ms. Louderman's office as well. There's just one question I have for you right now."

"Yes?"

"Why didn't you actually call me when you threatened to?"

"Well," I said with a little laugh, "I meant to. But I couldn't actually look properly at my phone, and my finger hit the wrong number. I'm just glad he didn't notice."

"Lucky for you," she said. "We could've been there by now otherwise."

"Yeah, that would've been preferable."

"And then maybe terrorists wouldn't have taken Miss Louderman's ghost. Which you're still bound to, isn't that right?"

"Uh...that's right. But I can't feel her now. The ring must still be in the ghost-proofed box."

"Mmm." That was an "I'm not sure I believe you" sound if ever I've heard one. "Well, Mr. Kim, it looks like you dodged a bullet, or worse. I've got agents out looking for Zawada, and I have to ask you not to talk about this incident except to us until we get a better handle on what's going on."

"Right," I said. "Of course not. And for the other work..."

"Oh, of course, we'll have you start that. I think that this incident will only raise your credibility among extras. As long as you don't mention having called the FBI."

"Of course not."

"And Jae?"

"Yes?"

She paused. "Don't give me another reason not to trust you."

The word "another" wasn't lost on me. "I understand," I said.

———

Outside, Czoltan stood a little way apart from the other three, checking his phone. He looked up when I came out, ears splayed. "Everything okay?"

"Depending on your definition of 'okay,' I think so," I said. And then my legs wobbled a bit and I kind of fell against him as the adrenaline and tension all left my body, and I didn't mind having to lean on him or his arms around me, because I could still feel the memory of Russell looking out of his eyes, of full-wolf him looking curiously at me as I tried desperately to guide him back, and I was afraid and thankful for him all in an overwhelming rush of emotion.

"Hey," he said. "We got out."

"Yeah." My voice was muffled against his chest.

"So what did the FBI say?"

As the others looked my way, I raised my voice to include them all. "The FBI's going to want to talk to us about this incident, so expect a call, and don't talk about it to anyone else because it sounds like this is going to become an ongoing investigation."

Ms. Louderman's mouth twisted, but she nodded sharply, once. "As well it should be," she said, and then turned to her security guard. "Mr. Kim and his boyfriend are going to escort us to the Visitor Center. Please hang back from us to make sure that Agent Zawada or his people don't ambush us."

"Yes, ma'am." He dropped back immediately.

Holding onto Czoltan, I took another look at the Wolftown wall, the graffiti, the silhouette of the werewolf behind bars. My legs had steadied, so I lifted my face to his for a kiss, then stepped back and walked with the others back down the street. It wasn't crowded, but several werewolves gave us curious looks. None of them asked if we were lost, though; probably Czoltan's presence reassured the other wolves.

"That was crazy, wasn't it?" Jake said. "Was that guy really going to kill us?"

Ms. Louderman didn't answer, and I said, "Seemed like it. It's illegal to order a ghost to possess someone, and illegal to force an extra to change form, but..."

It shouldn't have taken an encounter with a corrupt BEA official to make me feel how vulnerable extras were. I'd always known they walked a more precarious line than humans, but I thought we had plenty of laws in place to protect them.

Nothing like a little personal experience to radicalize you, Penny said as Jake and Ms. Louderman discussed Rock's crimes further.

You walked the same path, with your friend's dad and all.

First of all, I was fourteen when that happened, and second, yeah, I know. I wasn't being sarcastic.

That let me open up a little more. *It doesn't feel good, not knowing what Czoltan was coping with.*

I'm not gonna excuse you, Penny replied, *but look, he was dealing with a lot of shit, and he's better off here. So...you're learning. Like we all are.*

Ms. Louderman broke in on my conversation. "Mr. Kim."

"Yes," I said. "Sorry, what?"

"I wonder if you'd tell me the truth about the ring now. Why did they want it so badly?"

"Check your jacket pocket."

The corner of her mouth quirked up, and she gave a small snort. One hand slipped delicately up and patted her jacket. When she felt the outline of the ring in her inside pocket, she reached in and grasped it. "Very clever," she said. "But I—"

Her face froze and she stopped walking. Jake and Czoltan carried on for a few steps before noticing, then stopped and turned. I stayed at her side, and we waited for her.

She had a faraway look in her eyes. "Penny?" she said.

Jake met my eyes with a smile. I nodded, and we waited while Penny's mother listened to her daughter. "But where *are* you?" she said after a moment. Then she frowned and said, "I can?" and then she was silent.

Czoltan pulled out his phone and checked it, but Jake and I kept an eye on Ms. Louderman, while her security stood ten feet behind us, alert. Finally, she pulled the ring out of her pocket and held it out to me, her eyes glistening.

"I think you should keep it," I said.

She pushed her hand out again. "No," she said. "I under-stand why that agent wanted it. The magic to listen to thoughts and convey them is amazing. But this ring...is not mine."

I held out my hand, reluctantly. "But your daughter..."

"Is gone. I was taken in back at the house, but this is clearly an actress. Well-coached, but a mother can—can tell." She dropped the ring into my hand. "If Penny was involved in something illegal, about this ring perhaps...that's all the more reason I don't want it."

"But legally—"

I didn't get more than those two words out. "I do not believe I have any legal title to that ring, but if you insist, it will not be too much trouble to have Jake contact Mrs. Pulaski and draft a legal transfer of ownership of the ring to you."

"I don't—"

"At your expense, of course." She fixed me with a steely gaze.

Jake stepped in. "I'll make sure the transfer includes all the contents of the ring," he told me. "Let's leave it at that."

Only then did I take the ring from Penny's mom. I closed my hand around it and asked Penny, *Are you okay?*

There was a long pause before Penny said, *Yeah. Somehow I'd rather she not believe this is me than get back on her bullshit.*

I think she was faltering. She's not going to give up her beliefs overnight. Maybe with time—

Maybe. But I'm not interested in waiting around for it. She's giving you custody of me, and that's fine.

Yeah. Her mother continued to walk down the street, and asked Czoltan, "How do you fit into all this?"

"I'm Jae's boyfriend," he said.

"I understood that," she replied. "Do you live here in Wolftown?"

I let their conversation fade into the background and focused on Penny. *So...do you want to be my partner? I could train you...*

God, no. I mean, no offense, but I want to do something that makes a difference.

That stung a little bit. *I make a difference. I saved you, didn't I?*

Hey, I said no offense. I'm sure you do really important work to like, find guys the feds are looking for.

I didn't turn in Marta.

Yeah, I noticed. S'pose you want a medal for growing a pair?

No, I just— I didn't really want her to stick around as my partner anyway. *Baby steps, right?*

Penny's mother was talking to me. "Hm? Sorry," I said, "can you repeat that?"

"You look like you were a million miles away again. I suppose you were talking to that—that actress." I nodded, unsure what words to use, and that satisfied her. "I asked you what your line of work is. Do you work with the Wolftown peacekeepers?"

"Sometimes. I'm a private investigator. I help process servers a lot. My specialty is finding people in Wolftown. Lots of humans aren't comfortable in here."

"But you have an extra for a boyfriend, so you are," she said. "Commendable. I don't get into Wolftown as much as I should, but I do have occasion to do business there, and on rare occasions our office needs to find people. Jake, take down Mr. Kim's info. We will call on him in the future."

"Yes, ma'am," Jake said, and hung back to get my number and email to put in his phone.

That'll get you some more business, Penny said. *Maybe you won't have to take that FBI job.*

That'd be nice, I said, *but I think I owe them now. They saved Czoltan from the BEA.*

Oh yeah. Well, shit. You're fucked, I guess.

Thanks.

"Now." Ms. Louderman turned to Czoltan. "Tell me more about your representation in Detroit."

He told her the name of his city representative and about some of the initiatives she was working on, and Ms. Louderman responded with a politician's hunger for connections and networking. They got a bit ahead of us, and Jake didn't seem inclined to catch up. He kept eyeing them, and when they were some ten feet ahead and absorbed in their own conversation, he lowered his voice. "Don't worry too much," he said.

"About what?" I asked, because I'd been thinking about the FBI and the conversation I was going to have with my boyfriend about it.

He nodded toward Ms. Louderman. "She's spent years building up this belief. I think she'll come around, but it's gonna take time, is all."

"The problem is," I said, "she thinks Penny is dead. And it'll be hard to accept that she's alive only to realize that she might lose her again any moment. Especially if Penny's business has to do with her mother, their reconciliation might be the thing that releases Penny."

"Ooof," Jake said, nodding. "Like in Final Words."

I grinned. "I try not to see ghost movies because they almost always fuck it up somehow. But yeah, I think that was the plot of that one."

"It wasn't bad," he said. "For a ghost movie. But yeah. Wife's husband dies and she mourns him and then discovers he's remained. Oh, and she has a new boyfriend. Anyway, he'd cheated on her and the way he died was he was on his way to see his mistress, and he always felt bad about that, so he had to stick around until he could make it up to her. And she forgives him and then that releases him."

I listened patiently to this summary. "Sounds about right," I said.

"So something like that could happen?"

I nodded. "It's hard on the remained when their unfinished business is with a living person, but it's often hard on the person because they have to basically experience the death of a loved one twice. I can recommend therapists when it gets to that point."

His mouth twisted up. "She's not big on therapists."

She thinks going to therapy is for sick people only.

"When it gets to that point," I repeated. "Desperation drives people to places they might not go otherwise."

I'm not interested in patching things up with her.

Give it time.

"I hope you're right," Jake said.

Penny snorted. *You know what it sounds like when you say dumb stuff like that.*

Kids, I said.

Ugggggggh, you old people.

All right. You know about Moving On, right?

Yeeeeah. I'd rather be with Marta.

Let me at least take you by there and we'll get you a counselor. You don't think therapy is just for sick people, do you?

You probably think it's clever throwing my own words back at me like that, don't you?

That depends, I said. *Did it work?*

I'll go by and talk to them.

I grinned at Jake. "What?" he said, looking up from his phone.

"Ah, nothing," I said. "Just thinking about how hard it must be to be a parent."

"You thinking about having kids?"

I looked ahead at Czoltan. "We're not at a stage where that's a question yet. We need to both be in the same city first."

"Ah well." He smiled. "I know it's an individual journey for everyone and all that, but Bill and I found it really rewarding."

"How old's yours?"

"Just two. Bill works from home, so he can parent during the day, and I take the evening and morning shifts. But I go home for lunch sometimes too. When I'm not escorting the Alderman into Wolftown on a bizarre mission to rescue her remained daughter."

I smiled back at him. "Mind if I ask, did you adopt, or use a surrogate or what?"

"Oh, uh." His face clouded for a moment. "No. I, uh, I carried the child."

"Oh. Oh, got it. Cool."

The clouds in his expression parted and relief shone through. "Ms. Louderman has been so supportive," he said, more easily. "I know the whole business with Penny makes her seem shitty, but she can be really caring. If Bill didn't have an Aunt Teri, I might've asked her to be the godmother."

Really? Penny asked.

"Really?" I echoed. To Penny I said, *You didn't know?*

I knew he had a kid. I didn't know how involved my mom was.

"Yeah." Jake bobbed his head. "I didn't want to get between her and Penny, so I tried to be a friend to both of them separately."

Nice to know she was a good mom to someone, Penny said acidly. *He even believes in the remained and that didn't bother her.*

"She didn't mind that you believe in the remained?"

"Well, ah." He glanced at the ring on my hand. "I don't call her a 'catastrophically stupid pig-stubborn bitch' when we talk about it, and I think that helps."

I only said that once. Wait until his kid is a teenager.

"Penny says, 'Wait until his kid is a teenager.'"

Jake laughed. "Don't I know it. But that's eleven years away, and we have a lot of time to, you know, build bonds that will withstand some philosophical disagreements."

"Good luck," I said.

He smiled. "Thanks. And good luck with Penny."

Penny snorted. "I'm going to take her to Moving On," I said, wary about talking about Marta in public, "and then she's out of my hands."

Jake's smile faded, and he nodded. "I wonder if you could find a way for me to keep in touch with her, until she does move on. Once a month, you think?"

"Now that she can manifest, I'm sure she can do that," I said. "We can work something out." *If you want to,* I added to Penny.

I do, she said.

"Good." Jake exhaled. "Hey, Mr. Kim, you know more about this than I do, but...isn't it weird that Penny was working on this activist stuff, and she had something she had to tell that otter..."

I waited. Jake glanced at me to see if I would jump in, but I let him keep going. "Anyway, it's weird that she died right at that time, right? She was only seventeen."

"Seventeen-year-olds have heart attacks too," I said. "And they sometimes drink too much or take the wrong pills."

"Yeah, that's what I thought, until I saw that guy try to—I mean, it sure seemed like he was trying to kill us. Do you think..."

Penny remained silent. I wasn't sure how much I wanted to share with Jake, so I stayed cautious. "He might have just been trying to scare us," I said. "To provoke Marta into acting somehow."

"Oh, that makes sense," Jake said with a wash of relief. "I mean, I know the government does some terrible things, but I can't imagine they would actually murder civilians. Don't you find that hard to believe?"

I closed my eyes, but that only brought back images from Kosovo, so I opened them again to impress myself back into my surroundings, amid the very ordinary row houses of Wolftown, in the crowd of werewolves and vampires and gumiho and there, a kishi. Here in Wolftown Chicago, half a world away from the horrors of war I'd seen, it was tempting to believe in a world where everyone treated each other more or less with respect, where violence and aggression remained on an individual level and weren't government-sponsored. Here on a quiet street, where werewolves chatted on their phones or laughed together, where the houses had stood for fifty years and might stand for fifty more, I did find it hard to believe. But the part of me that had never left Kosovo, the part of me that had seen what governments did when they were at war, when they thought nobody was watching, that part of me whispered, *Is it hard to believe? Is it really?*

"Mr. Kim? What's Penny saying?"

Jake looked at me anxiously. I guess a reverie looked a lot like talking to a remained person. Now I had to decide whether to comfort him or open his eyes. I turned the ring on my finger. He was already devoted to remained person rights, and would no doubt redouble his efforts now that Penny was one of them. I didn't know that casting the BEA as the villain they were would make much of a difference.

But as a private investigator, I'd promised to uphold the truth. And even though Jake hadn't hired me, we'd gone through a harrowing situation together, and that creates a bond. "She finds it hard to believe too," I hedged.

Not that hard.

You think I can tell him the truth? I asked Penny.

So you do think they killed me.

Don't you remember?

I remember getting into the offices. I remember feeling really weird, and I was in bed at the USA house but I didn't remember how I got there. But it could've been an aneurysm or a breakdown or something, right? I was under a lot of stress to get that stuff.

"I'm asking Penny what she remembers," I told Jake, who was still waiting for an answer. To Penny, I said, *Russell said they had a remained person—not him—possess you, but he didn't say what they'd done. Don't you hate the BEA? Don't you think they would've killed to protect that information?*

I know they're murderers, she said. *I just don't want them to have murdered* me.

I drew in a breath, collected my thoughts, and let it out. "Me? I don't think it's hard to believe," I said. "I don't have any specific knowledge of what the BEA does. But the stuff Penny found there, that they're binding suspected terrorists—that I believe. And if I believe that, then I have to ask if I believe they just happened to be around when those people died to collect their spirit. That seems like a bit of a stretch. So if they killed those people, then is it likely they also killed Penny?"

Jake's earnest face fell. "Bastards," he said.

"We don't have any proof," I reminded him, conscious of the fact that I couldn't tell him I'd spoken to Russell while he'd been frozen. "Penny doesn't remember clearly what happened to her. But it's suspicious as hell that she broke into their offices and died the next morning, isn't it?

"I just...that's the government. I work in the government." He shook his head. "It's the feds, though, we know they're different. Always come in like they're the shit, think they know best even though we're the ones who know this town and these people."

I didn't know how well Jake and Ms. Louderman could know Wolftown from their office outside its walls, but that was a bit of truth to maybe save for later. So I said, "There's also good people at the BEA. Czoltan says he knows some that help extras get their benefits and stuff like that. And Zawada only had two other people from the BEA office helping him. Probably most of the ones who work here don't know anything about it."

"Sure, but, I mean..." He looked ahead at his boss. "If I do nothing but help people, and my boss is going out at night murdering them, am I really innocent?"

"Maybe if you don't know about it." I squinted. "Does she go out and murder people?"

Ha, Penny tossed in.

Jake shook his head. "I mean, I don't watch her every minute. But I seriously doubt it. She really does care about her district."

Cares about her position in it, he means, Penny said acidly.

"And she cares about Penny," Jake went on. He glanced at my ring. "Even if Penny finds it hard to believe."

"I know she does," I said. "I think Penny will come to see it too, in time."

"I hope so. I hope she can find peace."

"I'd like a little peace myself," I said.

Jake gave me a sad smile. "Nah," he said. "Peace isn't for the living."

CHAPTER

NINETEEN

P eace isn't for the living.

I didn't like when Jake said that, because I didn't want it to be true. I can find peace, I argued. I can settle down with Czoltan and I can work my cases to bring small measures of peace to others, can't I?

I could, that's true. But I would also always be thinking about Penny, about Russell, about the remained in BEA custody somewhere around D.C. And I wouldn't have peace knowing that there might be something more I could do for them.

Not to mention all the problems extras still faced in this country, including the question of whether the Wolftowns were a good or bad thing, and why the people in charge of them weren't the people who were living in them. When problems like this face the people you love, peace can only come through ignorance, whether genuine or chosen.

Or, in my case, by calling the FBI. Which you could make a good argument for being either.

When we said good-bye to Ms. Louderman and Jake and

the other guy, the guard whose name we were never told, at the Visitor Center, then it was just me and Czoltan (and Penny). We stayed inside the air-conditioned lobby for a moment before venturing back out into the summer heat. The sun had not yet set, and it seemed impossible to me that just that morning, I'd set out to meet Ms. Louderman for the first time.

"You hungry?" Czoltan asked as we stepped outside and the hot afternoon air rolled over us. He stayed in wolf form because he didn't have an extra shirt to put on, and a werewolf was less conspicuous than a bare-shirted man (if only a little, at this time of year).

"Yeah. We can grab something on the way home." The ordinariness of the conversation felt wrong also. "Listen, about all that. How are you doing?"

His muzzle dipped toward his chest. "Uh, I feel bad because...I feel like it was a lot worse for the rest of you. I didn't really know until you said it there in the house exactly what happened. I was standing next to you, and then I felt like I was dreaming about turning into a wolf, only when I...woke up, it wasn't a dream, and you were staring at me trying to bring me back."

Wait, he turned into a wolf? Penny said. *Like a real full wolf? Isn't that dangerous?* I didn't have time to form my response of "hold on, I'll tell you later" into words before she got the feeling. *Right, sorry, I'll just listen.*

"I'm glad you came back," I said. "Obviously."

"Yeah, uh, me too." He looped an arm over my shoulder. "It's hitting me now, but at the time, when I was..." He looked around then at the other people on the sidewalk, but nobody was near us or even paying attention. He lowered his voice anyway. "When I was wolf, there wasn't any of that. It wasn't scary, I mean. There was just...I was hungry, and I was curious about the world, and there was kind of a peace to it. I can see how people fall into that shape and never want to leave. But I'm glad I did," he added hurriedly, giving my shoulder a squeeze.

I leaned into him. "I'm sorry for dragging you into this. And involving the FBI, and all the other stuff. When I thought they might deport you, I thought that was the worst thing Rock could do, and then..."

That snapped his ears up, and we missed that the light had changed until people started flowing around us. Then we walked along with them, keeping our voices down. "Deport me? But I'm here legally. I'm eligible for citizenship next year."

"What he said specifically was, ah, something about 'associating with known terrorists.' That's enough, I guess, if they want to press it."

"And he called Marta a terrorist. And..." Czoltan dropped his gaze to the street and I saw him running through his list of friends in his head. "Fuck."

"Yeah."

I waited until we'd crossed and the crowd had thinned a little before I said, "So I guess we should talk about the, ah..." Now it was my turn to look around, and then for good measure I took my phone out of my pocket and powered it off. I didn't know if that disabled the microphone fully for anyone listening, but it felt like the best I could do. "The Feds."

He nodded as I slipped the phone back into my pocket, watching what I'd done. "Yeah, you said you called them when Zawada took me? I guess you told them some of what was happening. Glad you didn't give up Marta."

Me too. Sorry, just listening here.

"Just because they offered me a ton of money doesn't mean I trust them," I said. "But they did get Zawada to release you, earlier."

"Ah." He looked down at me. "So now you owe them. Now you have to take that contract."

"Kind of. I mean, yes, I agreed to do it if they'd help you. I couldn't think of any other way to get you out of there, and that was the most important thing on my mind." We paused at a corner waiting for a light, and I looked up with my most heartfelt expression. "But I did it for you."

And the Oscar goes to...

Quiet, I said to Penny. *This is as real as it gets.*

"Christ, Jae." He ran a paw over his head. "I'm mad at you but also I love you and I don't know what to do with that."

"Well," I said. "I'm a little mad at me too, and if you wanted to take a break for a while, at least until this contract is up, I'd understand."

He didn't say anything for the rest of the block, until we were about to turn onto the street where my apartment was, leaving me agonizing about what his answer was going to be. Penny, surprisingly, said only, *That was the right thing to say,* and I felt her sympathy.

Finally, at the curb, Czoltan put a paw on my shoulder. "I guess this is the situation we're in now," he said. "So maybe we don't have pre-march meetings at your place anymore. At least for a while."

"That might be best." I squeezed my hands into fists and then released the tension. "So...you don't want to take a break?"

He blinked down at me. "Fuck, no, Jae. Sorry! I was working out in my head what I needed to change with this new job of yours. I don't want to take a break."

"I'm sorry about that."

We crossed the street, shedding more of the crowd. Now it was just us and two guys in shirt and tie, probably coming back from a late lunch to one of the offices on this block.

Czoltan slowed to let them get ahead of us. "You know," he said, "I hadn't really thought about my activism maybe getting me in trouble. It's good that we have some people with power on our side, I guess, but...maybe I shouldn't go to marches at all."

My answer came quickly and automatically. "No," I said. "Fuck that. First off, if you're afraid of Agent Rock Zawada and what he might do to you if you step out of line, well, you've already done that. Nothing more you do is going to make it worse than it already is, in his eyes."

He looked at me with surprise, his ears coming up. "I'm not worried about Zawada," he said, "cause it seems like he's in more trouble than I am."

"And if you're worried about me," I said, "don't be."

"I'm not," he said, and reached over to pull me against him as we walked. "I don't like this."

"I know." I grinned, buoyed by the embrace. "You've been clear about that."

"But I get why you're doing it. And so...I guess...we'll just keep talking about it."

"For sure." We got to the apartment door and in the glass our reflections looked back at us, still held together with one grey-furred arm, both serious but also with the hints of smiles there, happiness leaking out despite the problems.

I took out my card and swiped it over the magnetic reader, staying in Czoltan's embrace. Only when the door clicked open did we reluctantly separate to walk through into the cool of the lobby.

"What does Penny have to say about all this?" he asked when the door had swung shut.

"She's been quiet," I said, but put the hand with the ring in Czoltan's paw so she could talk to both of us.

None of my business, she said. *But I'm glad you guys are staying together and still trying to change the world. At least, one of you is.*

Czoltan and I looked at each other and I raised my eyebrows. *Look,* Penny said, *I still don't think you get it. But I think you're trying, and that's worth something. This wolf is pretty cool and he wouldn't be staying with you if you were as dumb as you seem.*

"I'll take it," I said.

Back in the apartment, I finally took my phone out and turned it on. Agent Jefferson had sent a terse, *Thanks,* and then, *Check your email.*

She'd sent the contract along, password-protected so that it took me actually something like ten minutes to get the Authenticator app they used, register with it, then get the code and open the document. I read through it, which took another half hour, and absorbed all the consequences of me fucking this thing up: prison time, more prison time, prison time in one of those black ops sites that don't show up on maps (this wasn't spelled out but my imagination supplied it).

Czoltan put a paw on my shoulder and I switched the window instinctively. "I'm not looking," he said. "But you gotta sign it now. Would be nice if there were an easy way out of it, but there's not, is there?"

"No," I said. "The email said, 'per our discussion and the work we did on your behalf,' so if I don't agree to do this, they'll find something worse for me to do, I'm sure. I owe them now."

"*We* owe them," he said. "Go ahead and sign it."

As I clicked through to sign it digitally, he said, "And then call your mother."

"Christ," I said. "How do you know?"

"Because your phone's on silent and she called twenty

minutes ago." He patted me on the back. "I'm going to text Carla and see if we can set up another meeting with Marta so we can give Penny over to her once her mom does the legal part."

"Fine," I said. "I'll call Mom when I start dinner."

"I'll stay in the bedroom."

"No." I looked up at him. "Stay out here. It's time she met you."

"You sure?"

"Yeah." It didn't seem necessary to explain that I was afraid I might've lost him without my mother ever meeting him, or that I'd had to think a lot about the situation extras suffered through in general over the last few days, or that if (God forbid) he did get deported, I'd rather have Mom fighting on my side. It didn't seem necessary to explain that I was doing something I should've done years ago.

Czoltan nodded and shifted back from wolf to handsome (I thought) human, dark hair and moody eyes. But his smile lit me up inside before he hurried to the bedroom to find a shirt to put on, even though there was a twinge—more than a twinge —that I was asking him to hide part of himself.

He is handsome as a human, Penny observed. *The hot ones are always gay.*

I'm flattered.

She coughed. *I didn't say that all the gay ones are hot.*

Maybe I'm flattered that you were complimenting my taste in men.

Right.

Penny offered to let me put the ring in a box for privacy, but I didn't want to isolate her. I'd met her mother, so she might as well meet mine. Also I was going to tell Mom about Czoltan, and in a weird way I wanted Penny's approval.

"Jae! It's so nice to finally hear from you."

"It's been a busy day, Mom."

"I've booked the flight I told you about. I get in the 28th, that's a Thursday, and then I leave on Tuesday. I thought it would be nice to have a few more days. I got a good deal on the flight, too. You know, usually when I have to wait this long to book a flight, it's more expensive, but I saw a deal come through on Alaska, so I took it. I'll send you my flight so you can come pick me up."

"Sure, Mom," I said. "Sounds good."

"How did that job turn out? Did you find the guy?"

"Yeah. I found him. It's wrapped up now, except for a couple loose ends."

"Good. Why can't I see you?"

"I'm making dinner," I said. Even that simple statement was a little charged, because she would absolutely ask—

"Just for yourself, or do you have company tonight?"

Here we go. "I've got company." I sliced the ends off of snow peas to throw in the steamer.

"Oh, lovely! Who is it? Is it your friend on the CPD, what's her name, Jo?"

"No. Actually, Mom, I wanted to tell you I've been seeing someone."

"Jae! That's wonderful!" Delight shifted instantly into concern. "You've 'been' seeing someone? Why haven't you told me? What's wrong with him?"

"Well, he's not Korean." I tossed the peas into the steamer and pulled carrots onto the cutting board.

She drew in a breath sharper than the knife I was holding. "Where did you meet him?"

"I met him when I was over in Kosovo. We dated for a

while there, and a bit when we came back, and then I broke it off." I held "because I didn't think you'd approve" in reserve. "But we reconnected again when I was in Detroit a few months ago, and we've been taking it slow, but it's going really well."

"I see."

She's not as much of a bitch as my mom, Penny said. *My mom would've told you to stop seeing him or she'd disown you.*

Shh.

"I didn't want to tell you until I was sure it was going to be something, because I knew you'd be upset, but it really is something."

"Is he there now? Is that why we're not on video?"

Czoltan stood across from me, in a blue polo shirt with white horizontal pinstripes. "He's here, yes."

"Put me on video."

"It doesn't work that way, Mom. I have to call you back."

I set up the phone on the stand while Czoltan came around to my side of the kitchen, then called Mom back. "Here you go," I said. "Now you can see me." I showed her the peas and carrots. "Making beef and veggies."

"Don't you ever cook Korean food?" she sighed.

"I got Korean barbecue sauce for the beef. Not the cheap brand, the one you like."

That mollified her a little. "So show me this man of yours. What's his name?"

"Czoltan," I said, by way of answer, and nodded to him.

He came over to stand next to me as Mom tried to pronounce his name. "Zol-tan?"

"That's close enough," he said with a smile. "Hi, Mrs. Kim. It's nice to meet you."

"How old are you?" she asked.

"I'm twenty-eight," he said.

"Hmph." I watched her do math in her head. "How old were you when you met Jae?"

"Twenty-one," he said. "I grew up in Kosovo and lost my family in the war. Jae was working at the Red Cross camp and was a big help to me. I might not have made it through if not for him." I kicked his ankle under the counter and he gave me a startled look, then remembered what I'd told him to say. "You raised such a wonderful son," he said. "He's so caring. It wasn't only me he helped over there, but we just...clicked."

The compliment to her mothering skills landed. "He's always been that way. I just encouraged it," she said, deflecting the compliment without outright denying it. "You don't have *any* family?"

"I have found family in Detroit," Czoltan said. "Other refugees who lost relatives in the war. We have a good group that's helped keep each other going."

"And what do you do?"

"I work in a call center."

Ah, he was doing so well, too, Penny said.

I intercepted the frown on Mom's face before it could deepen. "He's been promoted to level three support. That's better pay and he works directly with the engineers. He's not just answering phones."

"Hm."

"And," Czoltan put in, "I'm in the training program to move up to junior engineer. I've got to take a couple years of college classes, but the company is really good about promoting from within."

"You're already twenty-eight," Mom said.

"Mom. His village was bombed when he was a teenager. You supported me when I went over to help people, right? This is also part of what that looks like."

"I'm sure the Army didn't ask you to date a refugee," she said, but not sharply.

You're doing pretty good too, Penny put in.

"It just happened," I said. "I know you wanted me to marry a Korean guy, but we don't choose who we fall in love with."

"Whom," she corrected me. "Jae, I just want you to be happy."

"With a Korean man."

"Yes, if possible, but I know how picky you are, and if you found someone who makes you happy, then I can't object to that."

Knowing her, she'd find ways to object to it anyway, but hearing that gave me a wash of relief. Czoltan leaned in. "I'm looking forward to meeting you in September, Mrs. Kim," he said.

"Yes, well, maybe I shouldn't stay at your house. I'll ask Vella if her room is still available. And I'll buy some earplugs. Are you bringing him to the wedding?"

"Oh," Czoltan said, "I don't think I'm ready to meet the rest of the family yet. But I hope you'll have some time while you're here."

This had the dual effect of relieving my mother's worry that she would have to explain my non-Korean boyfriend to the rest of her friends, and making her feel special for getting to meet him first. "I will definitely have time," she declared. "I would stay an extra few days, but I don't think my flight is changeable."

"I'll make sure to take that Monday and Tuesday off," Czoltan said quickly.

"All right then. Good. Good!" Her face brightened.

"Thanks, Mom," I said. "I'm really glad you took it well."

"You know," she said, "Kelly Park's boy just had a baby. I

think he used a surrogate. I'll ask her. Maybe she can refer you to her."

"Oh yeah, when we're ready to think about children—"

She cut me off. "You're in your thirties, Jae. If you don't think about children now, when will you? I'll let you know what I find. When I come for the wedding, we can look at some pictures."

"All right," I said faintly. That was a month away, and we'd accomplished the most important goal of this call anyway.

"It was nice to meet you, Mrs. Kim," Czoltan said. "I'm gonna let Jae get back to making dinner."

I'd finished the carrots and now pulled the chicken over to cut. "Oh, I'll leave you alone," Mom said. "Jae, call me tomorrow."

I tapped the End Call button with a clean knuckle. There would be a more thorough cross-examination then about my relationship, but I could stand that. We'd taken a first step, and that felt good. For a moment, my knees weakened, but they didn't give way. I leaned against Czoltan anyway.

If I could've lived in a different city from my mother, I think I could've gotten along with her better too, Penny said.

Czoltan put an arm around my waist as I continued to cut. "You doing okay?" he asked, shifting to wolf. Fur sprouted next to my shirt, and a moment later his tail brushed the back of my leg.

"Yeah," I said. "Oh man, I don't think I've ever seen you wolfy with a shirt on."

He stuck his tongue out, pulled the shirt over his head, and threw it into the living room. "I thought that went pretty well."

"I feel good that she got to meet you finally, but also...I wish I could tell her everything."

"If she lived nearby, it might be a problem," he said. "But

246

it'll be fine. We can get her accustomed to extras and to me, and then..."

"And then maybe it'll only give her a minor heart attack when we tell her." He made a worried face, and I forced a laugh. "No," I said. "No, it'll be fine. Eventually. I'm sure of it. I'm sorry I'm asking you to hide part of who you are."

He squeezed my waist. "You didn't ask. I offered."

"Yeah, but I put you in this situation."

"Your mom did. We're trying to take it easy with her. And you're doing the right thing. To overcome prejudice, she's got to meet real people, not just believe what she reads."

"I know. I've tried that before, though. I had extra friends in college and tried to get her to meet them and...it didn't go well." I finished cutting the chicken and stood there staring down at it.

"People change. Have you actually talked to her about extras in the last...ten years? How long ago was college?"

I laughed through the emotion in my throat and elbowed him, then tossed the chicken into the sauté pan and started moving it around. "My sophomore year, I tried to bring home a gumiho friend. I thought because she was Korean, Mom would be more okay with it, but she wouldn't even let her in the house."

Czoltan let go of my waist and stepped back from the spatter of oil, his smile gone. "Ah, I'm sorry. That sucks."

"Yeah, it did. I think that was the last time I really tried. Then after college I went to the Army and that solved a lot of the problems."

He rested a paw on the small of my back. "And created more."

"Yeah, but these are the good kind of problems." I turned to smile. "And it helps that I don't have to solve them alone."

His whiskers brushed my cheek and then he kissed me. "Not any more."

Penny, considerately, remained silent.

EPILOGUE

Yumi accompanied us so we would have some protection, but no BEA agents bothered us on our way to or through Wolftown. I suspected Rock and his two colleagues were long gone from Chicago, but it didn't hurt to be sure. When we got to the Unified Society Alliance house, Yumi stayed outside, though. Plausible deniability, she said. Same reason I left my phone at home, I said.

The room Penny had been staying in was still closed off and Gina Przybyla, the head of the USA, wouldn't let me look in there. Not that I had a reason to, but I was somewhat curious. Penny's body had been removed, but I wanted to see the place she'd lived.

Penny didn't want to see it again, at least not with me. *There's a lot of cringe in there*, she'd said as we were walking into the USA house.

I wouldn't think you would be into cringe.

My attempt to tease her, like all the previous ones, did not land. *Ugh.* She had a way of saying that that made me envision her eyes rolling. *Everyone's into cringe, it's only cringe if other people see you into it. God, you're old.*

But Gina did have Penny's phone, and Penny asked her if I could hold it. *I've got a favor to ask,* she said to me. *Well, the first one is don't look at the journal when you open it.*

At all?

You can read the last entry, but don't scroll back.

Ok, I said.

There was a pause, and she said, *I journaled about a lot of stuff, and some of it might get friends of mine in trouble. I trust you, but it's not...*

It's ok, I said. *I don't need to scroll back. What's the last entry?*

I don't really remember, she said. *I want to read it too.*

So she gave me the password and the phone opened to a home screen. She told me which app held the journal, and together we read the last entry:

I'm so tired I can't stop yawning so I'm dictating instead of typing. I went into the BEA office today and signed in as a visitor and then Marta's friend signed out while the regular guard was on a break and signed me out too I hid in a restroom until the office close and then found the office I was looking for I picked the lock in aaaa elf segments and started to clone the hard drive but while it was cloning I opened the filing cabinets and found the papers so I just took them and then because I could tell where they were being held I thought maybe I could rescue them so I went looking but I didn't find anything period I want back to the office to wait for the drive to finish and I must have fallen asleep there I woke up before the drive was done though and got it and the papers and then went out through the fire door which set off alarms but I hid across the street I was getting tired so I put all the stuff in one of the tourist lockers along the plaza just in case some of the people came looking for me or I passed out on the street this was the backup plan Marta taught me I put it in locker 34 combination 1 2 1 9 and then I came home I wasn't sure I was going make it

We were quiet for a moment and then I said, *Bastards.*

To my surprise, Penny sounded more proud than angry. *Yeah,* she said, *but I did it, didn't I?*

You did. I found myself swallowing against the emotion in my throat for this brave girl who'd died to help people. *I'm proud of you.*

You're not my dad, she said, but it was affectionate, not angry. *Go to my messages. Look for David Wolf.*

There, second down in her Messages list, was the name David Wolf next to a picture of a handsome young werewolf. *Open it up, get his number,* Penny instructed.

The page of messages I saw were the banter of young people comfortable enough with each other to make terrible jokes. David had said, gotta go or mom will skin me alive, and Penny replied, at least then she'll have a nice rug, and he said really?? but with a heart emoji, and then had added, better than a pile of disgusting human skin, and Penny'd said ew gross but also with a heart emoji and then ttyl, which he'd replied to in kind. Then from yesterday there was one message from him: sup?

Was he your boyfriend? I asked, trying to cover the ache I felt looking at that conversation and knowing it was over forever.

No, she said. *Might have been one day. Just get his number.*

I scribbled it down on a piece of paper, since I didn't have my phone. Of course she wouldn't want me to text him from her phone; that would've been weird.

So weird, she said, listening in on my thoughts. *Can you just tell him I—tell him I died?*

Sure. If someone dies, it's standard practice to notify the people in their messages. Or at least I can tell him that. You don't want him to know you've remained?

Not yet. Maybe if I'm still around in a bit, but...I want to settle myself first.

No problem, I said.

Thanks. And can you wipe the phone?

I turned it off. *I'll send the phone with you. You can learn to operate it, and maybe if you stick around, you'll want it.*

I'm worried the BEA will get it.

I don't think you have to worry about that. Rock is not going to be a problem. Although it was true that the FBI had been cagey about whether they'd caught him yet when they'd debriefed us, so he might still be out there. I just didn't think he'd be here. Penny had delivered the information he'd wanted to keep secret, so he shouldn't care about her anymore.

She took the mental equivalent of a deep breath. *All right. I know Marta won't let that happen.*

Listen, Penny. About Marta...

What?

I'd had this thought a few times over the last couple days, and Penny had only gotten that maybe I didn't like Marta very much, because I'd kept the worry down. But I had to tell her before we said goodbye. *It's possible that she knew what was going to happen to you. That it was likely, I mean.* She didn't say anything. *That she sent you deliberately into danger and got you killed.*

No, Penny said in a small voice. *She told me it was dangerous, but she thought I could do it.*

I know she cares about you, I said. *But I just want you to be careful.*

There was a pause, and then she laughed shortly. *What else can happen to me now? I'm already dead. And I know who killed me, and it wasn't her. So...I'm gonna go with her. Okay?*

I wouldn't have brought you here if I thought it wasn't okay. Just—

I know, I know, I'll be careful. And I know how to get in touch with you.

You want me to put my number in your phone? I asked, and got a snort in response. *All right. But call anytime.*

When I told Gina we were ready, she led me to another room on the second floor, one with the windows boarded up, lit only by a small incandescent lamp. I had a feeling this was for more than just her comfort as a vampire out in the daytime, but I didn't ask.

Waiting in the room, seated at wooden chairs around a plain wooden table and looking at their phones, were two other people. They stood as we entered, and the nearer one proved to be almost as tall as Gina, who towered a foot over me. But where Gina had a small, round face, straight brown hair, and a build like a skeleton in a black t-shirt and jeans (I have never seen a vampire anything but underweight), this other person's rectangular face mirrored their thick, rectangular build. The short-sleeved collared shirt they wore, pale blue, had visible sweat stains under the arms—reasonable considering this closed-in room felt as stuffy as an oven—and their black necktie had a picture of Casper the Friendly Ghost on it. "Terrence," they said, extending a dark brown hand and giving a bright smile. "I'm the remained persons expert."

I shook Terrence's hand and glanced at the other person, chair pushed back from the table and not looking at me. Their brown skin and black shoulder-length hair were set off by more pieces of jewelry than I could count: ear studs, eyebrow studs, a nose piercing, two necklaces, a silver armband decorated with colorful swirls, some number of rings on each hand. What I'd thought was a plain white t-shirt while they were seated now revealed itself to be body-length, like a night-shirt. Then I noticed their slight rocking movements, saw the scaled tail on the floor behind them, and realized they were a Naga. The full-length shirt can be worn when they're part-snake or when they're fully human—they have a human torso even when shifted.

The Naga didn't meet my eyes. "This," Gina said gently, sitting down, "is Marta's friend. They prefer to remain anonymous."

I sat, and Terrence did too. The Naga lowered themself until they were at eye level with us, and then closed their eyes. A moment later, Marta appeared between Terrence and the Naga, webbed paws clasped in front of her. She opened her eyes and let her arms fall to her sides, and a smile blossomed. "Hi, Gina," she said.

Ah, the Naga was the corporeal person who'd bound Marta, but allowed her to act on her own. I understood the functionality of all the jewelry now: either they had a lot of remained persons bound or they wanted to hide the one piece of jewelry that was important by surrounding it with others. Effective.

Marta's whiskered otter face turned to me. "Detective Kim, isn't it? I understand you have been a kind guardian to Penny."

You wanna answer that one? I asked Penny.

Should I manifest? Will that screw up the transfer?

I'm sure they'll walk us through it, I said. *Go on.*

Penny wavered as she manifested, but after a few seconds, held her appearance steady. She looked right at Marta and said, "Hi."

"It's good to see you again, Penny. I'm so sorry for what happened."

"It's okay. If what I did helps, then I'm glad."

"It has helped. It will help more."

Now Penny did look my way. "Mr. Kim's been cool, I guess," she said.

"If not for his quick action, you might be in the hands of the BEA, so I'm glad he's also treated you well."

I shifted in my seat. "Yumi told me to come to the scene," I said. "She deserves some credit. I don't think she'd have just handed you over to Rock."

"Take the credit, jeez," Penny said. "You fuckin' allergic to compliments or what?"

"Kind of," I said.

"Fuckin' gen X."

"I'm a millennial."

"Even worse. Everything's your fault, you realize."

"I've been told."

"All right." Marta smiled tolerantly. "Terrence, would you begin the transfer?"

"If everyone is ready?" Terrence leaned forward.

I held out the ring. The Naga held out a slender, attractive copper bracelet. Terrence grasped my hand, making sure to touch the ring, and placed his other hand on the bracelet.

He didn't make an attempt to hide the incantation. I followed a little of it; I'd learned the transfer spell a long time ago, but I'd never used it nor had much reason to memorize it. You've got to have the binding memorized because it's so tricky dealing with unbound ghosts, but transferring a bound ghost from one person to another is just a little balancing act.

I slipped into the trance as the spell took effect, and came to on a wooden deck above a beach. Not too far away, the sun sparkled over a gentle procession of swells making their way to shore, and a soft breeze brought the rustling of sea grasses to us.

I stood next to the railing, with Penny to my left and the Naga on the other side of her. Standing on the other side of the deck, reflected in the closed glass windows that led to a darkened interior, Terrence smiled and held out his arms.

"It's so lovely to see you all here," he said. "Penny, are you ready to move from Jae to our friend?"

She looked at me and reached out a hand. I took it in mine, and she gave it a squeeze. "Thanks for everything," she said. "Take care of Czoltan."

"I will." It felt strange to feel her hand for "real," to look into her eyes and see her smile. Smell was missing from this unreality, but that was common with humans; we rarely thought about how we smelled to others. Also, our voices in dream projections sound like they do in our heads, not to others. Just a little point of interest there. I didn't know what Penny's voice sounded like corporeally, and I might never, unless I found some Internet video of her. "Hey, I mean to ask... why the Cobain shirt?"

Her smile got bigger. "I caught Nirvana on oldies stations. Pretty punk. Plus it pissed off my mom."

Nirvana on "oldies" stations was a knife in my gut, and from her expression, she knew it. "Well, you take care of yourself, and, uh. Fight the power."

Her mouth twitched. "We can use all the help we can get."

"Yeah, I know. I'll be...I'm gonna do more."

"Good." She gave a nod, let go of me, and then turned to the Naga. "I'm ready now."

Terrence beamed. "Take their hand."

Penny reached out to the Naga, who in this dream-state wore a waist-length beaded shirt with a floral pattern that left their entire lower half exposed, a beautiful snake's body with a tan underside and black scales around the rest, yellow lines running through them. They didn't speak as Penny took their hand, but smiled with graceful ease.

Terrence intoned the words of the transfer spell again. I felt nothing, but a small glow sparked between Penny and the Naga. I stepped back, feeling suddenly like an intruder here as the two of them spoke via their minds. Terrence caught my eye and smiled. "Thank you for being a caretaker," he said. "You have the spirit of a protector."

"Oh," I said, "I don't know about that."

The world frayed at the edges and wobbled. Penny turned to me and grinned. "Take a fuckin' compliment," she said.

I tottered back on my heels, blinked, and opened my eyes to the dark room. Penny was gone, but Marta remained, eyes closed, between the Naga and Terrence.

Terrence was the first one to stand. Gina followed suit quickly. "It's done?" she said.

"It's done," Terrence confirmed, and reached out to me. "Come on," he said. "Let's leave them."

He and Gina and I walked downstairs and out, where we rejoined Yumi. Gina stayed in the shade of the porch, and smiled at Yumi. "You don't need to be invited in," she said.

"Better if I'm not seen going inside," the yuki-onna replied. "Unless there's a death."

Yumi grimaced and made a small gesture with one hand. "Right. Everything go okay?"

That was to me, or maybe Terrence, but I answered. "Went great." I turned the empty ring on my finger. "Penny's safe."

"As safe as we can make her," Gina said. She raised a hand. "Thanks. Say hi to Zo for me."

"I will," I said as she went back inside.

"Oh," Yumi said, "speaking of, he texted me, said you

should call him." She offered her phone, with his phone number up and ready to call.

"Hey," I said when he picked up. "What's going on?"

"You get Penny sorted out?"

"Yeah. You need me to pick up something on the way home?"

"Nah. You got three calls from Desiree and a couple texts saying to call her."

Prickles of warning spiked down the back of my neck. "Shit. That doesn't sound good. Read me off her number?"

I put him on speaker and typed the phone number into Yumi's phone while she watched. "What happened?" she asked.

"Nothing good," I said. "We usually talk after her workday. Thanks, Czoltan, I'll let you know what she says."

"No problem," he said. "See you soon."

"Mind if I make one more call?" I asked Yumi, finger hovering over the phone number.

"What kind of asshole would I be if I said 'yes'? Go ahead." Her creased brow belied her light tone.

Fortunately, Desiree picked up. "It's Jae," I said. "I'm on a friend's phone. What's up?"

"Jae," she said, "I thought you were going to work out a solution. Why did you turn Richard over to the government?"

The prickling got worse. "I didn't," I said. "What happened?"

Yumi's concern deepened at my tone. Desiree said, "This agent came and took him, just bound him. I said you had to be there because you'd bound him, but he said he could do it and I guess he did. And then he told me that you asked for this. Was he lying?"

"What was his name?" I asked, though the hackles on my neck already knew.

"Rock something. Isn't that weird? Let me get his card. Jae, was he really with the government?"

"Zawada," I said. "Yeah. He's really with the government. At least, he used to be."

Yumi's face held the question she wasn't asking. "So why did you ask him to take Richard?" Desiree asked, anguish creeping in. "I thought you were going to take care of him."

"I was. I am. Listen, this guy—I rescued someone from him and he's doing this for revenge. That's what he meant. But we'll get Richard back. I'll get Richard back."

"All right." She calmed. "How?"

"Give me some time to work on this. I'll keep you updated."

"Thank you, Jae."

I put my phone away and met Yumi's eyes. "Well, shit," I said.

ACKNOWLEDGMENTS

This novel was serialized on my Patreon page at http://www.patreon.com/timsusman, and has been supported by the following members, to whom I owe great thanks: Doug Kelly, Fen, glassan, Kario Tojima, Mevolas, qazwsx7946, Stephan Harmann, sunkawakan, and tav fox.

Alisa Alering, Dayna Smith, Brooke Wonders, Becky Wright, Ryan Campbell, David Cowan, Watts Martin, Mark Brown, Jack DeVries, Malcolm Cross, and Melli Yoon all read the novel in various stages. Their feedback has helped immensely to improve the story, and any flaws that remain are entirely my fault. Thanks also to Salt & Sage Books for their editorial help.

Thanks as always to Mark Harrison at Argyll Productions, whose dedication to recognizing underrepresented voices inspires me every day.

And none of this would be possible without Mark and Jack, who have supported me in ways great and small for so many years now. We were deeply sad to say goodbye to our dog Kobalt, who passed away during the writing of this book. He was the very best boy, and though he has undoubtedly finished his business here and moved on, we still feel him with us every day.

ABOUT THE AUTHOR

Award-winning author Tim Susman began his writing career while pursuing degrees in chemical engineering and international business at the University of Pennsylvania. He later earned a master's in zoology from the University of Minnesota, where he worked with primatologist Jane Goodall.

After relocating to the San Francisco Bay Area, he embraced writing full-time. Tim co-founded Sofawolf Press, co-established RAWR workshop, trained at Clarion and CSSF workshops, and completed Stanford Continuing Studies courses to further hone his skills.

His stories have appeared in *Apex* and *Lightspeed*, and he's authored 40+ novels under both his name and his furry alter ego, Kyell Gold.

You can visit his alter ego's Substack, Dispatches From Kyell (kyellgold.substack.com), to sign up for newsletters about new releases, writing tips, work in progress previews, and more.

facebook.com/timsusmanbooks

bsky.app/profile/kyellgold

x.com/writerfox

furries.club/@kyellgold

Also by Tim Susman

If you would like to get monthly updates on upcoming publications, excerpts of works in progress, and writing tips, sign up for his mailing list at *http://kyellgold.substack.com*.

Wolftown

Unfinished Business — A detective uncovers a plot against him and must turn to his werewolf ex-boyfriend for help.

New Tibet

Breaking The Ice: Stories from New Tibet (editor) — On a hostile ice planet, survival is guaranteed to nobody.

Shadows in Snow (editor) — More stories from the unforgiving ice world of New Tibet.

Common and Precious — A kidnapped heiress comes to sympathize with her desperate captors, while her father discovers the limits of his power in trying to rescue her.

The Calatians

Book 1: The Tower and the Fox — Kip and his friends encounter prejudice and mysteries in their first few months at Prince George's College of Sorcery.

Book 2: The Demon and the Fox — The forces of revolution grow in Massachusetts as Kip and his friends rush to solve the mystery of the attack on the College of Sorcery.

Book 3: The War and the Fox — Kip and his friends are drafted into the fight for independence from Britain, but there is more at stake.

Book 4: The Revolution and the Fox — Two years after the war, Kip and his friends face their greatest threat yet.

Other books

The Price of Thorns — A down-on-his-luck thief meets the actual evil queen from many fairy tales when she offers him the job of a lifetime.

Writing as Kyell Gold:

Love Match

Love Match (vol. 1, 2008-2010) — Rocky arrives in the States from Africa and navigates the treacherous worlds of professional tennis and high school.

Love Match (vol. 2, 2010-2012) — Rocky begins his professional career, at the cost of his family and romantic relationships.

Love Match (vol. 3, 2013-2015) — As his career trends upward, Rocky's romantic life becomes less stable.

Out of Position (Dev and Lee)

Out of Position — Dev the football player and Lee the gay activist discover how to navigate their relationship. *(mature readers)*

Isolation Play — The continuing story of Dev and Lee, as they contend with family and friends in their search for acceptance. *(mature readers)*

Divisions — As Dev's team fights to make the playoffs, Lee fights to keep his sense of self. *(mature readers)*

Uncovered — The playoffs are here, and Dev needs his focus more than ever. So when Lee becomes too distracting, something has to give. *(mature readers)*

Over Time — Dev and Lee try to plan their future while dealing with crises all around them. *(mature readers)*

Ty Game — Dev's teammate Ty navigates an arranged marriage while also falling in love. *(mature readers)*

Tales of the Firebirds — A collection of stories exploring the lives of some of the other characters from the Out of Position series. *(mature readers)*

Titles — In the two weeks leading up to Dev's third try at a championship, Dev and Lee face new challenges and changes in their lives. *(mature readers)*

Dangerous Spirits

Green Fairy — A gay high school senior struggling through his final year finds a strange old book that changes his dreams and his life.

Red Devil — A gay fox who fled his abusive family in Siberia seeks help from a ghost who demands he give up his gay lifestyle.

Black Angel — A young otter struggles to understand her sexuality as her friends prepare for post-high school life and dreams of women in other times plague her.

Argaea

Volle — The story of how Volle came to Tephos, a spy masquerading as a noble, and the first adventure he had there. *(mature readers)*

The Prisoner's Release and Other Stories — The story of how Volle escaped from prison, and the story of what happened after, plus two other stories following characters from "Volle." *(mature readers)*

Pendant of Fortune — Volle returns to Tephos to defend his honor, but soon finds himself fighting for much more. *(mature readers)*

Shadow of the Father — Volle's son, Yilon, must travel to the far-off land he is meant to rule, but he will have to fight treachery to take the lordship. *(mature readers)*

Weasel Presents — Five short stories from the land of Argaea, including "Helfer's Busy Day" and "Yilon's Journal." *(mature readers)*

Return From Divalia — Years after a night of adventure ruined his life, a young wolf gets a chance at redemption. *(mature readers)*

Forester Universe

Waterways — The full story of Kory's journey to understand himself and what it means to be gay. *(mature readers)*

Bridges — Hayward seems content to set up pairs of his friends. But what does he really need for himself? *(mature readers)*

Science Friction — Vaxy never took sex seriously, until he found out the professor he was sleeping with was married... *(mature readers)*

Winter Games — Sierra Snowpaw was an unsure high school student when someone he thought was a friend changed his life. Now he's fifteen years older and still looking for answers. *(mature readers)*

The Mysterious Affair of Giles — A servant in a British manor house tries to solve a murder.

Dude, Where's My Fox? — Lonnie chases down a fox he hooked up with at a party as a way to get over his breakup. *(mature readers)*

Dude, Where's My Pack? — Lonnie tries to navigate relationships old and new. *(mature readers)*

Losing My Religion —— On tour with his R.E.M. cover band, Jackson mentors the new guy in the band as his own life falls apart. *(mature readers)*

The Time He Desires — A Muslim immigrant struggles with the betrayal of his son and the dissolution of his marriage, as well as his own long-past trauma.

Camouflage — When Danilo is sent 500 years into the past, he must choose between safety in an unfamiliar world and his own sense of what is right. *(mature readers)*

Other Books

The Silver Circle — Valerie thought the old hunter was crazy when he warned her about werewolves—until she met one.

In the Doghouse of Justice — Seven stories of superheroes and their not-so-super relationships. *(mature readers)*

Twelve Sides — Twelve short stories about side characters from the above books. *(mature readers)*

Do You Need Help? — Writing advice for furry (and non-furry) writers.

www.ingramcontent.com/pod-product-compliance
Lightning Source LLC
Chambersburg PA
CBHW071824020726
47502CB00004B/1226